HOW M GOT ARRESTED

MW00936893

by

Leslie O'Kane

Book Club Trilogy Book 1

To Lynn Post,

whose very presence brightens our
book club, as well as the lives of all of us
fortunate enough to know you.
Rock on, my dear friend!

How My Book Club Got Arrested

Books by Leslie O'Kane

Foreword
Important Note from the Author
Please Read This
(Speaking for myself, I tend to skip forewords.)

Getting a book published has been my lifelong dream. Several years ago, I attended a bookstore signing at which the author was late to arrive, so the store owner led the audience in a group discussion by asking: "What do you most want to see in a book?" My answer was: "My name as its author on the cover." Although publishing HOW MY BOOK CLUB GOT ARRESTED was the realization of my dream, having my name on the cover has proved to be problematic.

Due to my book-club members not wanting to get hauled into court yet again, all of the names herein have been changed, including my own. All of the *events*, on the other hand, occurred as written and were witnessed/perpetrated by one or more of us. Most of our conversations were recorded by a prototype voice-to-text app (which, btw, my computer-whiz son designed; {my publisher didn't want me to include the name of this software program, but if you ask a computer expert to recommend the best voice-to-text app on the market today—with such first-rate voice recognition that it can identify up to eight different speakers—that will be my son's}) :). (Okay, yes, that's a happy face, which is amateurish. I was having fun with punctuation.)

It is an understatement to say that, in my telling of this story, feathers were ruffled. Feathers were plucked and jabbed into sensitive places where no feathers belong. Countless times none of us book-clubbers wanted to believe that we actually *said* the things the app recorded. This led to a sentence-by-sentence dismantling of initial drafts of this book, even though the text and the software application that produced the text were thoroughly vetted and have been declared accurate by no less than the entire freaking State of Missouri! (I'm a bit touchy on this particular subject.)

Many book clubs are basically wine and cheese parties named after a different book each month. That sounds fun. Cheers! *My* merry band of book lovers, however, can criticize the daylights out of a book. To date, we've discussed some 128 titles and have yet to find a single book that we all held in precisely the same regard.

Imagine, if you will, how things played out when I asked them to critique a book about *them*—my beloved-but-opinionated friends who were traumatized by the very events described within said book. Are you picturing something along the lines of me as a metaphoric sirloin patty that's been dropped into a tank of hungry piranhas? If so, that's not quite right. Out of a complex need to protect one another's feelings and yet assuage our own guilty consciences, it was more along the lines of five underfed piranhas—myself included—trying to simultaneous eat themselves plus one another, along with the aforementioned metaphoric sirloin patty.

The only thing that presented an even greater challenge was when I gave my manuscript to the *sixth* member of the book club—my adult daughter. Fortunately, she handled the matter with grace and maturity. (Because I've bragged about my son's software application and I don't play favorites {which neither of them believe}, I'm joyously announcing that my daughter's singing, dancing, and acting skills have recently led to her being cast in a musical on Broadway! Yet another reason that pseudonyms were required for all concerned.)

Even though it's fair to say that the state of Missouri agrees with the narrative herein, it is also fair to say that an average of two points of significant contention regarding accuracy arose on every single page of this book from one or more of my fellow Boobs. (And, no, the word *Boobs* is not a typo. An explanation can be found in Chapter 1.) Even so, we talked everything through, and the book club remains intact.

A couple of months have passed since everyone in the group was given the opportunity to read and comment on my eighth draft. There will not be a ninth, because one of the members, whose real and fake names shall remain anonymous, threatened to strangle me—and honest to God, at this point, I'd be more than happy to provide a hemp-based (see Chapter 2) rope.

At the onset of the road trip from Boulder, Colorado, to Branson, Missouri, I had envisioned this book as a travelogue. In my capacity as a beta tester for the voice-to-text software, I requested and was granted everyone's verbal permission to record them. I kept the app running on my mini-iPad in my purse, except while recharging it at night, and my purse was usually with me. What none of us knew at the time was that these recordings would be key evidence in a trial.

And so, dear readers (assuming more than one person buys this book), here is what actually (sort of) happened. :) (My last happy face. I promise.)

Chapter 1
Having a Ball...

"Move the catsup bottle, and scoot your chairs closer together," Susan, our book club leader, instructed from the iPad screen at the far end of our restaurant table. "I can't see Abby."

"I'll just lean in front of Leslie whenever I have anything to say," Abby Preston suggested, rising enough to do exactly that and waving at Susan's screen image. I took a deep breath and blew on her wispy, sandy-brown hair. Laughing, Abby said, "Cut that out," and sat back down. After a few moments of adjusting our chairs, the computer, and the catsup, Susan said, "Let's begin."

"You sound like we're commencing a deposition," Jane Henderson teased. (Jane's a lawyer.)

"Well, she *is* wearing a *robe*," I said.

Kate Ryan chuckled. (She's kindhearted and laughs at everyone's jokes.)

"We can call her 'Judge Susan,'" Abby said.

"I'm a little nervous," Susan replied. "It feels weird talking to a screen."

Yesterday morning, Susan Tyler had fallen off her bike at CU Boulder—where she is a professor in American history—while trying to avoid a squirrel on the path. She saved the squirrel, but broke her ankle. Susan was forced to stay home from our group road trip.

Susan grinned. "Okay, Boobs, what's the first thing that hit you as you read Wilder's book?"

"This was my first time reading Laura Ingalls Wilder," I said (jumping right in per usual), "and I was really impressed. I thought it was great when Laura said how disappointed she was that Pa had missed shooting the bear that was trying to eat their pig. And that she loved bear meat. If ever there was a statement about how much times have changed in America, that had to be it."

The waitress did a double take as she passed our table. I gave her a sheepish smile. She'd cleared our plates a few minutes earlier. It was eleven thirty a.m., and this diner in Burlington, Colorado, was less than a third full. I'm sure it was strange to see four thirtyish-looking women jammed shoulder-to-shoulder at one corner of their table, talking at a mini-iPad at the opposite corner. (FYI: Not counting my daughter, Alicia, Kate Ryan is our youngest member at forty-six. The operative word in the previous sentence was "looking." Plus the suffix "ish." And possibly an iamb of poetic license.)

"I liked how Mary got to play with the pig's bladder like a balloon," Kate said. "I loved reading this book again. Wilder's language is just so soothing. It makes me want to cuddle with a child in front of a fireplace and read it aloud."

"So that's two possible activities for us to engage in before we reach Branson," I said. "Provided we can find a store that sells pig bladders. I'm certainly happy to volunteer to fill the role of the child being read to."

"I don't remember anything about a bear and a pig in the book," Jane said. She was a striking-looking woman—tall, athletic, with long, wavy auburn hair—but today her blue eyes lacked their sparkle; she looked like she had a headache. "I must have missed that section when I was speed-reading. I thought the writing was terrible."

"I found her writing style utterly charming," I replied, surprised at Jane's reaction. We typically agreed about the quality of the writing in books, if not the book's plot, characters, theme, and overall quality.

"Oh, dear," Kate said to Jane. "Maybe it was just the childlike tone that didn't appeal to you."

"No...I really think it was the crappy writing."

"So, who was your favorite character?" Susan asked, after glancing down at her notes. (Well-organized people are such a blessing to those of us who can never as much as find the same dedicated loose-leaf notebook twice in a row.) Instead of giving any of us the chance to answer, Susan launched into a lecture about Ma and Pa Ingalls' relationship.

We are the Second Saturday of the Month Book Club, also known as: the Boobs. Nine months ago, in September of last year, Susan had made a typo in our group email. Since then, we would occasionally say something like: "Are we missing any Boobs today?" which led to silly responses such as: "Left boob's here, though she seems a little flat today." I continue to suspect that my fellow Boobs were eager to do anything and everything to cheer me up in the wake of my husband's death, last August. He'd been only 57. I was devastated. We'd had a highly imperfect marriage that worked almost perfectly for us. I wasn't even sure that Susan's "Boob" in the email was unintentional; a deliberate typo a mere month after my loss was in keeping with the wonderful way our club ebbed and flowed. We were well aware of one another's faults, but we were fiercely loyal. In one of our less-than-sober moments at our annual Christmas party, we'd declared our motto to be: *Don't mess with the Boobs, because we've got each other's backs!* There were six of us in the club, counting my adult daughter, who'd joined us seven or eight years ago when she was still in high school. Now that she'd moved to Branson, Missouri, she—rather than Susan—had been the member who attended our meetings via telecommunication.

Our only rules were that the host of that month's meeting led the discussion, which consisted of asking us a couple of book-related questions about the storyline and characters. From there, we'd discuss the book, as well as our childhoods, recipes, jobs, Zumba, spouses, vacations, movies, stain removal, politics, racism, life philosophies, North Korea, God, hair, sports, cavities, gum, plastic wrap, and mascara, which would organically lead us back into an analysis of the author's writing style, and sometimes into my pet rant—new-age writers who refrain from using punctuation. That discussion would then delve into taxi drivers, Uber, grocery stores, insurance rates, allergies, swimsuits, wealth distribution, child rearing, Adele, and coconut oil, then into the reminder about the upcoming month's book club. Finally, while Susan (typically) kicked off our thank-yous to this month's host, Jane would learn, as if for the first time, which book and which hostess was scheduled for next month. Abby, in turn, would promise she'd start reading tomorrow and would complete *next* month's book. Kate would say something sweet and reassuring along the lines that there was no need to apologize, even though (in a typical meeting): 1) Jane vehemently disapproved of our next book choice, 2) Abby had gotten sidetracked from reading last month by the burbling in her condo's plumbing, 3) Kate and Alicia (my daughter) hadn't talked as much as Jane, Susan, or I, and 4) I had eaten more than my fair share of the snacks.

Getting back to *today*'s meeting, however, Susan's current treatise on Ma and Pa had dabbled its toe into the changing role of women's rights and marital relationships in modern times, but then hopscotched into how moved she'd been upon seeing the actual fiddle that Pa played the first time she'd visited the Laura Ingalls Wilder Museum in Mansfield, Missouri (our final destination on our road trip). Susan suddenly broke off and said, "Whoa. I've been rattling endlessly, haven't I? Is the computer still on, or did I break its little speaker?"

"We're still listening," I replied.

"Excellent points, Susan," Kate said. "It's enlightening to hear about husbands and wives relationship from a historical perspective. You're just such an asset in our group." (Kate Ryan is from Kansas, teaches fourth grade, and is a joy to be around. She's also beautiful and has an amazing singing voice. If this book was fictional, I'd never have chosen her to appear within these pages, because she doesn't have any interesting character flaws.)

"I wonder what blind-people's dreams look like," Abby said.

Jane and I exchanged grins. We enjoyed playing hide-and-seek with Abby's non-sequiturs.

"You're thinking of Mary, Laura's blind sister?" Jane asked. "She wasn't blind at birth, so I'm sure her dreams are probably like anyone else's."

"But what about Stevie Wonder?"

"He wasn't in *Little House in the Big Woods*," I quipped. "Stevie makes his first appearance in the Little House book six, doesn't he?"

"*Little House in the Big Woods*?" Jane repeated as if confused, while Abby, speaking over Jane's voice, said, "Stevie Wonder *was* blind at birth. So does he dream about people like we do? With regular faces? Or are their features all blurry?"

"He probably hears lots of music in his dreams," Kate said.

"I kind of like the thought of Stevie lying in bed, hearing 'Isn't She Lovely?' as he sleeps," Abby said wistfully.

"All of us are sighted," Susan said, "so we can't answer that question. Somebody who was born blind but gained sight later in life could probably answer."

"Let's get back to Laura Ingalls," I said. "My favorite character is—"

"I'm going to ask Siri," Abby said.

I put my hand on top of her purse to block access to her cellphone. "Let's get her input later. Siri isn't a Boob." (I'm sorry to say that I can get snarky sometimes, and "Let's ask Siri," is one of my least-favorite phrases. That is, unless I'm driving and need directions, or I've been drinking and am in a jovial mood.) "My favorite character is Laura," I persisted. "It's just so interesting to see how loving and happy about household chores she is, without all of the luxuries and time-savers we have now. She *did* slap Mary for bragging about her blond hair, though. At the same time, I wonder how accurate her story really is. She started writing the books in her middle age, and she's only four or five in the first book."

"She's *four*?" Jane asked. "Geez. No *wonder* none of you are making any sense. I read the wrong book. I thought we were supposed to read the *first* book in the series."

"We *were*. Didn't you read my email?" Susan said, her voice a little testy. "The note in which I reminded all of us to read *Little House in the Big Woods*?"

"'Fraid not. *Mea Culpa*. I just assumed the first book was: '*The First Four Years*,' because of its title. Naturally, I thought that meant the first four years of her life."

"The title refers to the first four years of Laura's marriage to Almonzo," Susan said.

(I resisted my urge to joke that *I* thought she'd married Stevie Wonder.)

"My favorite character is Michael Landon," Abby said. "Or his character, rather. What a cutie he is! His big smile. His gorgeous hair." She sighed as if picturing the actor in front of her.

From the computer screen, Susan was forcing herself not to comment. When Susan committed herself not to say what was on her mind, her mouth became a straight line as she bit both of her lips.

"It was so touching when Mary went blind and everyone was sick," Abby continued. "She had to drag herself across the room to fetch her parents a cup of water."

"That didn't actually happen until book five or so of the series," Kate said. "*On the Shore of Silver Lake.*"

"She went blind on the shore of a lake?" Abby asked earnestly. "I thought it was scarlet fever."

"That's the name of the book."

"It's named *Scarlet Fever*?" (*Authors note*: Abby was much spacier than normal. That said, none of us were pleased with how goofy we sounded when we read our conversation on these pages; we typically get into intelligent, thought-provoking discussions. Months later, after much discussion, our agreed-upon excuse for this particular conversation is: reviewing a children's book put us into juvenile mindsets. On the off chance that we *are,* in fact, a bunch of nitwits, we also agreed to never again record our future meetings.)

Jane started fidgeting—simultaneously stirring her soda with a straw and rocking in her seat.

"Did you *read* the book, Abby?" Susan asked. "Not counting watching old episodes of *Little House on the Prairie*?"

She shook her head. "I ran out of time. I'd forgotten how we'd switched mid-month to *Little House*, from the book about the invisible light."

"*All the Light We Cannot See*," Jane grumbled. "*That* one, I read."

"It was fun to read a children's book for a change," Kate interjected. "I hope we choose to do this again sometime."

When Kate changes topics suddenly, she is sensing hostility. I glanced at the screen and saw that Susan's mouth was once again a lipless line.

"Do your students read the Little House books?" I asked Kate.

"Yes, although early readers can start on them in second or third grade."

"Sorry to interrupt," Abby interrupted, "but I need to go check on Red again." (Red's her dog.)

"Do you still have the car keys?" Kate asked.

"Sure do. Thanks," Abby answered.

"Hang on a sec," Jane said. "I think I left my wallet in the car." She swept up her Coach bag from the back of her chair and strode toward Abby. "But don't let us hold up the discussion."

She and Abby rounded the corner, chatting quietly. Jane's abrupt departure worried me. Had I been talking too much? Or offended Jane somehow? I knew Kate or Susan couldn't be to blame. Most likely, this was mere paranoia on my part. With my husband's death and my daughter's recent long-distance move, my book club *was* my family; I shuddered at the thought of anything jeopardizing our group.

"How much longer will your leg be in the cast?" Kate asked Susan.

"At least two months."

"Are you in pain?" I asked.

"Not at all. I'm on OxyContin. Thanks to the drugs, it barely even bothers me that only the three of us read the book. And that I won't get the chance to see the Laura Ingalls Wilder Museum with you."

"I'll make it up to you as best I can," I said. "I'll not only give you a copy of the printout from the Pocket Stenographer (not the app's real name) so you can read what we talked about, but we'll schedule another Facetime session when we're in Mansfield. I'll carry my iPad with me, facing out, the whole time we're in the museum."

Susan beamed at me. "That's so sweet. Thank you, Leslie."

"Plus, *I'll* text you whenever I think of how much I wish you were with us," Kate offered. "Actually, every tenth time. Otherwise, I'd be texting constantly."

Susan was getting choked up, and *my* kneejerk reaction to emotional moments is to reach for a laugh. "We'll have to insist that you sing 'A Hundred Bottles of Beer on the Wall' while you're driving then, Kate. It'll be unpleasant, but safer than texting while you're behind the wheel." (The operative word this time was *reach*; I'm well aware my remark wasn't funny. Kate chuckled anyway, rather than letting me ruminate about my lame comment.)

"I get emotional easily while I'm on such strong pain killers," Susan said, wiping her eyes. "Tell you what. Instead of texting me when you miss me, how about if you both text me when you see something that reminds you of a book we've read recently? That would be really fun for me."

"Great idea," I said, while Kate, too, expressed her enthusiasm. "Also, Susan, I might have already mentioned this, but even though they don't allow audio recordings at her theater, Alicia told me she thinks she can get permission for me to record a song or two of her and Kurt's performances."

Attending Alicia's performance was the key objective of our road trip. Her boyfriend, Kurt Winston, had taken a Freshman History class from Susan six years ago and became one of her favorite students. With some egging on by Susan, Alicia and Kurt met each other. Their second semester, they wound up getting roles in a student theater production. They fell in love. After graduating from

CU, they'd stayed in Boulder and moved in together. Kurt is from Branson, and his mother had arranged auditions for them for an oldies' show. Ergo, two months ago, they moved to Branson. Wednesday—four days from now—we had primo tickets to their show.

Susan looked at Kate with an inscrutable expression; the two of them had done most of the planning for this trip, including getting us tickets to a couple of other shows. "That'd be great," Susan said. "Fingers crossed." She looked at her watch. "I can see why Alicia struggles a bit now that she's attending meetings only virtually. It definitely feels a little like you're an outcast."

"You're never an outcast to us!" Kate hastened to exclaim.

"Our unusual meeting time today conflicts with Alicia's matinee," I told Susan. "I was hoping to angle two iPads so you two could see and hear each other."

Abby and Jane returned together and reclaimed their seats. I got a whiff of what smelled like alcohol on Jane's breath. I studied her features. She'd had a nasty divorce from a husband over a year ago and was struggling. Recently, I'd tossed a piece of tinfoil into her recyclables and was stunned at the number of empty wine bottles. A prickle of worry ran up my spine.

"Red's fine," Abby said. "He was sound asleep in the driver's seat until I woke him up. It's still nice and cool in the car, with the windows rolled down a little." She gave me a quick hug around the shoulders. "Leslie will be thrilled to hear that I also checked Siri. Basically, blind people's other senses are heightened, so their dreams are about smells and people's voices and the particular sensation of their touch. But they don't have any visuals."

I had no response. The waitress came over and gave us our check, but assured us there was no rush.

"So how was *The First Four Years*?" Abby asked Jane.

"Don't get me started. Twice in a row now I've been forced to read first drafts of books by talented authors who never wanted their manuscripts to be published."

"Laura Wilder didn't want *The First Four Years* to be published?" I asked.

"Nobody *forces* us to read any of the books," Susan pointed out. "But, yes. Laura Ingalls Wilder had already died by the time *The First Four Years* manuscript was discovered, and it was her weakest book, by a wide margin. Some readers think that's because this is the only 'Little House' book her daughter didn't rewrite for her. But others think it's just not as good as the others because it was her first attempt at writing through an adult's eyes, and she might have lost all her enthusiasm by then."

"In reality, it was probably the fault of some money-grubbing agent who found the first draft and published it without anyone's consent," Jane scoffed.

I groaned. (But quietly.) "You promised we weren't going to discuss Harper Lee this week."

Jane shrugged. "At least I didn't say her name."

"But you referred to a 'money-grubbing agent' for the hundredth time since we first put '*Go Set a You-know-what*' on our book list."

Jane spread her arms. "*Somebody* has to stand up for Atticus Finch."

(As you've probably realized, *Go Set a Watchman* was our club's previous book, which Jane had failed to object to when Susan sent the email list of suggested titles for the upcoming six months. As we discovered at last month's meeting, however, Jane's deep admiration for the character Atticus Finch was a major reason she had chosen to enter the field of law in the first place. In Jane's personal opinion, publishing *Go Set a Watchman* was elderly abuse, something she cares about so deeply, she does pro bono legal work for senior citizens in Boulder County.)

"Should we continue our book club meeting," Susan asked, "or are you eager to get to wherever you're staying tonight?"

"Oh, it's no problem. We're less than four hours away from the ball—" Kate stopped, blushing slightly.

"Ooh," I said, with a grin. "The cat's out of the bag. We finally know where we're going for tonight's surprise destination. We're going to the ball, where we can dance with the prince!"

"Goody," Jane said. "I've been brushing up on my Fox Trot!"

"I *meant* to say we're only four hours away from having a ball when we arrive," Kate said.

That made little sense. Puzzled, I studied her attractive features. Kate has what poker players call a "tell." Whenever she lies (next to never) she looks over your shoulder instead of meeting your gaze. Ever since we'd agreed on taking this trip to Branson, she'd spent quite a bit of time glancing over my shoulder.

My cellphone made a noise. I knew the noise signified something other than a phone call, but that's as techno-savvy as I get regarding my phone. I looked at the screen and saw I'd gotten a text from my daughter. After a couple of swipes and screen touches, I was able to read:

Getting ready to go on stage. Can't wait to see you!

So glad you're finally meeting Kurt's dad! Xoxo

"Huh," I muttered. "Alicia says she's happy that I'm going to meet Kurt's divorced father. I sure hope she's not trying to fix us up."

"She probably just wants both families to enjoy each other's company," Kate replied. "Which brings up a good topic for discussion. The Ingalls were pretty isolated. Did you think that they had lonely lives?"

"Not for that time period," I replied, too distracted to elaborate. Kate's vision had been focused over my shoulder when she gave an excuse for Alicia being excited about my meeting Kurt's father.

Chapter 2
...Of Twine

Four hours later, Kate was in the passenger seat, and I was behind the wheel. "How's the doggie?" Abby said in baby-talk tones, turning from her middle-row seat in the van to glance behind her.

At the sound of his master's voice, Red's collar started jingling, and I caught a glimpse of him in the rearview mirror. The mostly terrier mixed-breed had skinny legs and a skinny tail, perky ears, and a cute little pointy head. (*Author's note*: Abby changes this to "pointy ears...perky head" in every draft copy she's read. Although he's clever, in addition to having a terrific disposition, Red's skull is shaped like a dunce cap.)

Afraid Red would hurt himself, I winced as he leapt over the seatbacks and scrambled into Abby's lap, bouncing off Jane's shoulder in the process. "Watch it," Jane grumbled, but with a grin. We all loved the little guy. Even so, with the probable exception of Abby, none of us wanted Red to come on this trip. We'd managed to get last-minute permission for a dog from our B&B in Branson, Missouri, but not from wherever Kate had arranged for us to stay tonight.

"Red's sorry." Chuckling, Abby lifted the dog and bumped him against Jane's shoulder. "Give Jane a kiss, Red," she said, laughing heartily as Red immediately licked Jane's cheek. Jane squirmed away, laughing as well.

"I'm looking forward to seeing Alicia tomorrow," Kate said.

"Me, too," I replied. "Especially to seeing her show." For the countless time, I found myself wondering if Alicia had surreptitiously suggested this trip because she was so worried about my being lonely in my four-bedroom house in Boulder.

"That's going to be the highlight of the trip," Jane said. "But how much farther is it to tonight's surprise lodging?"

"Almost there," Kate said through a big smile.

"You said it's on this road, right?" (I tried to keep my voice from revealing my skepticism, but we seemed to be driving toward Nowhere, USA.) We'd passed a sign that read we were entering a town with just 468 citizens. I wondered if someone headed out to the sign with a Sharpie whenever the town had a birth or a death.

Kate pointed out her window. "There it is!"

"There *what* is?" I asked pulling over and parking. We all rotated in our seats to stare out at the brown blob inside a cabana-like structure a few feet from the sidewalk.

"The ball of twine," Kate said, as if gazing upon the Hope Diamond.

"*That's* what that brown thing is?" Jane asked. "A clump of twine?"

"Yes, and we're staying in the little house across the street," Kate said.

We craned our necks to look out my side of the car at a second square structure, in this case, with adobe walls.

"That's the Ball of Twine Inn. Isn't it darling?"

A pause ensued.

"It's *little*, all right," Abby said. "And kind of run-down." She chuckled. "Leslie can write the *next*

Laura Wilder book: *The Little House Opposite the Twine.*"

"Don't mock our lodging," Kate said cheerfully. "This is fun. Trust me. I'm from Kansas. I know all the hot spots."

We got out of the car and reassembled at the sidewalk, where we stood and stared at the ball for several seconds. Last week, when Kate had told us we were in for a real treat, I had envisioned a fancy hotel with a spa. I'd anticipated spending this evening with my closest friends, all of us clad in soft, luxurious robes, with soothing background music and glorious lavender-scented air, as we sipped chilled champagne and awaited our turns for our massage. Instead, I'd been presented with an impractically enormous roundish heap of icky, brown twine and a ramshackle "inn" on the side of a noisy road.

My need to adjust my expectations brought to mind a charming novel we'd read a year or so ago. I grabbed my cellphone and snapped a photo, texting to Susan:

"This *is Kate's surprise. Tantamount to:* The Unlikely Pilgrimage of Harold Fry."

My texting skills were too cruddy to expound on the matter, but imagining a luxury spa and getting The Ball of Twine Inn struck me as unlikely as how Harold left his house to mail a letter and wound up walking across England to hand-deliver it.

I glanced at Jane, who was shaking with suppressed laughter. Abby, too, was giggling up a storm. The sight made me smile. Kate led the way to the twine ball, and we followed.

"It's more a dome than a ball," Abby noted. Suddenly, she gave a happy little hop. "Hey! This could be my next business venture! I could go town to town, encouraging communities to start their own balls of used items. Like old balloons! I heard that one animal dies for every helium balloon that you release. I guess they tend to accidentally eat the popped balloons."

"How would doing that earn you any money?" Jane asked.

"Maybe the EPA would pay me for every burst balloon I collect."

"Why do you need a new business venture?" I asked. "I thought you started working part-time in the bakery section at King Soopers."

"I am, but now I'm spending too much of my earnings on buying the products I'm selling. I want to do something that gets me some exercise. Do you think I should maybe invest in a herd of goats instead? For landscaping?"

Not knowing how to begin to answer, I looked at Kate and Jane. They avoided my gaze. "I don't know anything about goats, although I'm willing to bet they shouldn't be fed balloons. But how about if you ask Susan instead of Siri? That way she'll feel included."

"Plus, Susan's a Boob!" Abby declared.

"And maybe even a goat lover," I said. (She *wasn't*, but with Susan's affection for research, we could be reasonably assured she would happily send Abby a Profit-and-Loss analysis and city codes pertaining to herds of goats.)

A car came to a screeching stop behind ours. A pair of young men emerged and ambled toward us. They both wore sandals, baggy shorts, T-shirts, and sunglasses. "Oh, man," one of them cried, pointing at the Kate's license plates. "Colorado. Is that where y'all are from?"

"Yes, we are," Karen said with a big grin.

"My name's Jim. Jimmie to friends." He had a slight southern accent. He rocked on the balls of his feet and maintained his huge smile. "And this here is Marcus. Guess where we just now drove from."

"Missouri?" Jane immediately replied, playing dumb; they obviously meant Colorado.

"Nope. Colorado," Marcus said. "But that's where we live. Missouri."

"And that's exactly where *we* are all heading tomorrow," Karen announced. "We're going to Branson. That's where Leslie's daughter is working. She's in a musical revue. She's a very talented actress and singer."

Jimmie was eyeing the ball of twine. In a dreamy voice, he said, "I wish this whole ball was made of marijuana, so we could light it up and breathe it in."

"You got any pot with you?" Marcus asked us.

"No, we do not," Jane said. "It's illegal to bring marijuana across state lines."

"That reminds me," Abby said. "Red is probably baking in the car by now." (Abby was a single divorcee with two adult sons who'd moved to Alaska. She loved her little dog as if he was her child.)

"Does she mean Acapulco Red?" Marcus asked Jimmie in reverential tones. He gave Jane a salute. "We will remove any and all not-Kansas-approved substances from your possession and dispose of it in a safe manner. No questions asked."

"*I* have a question. How old are you?" Jane asked, watching as Red galloped toward us, followed by Abby. Red was pulling so hard on his leash he was having a hard time keeping his front paws on the ground.

"Twenty-two," Marcus said, just as Jimmie was saying "Twenty-three."

"Dude!" Jimmie said, swatting Marcus. "'Red' must be the name of that dog."

"Bummer."

Across the street, an elderly woman was peering at the six of us below the brim of a hat that looked as if the fabric was originally a well-worn pair of blue jeans. She was ever-so-slowly walking past us on the opposite sidewalk. "Maybe that's the inn's owner there." I pointed with my chin.

Just then, Red lifted his leg and began to pee on the ball of twine.

"Oh, geez, Red!" Abby cried, sweeping up his skinny little frame and rotating in a half circle. His yellow spray formed an impressive arch in the air that was actually rather attractive, if you didn't know it was urine. The denim-hatted woman stopped in her tracks, arching her brow as if in surprise or indignation at Red. She eyed Kate's minivan and each of our faces, then she picked up her pace and turned the corner.

"That woman didn't look happy with us," Kate said. "I'm glad she wasn't the owner of the inn. She's supposed to meet us here."

"Unless the woman *is* the owner, and Red piddling made her decide not to rent to us," Abby said.

I continued to stare after the woman. "She looks familiar. I feel like I've seen a photograph of her recently."

"Let's hope it wasn't on a 'wanted' sign in the post office," Jane said. "She gave us quite the murderous look just now."

I texted Susan again.

Saw an old woman who reminds me of a book or movie, but can't place it. "Driving Miss Daisy," maybe.

Chapter 3
No Dogs at the Inn

While I was texting, a white pickup truck pulled up to the curb. The driver—a pleasant looking woman with brown, curly hair—rolled down the passenger-side window. "Welcome to Cawker City. I'm Patty Parker. Is one of you Kate Ryan?"

"That's me," Kate said, flashing her lovely smile.

"Wonderful! The beds are already made up for you." She emerged from her truck and looked at us, just as Jimmie and Marcus were taking photos of each other in the lotus position in front of the ball. "There aren't *six* of you wanting to stay at the inn tonight, are there?"

"Nah. We're not with them," Marcus said. "We just share a mutual appreciation for hemp." Again, they started laughing.

Just as I was about to grumble that Marcus should speak for himself, I realized that we often made a hemp-protein smoothie for breakfast. Susan had supplied the recipe at one meeting, and we had all become converts. (Not to interrupt my narrative, but I recommend it highly, and there's bound to be a recipe online.)

After a momentary pause, Patty replied cheerfully, "I'm so glad. Would you all like to add a length of twine to our ball?"

"Oh, absolutely," Kate replied, beaming. "Let's let Leslie go first."

Explaining that she kept track of the length of twine on the ball by measuring how much twine she had on her spool, she brought me a makeshift spool of twine that was at least two feet in diameter. The two young men, meanwhile, took seats on the nearby bench and declined the chance to add twine—or to sign the guestbook. I dutifully tied the end of Patty's twine onto an existing strand, and walked around the ball. Granted, adding to the twine ball was not like giving birth or getting a book published, but it had made my day. I passed the spool to Abby.

"Could I try to put my loop of string on the diagonal, so I can recognize it in the morning?" Abby asked Patty.

"If you'd like," Patty replied.

"Hey! I got an idea," Jimmie called out. "Tonight we can sit on top of the ball and party."

"As much as sitting on top of a large, round object sounds like a fun activity," Patty said pleasantly, despite her features tensing noticeably, "please do not climb on our twine ball. Your steps as you scramble up cause the twine to fall down."

"This ball of twine is just such a nice gift to the world," Kate said, ever finding the bright side to divert attention from a grievance. We'd yet to read a single book that she considered unworthy of considerable praise. Not even last month's original version (or "grandfather," as Harper Lee was quoted as calling it) of *To Kill a Mockingbird.*

Kate struck up a conversation with Patty about her Kansas roots. With some effort Abby completed her diagonal loop, and tried to put a couple of unique kinks in it before passing the spool to Kate. Kate and Patty continued to chat, with Patty strolling around the ball of twine with her.

"*All* towns really should do this," Abby said, "featuring materials that can't be easily recycled. *Including* used balloons. We could poke out the plastic on the windows of envelopes and spaghetti boxes and...crumple them together, maybe."

"That would leave us with a mound of envelope-window plastic," Jane said. "How would that be any different than the city dump?"

"Maybe we could melt down the envelope windows and form a sculpture of a unicorn," Abby suggested.

When Kate and Patty returned from circling the ball, Kate insisted on picking up the entire tab for our night's lodging and paid Patty Parker in cash. After pocketing the money, Patty gave Red a long look.

"My ex-husband was supposed to be watching my dog," Abby explained, "then he flaked out at the last minute, and I didn't have enough time to find an alternative dog-sitter. But, I don't plan to stay inside the Ball of Twine Inn. I'm going to keep my little buddy in the van with me. We go car-camping all the time, and he's very used to it."

"I live just a couple of blocks away," Patty said. "I'd be willing to board your dog there, if you'd like. It's just that the very next guests at the inn could be allergic."

"Oh, I understand," Abby replied. "We'll be perfectly comfortable sleeping in the van. Red needs to stay near me, is all, or he gets scared." (The reverse was true. Red has stayed at my house a few times. Abby had nightmares and was always shaky when she first arrived to collect him.)

"His name is '*Red*?'" Patty asked.

As if sensing a kindred spirit, Abby grinned. "He's named after the children's classic: *A Dog Named Red.*"

Patty matched her smile. "What a fun coincidence! The author of that book lives here in town!"

"Eugena Crowder lives here?" Abby and I cried in unison. Kate gasped in happy surprise, as well.

"That's the rumor, at least," Patty said. "The woman claims her name is Jean Smith. But we're all pretty sure it's really Eugena Crowder. We have a population of under five-hundred souls here, so we tend to know one another's business."

"Tell me everything," Abby cried. "I'm dying to hear all about Eugena Crowder. So is Red." She lifted him to eye-level and said to his furry face, "This woman knows the creator of your namesake!"

"How about if I tell you the story while I show you around the property?"

We eagerly agreed. Abby asked me for the keys so she could find a shady spot to lock Red in the car. Jimmie and Marcus were now lying supine on the lawn, grinning up at the sky. They gave us a wave and called out that it was nice meeting us, which we reciprocated. Patty, Kate, and I headed across the street. Jane paused long enough to exchange a few words with the young men, then trotted after us. (I suspected she was warning them that they were too obviously high to be driving.)

The house consisted of one bedroom, one bathroom, a kitchen, and a catchall room with bunk beds and a sleeper sofa. It was quaint and comfy—a well-seasoned bungalow with lots of little paintings from local artists on the walls. Patty gave us instructions about keys, the contents of the refrigerator, and details about what we needed to during our departure in the morning. Afterward, Jane said, "So tell us about this mysterious 'Jean Smith.'"

Abby came trotting through the door just then. "Wait. I don't want to miss a word."

Patty, Abby, Kate, and Jane settled into chairs at the kitchen table. I insisted I preferred to stay standing after the long drive. (I was just saying that to be gracious, which doesn't happen often enough.)

"Well, a 'Jean Smith' got a six-month rental on a house here in Cawker," Patty began. "Millie, who owns the hair salon and the auto-parts store, said her seven-year-old son saw her typing away at her computer through the window. Millie dragged out of her son that he'd spooked the lady when she shouted at her to ask what she was writing. That boy is something of a Dennis the Menace. I caught him tinkling on the ball of twine last year, and I doubt that was the only time he's done it. Anyway, Millie went over to apologize for her son pestering the woman. While they were talking, she spotted the 'Red' book beside the computer. Millie started saying how much she loved that book. The woman snarled, 'You and two-million *other* grown children. If you'll excuse me, I need to get back to giving the public what it wants.'"

"Is she an elderly woman? Short, thin, and a little stooped over?" I asked, all but breathless at the possibility that a literary idol of mine was nearby. "And does she wear a wide-brimmed hat, made from denim?"

"Yes, that's her," Patty said with a big smile. "She walks past here all the time—into downtown and back. Sometimes two or three times a day. I try to draw her into conversation but...the woman is just not chatty."

"I'll bet she's finally writing a sequel," Abby said, squeezing Kate's arm in excitement.

"Or maybe it's some copycat who thinks she can profit from reproducing Eugena Crowder's story," Jane said. "All she'll need to succeed is a crooked agent."

I rolled my eyes. (But quickly.)

"Right before you arrived," Abby told Patty, "Leslie had been saying the woman looked familiar to her."

"She became a loner after her first adult novel bombed," I said. "And then she followed that book by publishing a second novel, which turned out to have been plagiarized."

"Oh, my," Patty exclaimed. "That's terrible."

I nodded. "I've read a lot of articles about her. I use the opening chapter of *A Dog Named Red* in my composition classes. I teach at a junior college outside of Boulder."

"I read the opening chapter to my fourth-grade students almost every year," Kate said. "It's a wonderful book for reluctant readers." She gave me a sad smile. "I'm going to text the leader of our book club," she told Patty. "She's a history buff, and Ms. Crowder's book is set in the late fifties, when we still had a subculture of hobos...as we used to call the homeless...riding the rails."

"Has anyone *asked* Jean Smith if she was Eugena Crowder?" I asked Patty.

"Millie did. She brought over a couple of zucchinis and tomatoes, along with her son's copy of the book, and asked if she'd sign it. She answered that her name was Jean Smith, so she didn't see the sense in signing Eugena Crowder's book. She suggested Millie should ask some *other* stranger to sign it."

"Technically, that's not a denial," Jane noted. "The name 'Jean Smith' could be a pseudonym."

"I would *so* love to meet her," Abby said. "I worship that book."

"I'd like to meet her, too," Jane said. "I don't understand the motive behind a successful author stealing from somebody else's work."

"You want to be a vigilante of the publishing world." Although I based my pronouncement on Jane's fervent lecture on plagiarism at last month's meeting, my timing was inappropriate and brought the conversation to an abrupt halt. Embarrassed, I said to Patty the first thing that popped into my head: "You probably get ribbed a lot about your twine ball, don't you?"

"Quite often. But we don't mind. We're having fun with our ball of twine, and that's what matters." She rose. "I should get going. You might enjoy taking a walk around the town and checking out the ball-of-twine artwork."

"Artwork?" I asked, envisioning miniature statues made of twine. (Maybe of a unicorn, which would make Abby happy.)

"We have copies of famous paintings in the store windows, which have been enhanced by the addition of a ball of twine," Patty said.

"Oh, wow," I replied. It *was* easy to smile about a ball of twine. (Although, truth be told, a luxurious spa would have made my smile even wider.)

"Feel free to call if anything came up or you have any questions," she called over her shoulder as she left.

The instant the door closed behind Patty, Abby took a couple of joyous hops. "See? I *told* you it was the real Eugena Crowder. Right here in Cawker City," Abby said in a sing-song voice.

"We don't know for certain if Jean Smith and Eugena Crowder are one and the same," Kate said.

"My gut tells me they are," Abby replied. "I want to stay here long enough that we can meet her, before we head to Branson."

"We have to be in Branson by seven p.m. tomorrow," Jane countered. "It'll feel an hour earlier than that because we'll switch time zones. Plus, you'll probably have been sleeping in the car all night and will be dying to get to our B and B to spread out a little."

"Leslie? Kate? *You* know how wonderful a book Red's namesake is. You want to meet the author, too, don't you?"

"I'd *love* to, but I'm not going to knock on the woman's door," I said. "If she felt like tooting her own horn about the book, she'd have told this Millie person that she was indeed Eugena Crowder."

"Leslie's right. I don't want to intrude on her," Kate said.

Abby sighed. "Fine. We won't go knocking on doors, but we can comb the neighborhood and see if Red can spot Eugena. Or vice versa."

"*If* Jean Smith and Eugena Crowder are one and the same," Jane grumbled.

"They *are*," I said, my memory connecting a couple of dots. "Her nickname in the book is 'M.J.' because her schoolmates used to call her 'Mean Jean.'"

"But that—" Jane began to scoff.

"She used to hand sew her own clothing from scraps. Including a hat she made from her dad's old denim overalls."

Chapter 4
Vino Veritas Vamoose

Jane and I began a spirited discussion regarding Eugena Crowder's hat while we unpacked a few things for our overnight stay. (She and I were sharing the queen bed in the one designated bedroom.) Jane noted that if Eugena wanted to go unrecognized, she wouldn't wear M.J.'s signature hat. I felt that only indicated she was torn between wanting recognition and not wanting to be interrupted.

"Are we almost ready for a stroll downtown?" Kate called out before Jane could further the argument.

"Do you suppose we're *uptown* here at the inn?" I called back.

Jane promptly started singing Billy Joel's *Uptown Girl.* Abby and I joined in, and, with a little coaxing, so did Kate. Her beautiful soprano voice energized us. We added some choreography (two grapevine steps to the right with a kick, two to the left with a kick). Though we were hardly the Rockettes, we were in high spirits as we walked three blocks to the center of Cawker City, Kansas.

The artwork—juvenile-looking acrylic-on-cardboard paintings—was indeed in many of the shop windows. Although they weren't hard to locate,

Kate and I agreed that we felt the joy of an Easter egg hunt as we spotted each painting.

"This is all so silly and fun," Kate said.

"It's certainly *silly*," Jane replied, now looking less than enchanted. She was rubbing at her temples as if she had another headache.

After examining the last painting on display, we took a vote on which painting was the best. In typical Boob-club style, four paintings got one vote apiece. I voted for the "Mona Lisa," although I also liked "The Scream," "The Last Supper," and "Starry Night." (In retrospect, I wish I'd voted for the "The Scream." That particular painting used its ball of twine to the best advantage: it provided an explanation for the subject's terror. If I was being chased by a large ball of twine, I'd scream, too. Plus, if we'd had psychic powers, *all* of us would have felt that particular painting was eerily apropos.)

Abby suddenly stamped her foot. "I was certain we'd see Eugena by now!" She looked at me. "Remember that scene in her book when Red was tracking M.J. and followed her everywhere?"

"Yes, but the circumstances are very different. The original Red was a malnourished stray, so hitting on M.J. was his best hope to be fed."

"I know *my* Red wasn't actually *her* Red, but still." She shrugged. "It all felt like destiny. You know? We're here on a quest with our reading group, and Red's here, and my favorite-book's author's here...."

"It's not really a *quest*," I said. "We're mostly just going on a road trip to watch my daughter sing and dance...which Alicia herself says is kind of cheesy." Abby looked a little hurt, so I added, "This whole trip is really fun, and I'm grateful and flattered that everyone was so eager to do this, but it's not exactly the Holy Grail."

"Abby?" Kate said. "Should I call Patty and ask for Jean Smith's address?"

"I don't think so. We'd be putting Patty on the spot. She might feel bad that she told us about the woman who wanted Eugena to sign a book. There we'd be, knocking on Eugena's door, already knowing she's using an alias."

"I'll tell you what," Kate said, her demeanor brightening. "I haven't made the reservations yet for our Kansas surprise during our *return* drive from Missouri."

(I wondered what our second "Kansas surprise" would be. The Oz Museum? The world's largest octagon made with pipe-cleaners?)

"Let's see how we all feel in another week," Kate continued, "when we're leaving Branson. We can always opt to return to Cawker City. I'll talk to Patty, ask for Jean Smith's address, and assure her that we'll take care to honor Ms. Smith's privacy."

"Perfect!" Jane said. Her enthusiasm restored, she picked up Red. "We'll meet your Story God Mother yet, you good boy!" She set Red back down. "I don't know what to do with Red, though. I could bring his carrier, but they'll probably say it's against health regulations or something."

"When we go out to dinner tonight, you mean?" I asked.

She nodded.

"We can call around to find a dog-friendly restaurant," Kate suggested, "and if they say no, I'll come back to the inn with you, and we'll make dinner."

***

There were only two restaurants in Cawker City. One of them was closed. We called the other one and got permission to bring Red in his carrier. The four of us bipeds turned out to be the only patrons. A heavy-set young man with ruddy cheeks was watching the TV behind the bar and greeted us with: "Finally some people!" He glanced at Red's dog carrier that Abby had lugged with us. "You must be the lady who called me about her dog."

"Yes, I am. I'm Abby, and this is Red."

"As long as we're the only ones here, y'all don't need the cage. Just keep him under the table on his leash."

"Wonderful! Thank you so much, Bill!"

"Name's 'Bob.' You can take the big booth in the back corner." He gestured with his chin.

(*Author's note*: Cawker City, Kansas, *is* a real place and, at this point in time, still appears to only have the one restaurant. The one-man bartender, cook, maître d', busboy, and waiter was a nice guy. His real name is neither Bill nor Bob. I can report that our meals were inexpensive, cooked and served at appropriate temperatures, and tasted fine, although their menu is restrictive for vegans. {Susan is our only vegan.} I should also note that their beef patties, fortunately for me, were nice and tender. I'd taken the risk of ordering a burger, despite being only partway into getting an implant. My incisor was glued in place. My dentist had told me not to bite into meat, but I decided "ground" meat shouldn't apply.)

***

We are now jumping ahead to the end of our dining experience. The only notable interaction you've missed is that three of us ordered wine (Kate doesn't drink), and our options were: red or white. Unfortunately, *Red*, located himself directly under my chair (possibly after deducing his best odds of spillage), and believed we were calling for him whenever one of us ordered "red." He would leap up and bump his head on the bottom of my chair every single time. I was getting more and more worried about his cone-shaped noggin, which in my imagination, was growing like Pinocchio's nose every time the poor little guy's head hit the table on the same bruised spot.

Jane was lifting her empty glass, trying to get Bob's attention yet again.

"For the love of God, Jane," I cried. "Stop ordering wine! Or switch to white! Both you and the poor dog are going to be knocked unconscious at this rate!"

Jane stared at me, seemingly stunned at my outburst.

"Well? You've already had four glasses! Both the dog and I are counting!"

"We're all ready to go," Kate said. "Let's head back to the inn."

"Come, Red," Abby called.

I winced as he bonked his head on my seat yet again. "Keeping Red under a glass coffee table could be lethal," I grumbled.

Jane snorted. "I forgot what stick-in-the-muds you people are. But by all means, let's go back and get into our little beds. It's not a problem," Jane said in a voice that made it crystal clear it was very much a problem.

Bob must have overheard. He rushed to our table. Jane snatched the check from his hand and snarled, "My treat." She handed him cash and said gruffly, "Keep the change."

"Thank you, ma'am," he said, "Y'all have a great evening now."

"Thank *you* for the excellent service," Kate replied.

The rest of us left in an awkward silence, save for Red, who was yipping and tugging at his leash as if to challenge us to a footrace back to the inn.

"We can chat about books with our jammies on," Kate suggested. "We all read '*The Light We Cannot See*' before we switched to Laura Ingalls Wilder, right?"

"Ooh," I said. "That's a great idea! I think Anthony Doerr is going to prove to be the greatest writer of our generation. Which is not to say that I know what generation he belongs too, but I think we were born within the same decade."

"I'll ask Siri," Abby said. She smiled and winked at me. "It seems too late to bug Susan."

I rolled my eyes, but my lone glass of wine had mellowed me into not commenting.

A moment later Abby spoke into her phone in her tented hand to ask the man's birth year, then said to us, "1973."

"There you go," I said, trying to distract myself from Jane's laser-like glares. "He and I were school kids at the same time. I'd have been in high school while he was in grade school, but no sense splitting hairs. We get to claim a breathtakingly good writer as coming from our generation." I lifted my hand, and Kate gave me a high five.

"Oh, good," Kate exclaimed. "I'm so glad you enjoyed the book. I loved it, as well."

"Are you up for a second book-club meeting in the same day, Jane?" I asked.

To my relief, she'd regained her equanimity. "Sure, but I really liked the book, and so did the two of you, which is unfortunate."

"It is?"

"I want to hang on to my righteous anger for a while."

"You poor dear," I teased, patting her shoulder.

"The one time we agree on a book, and it has to be when I'm in the mood to pick an argument."

"I've only read the first half," Abby said, "but it's okay by me if you wind up spoiling the ending by talking about the second half."

"Oh, good," I said. "I have a lot to say about the ending, which is the one aspect that didn't work for me."

"I *loved* the ending," Kate said.

"There you have it, Jane. Different opinions."

"Well, so far, I'm just not into this book at all," Abby said. "I can't see what the fuss is about."

"By fuss, you mean his winning the *Pulitzer*?" I snapped. (What an annoying little literary snob I can be!)

"Doerr did?" Abby asked. "Really? Or do-er didn't? Get it?"

Ignoring her wanna-be pun, I said, "*All the Light We Cannot See* won the Pulitzer in 2013."

Jane grinned. "Yes! This is precisely the type of conversation I want to be involved in right now! Arguing about the worthiness of a World War Two epic novel about a blind French girl and a bright, underprivileged Nazi teenager."

"It's a shoo-in for a best-film Oscar," I added.

"I wish we could Facetime Susan for our discussion," Kate said. "She told us she expected to be sound asleep by seven, though. "By the way, Jane, she told me she had mixed feelings about *All the Light We Cannot See*."

"Did she mention the ending being anticlimactic and feeling tacked on?" I asked.

"No, just that she had mixed feelings."

I indulged my literary narcissism by thinking that *Susan* must surely agree with me about the loss of momentum in the final chapters. With Abby and Kate engaged in their own conversation, Jane said quietly, "It's not like I'm an alcoholic or anything, Leslie. I just like wine. A lot."

"But tonight's wine was awful. Yet you kept ordering, even so. Doesn't that mean you might have an addiction?"

"No. In this case, all it means is that I after the first glass, it started tasting pretty good."

I was skeptical and gave no reply. I kept replaying the vision of the dozens and dozens of empty wine bottles I'd seen in her recycle bin. The short stack of our local daily newspapers beside it led me to think the wine had been consumed within the last two weeks.

We had a fairly typical book-club meeting. Kate, Jane, and I lauded Doerr's lyrical writing style. (Abby called it "overblown.") Also his astonishingly well-drawn characters and the feat of making his young Nazi character so sympathetic. (Abby said she didn't find him physically attractive in her mind's eye, which caused a fork—with a very long tine—in our discussion.) We also disagreed at length about Doerr's choices regarding the romantic elements of the book.

Later, Jane and I indulged in a lovely ritual we'd developed over the years—each of us choosing and reading aloud our favorite paragraph in the book. (Last month, when discussing *Go Set a Watchman*, I'd passed. Jane had turned to the final page and read, "*The End.*")

To my relief, Jane drank only water throughout our book discussion. Meanwhile, Abby happily left us early to sleep in the roomy minivan with Red. She wanted to be sure to be with him by nine thirty, in case Red started howling, which he never did.

None of us detected anything out of the ordinary regarding Jane. We all expected her to still be in the inn with us when we awoke.

Chapter 5
A Dognapping

The following morning, I was vaguely aware that others were awake and rummaging about. I was experiencing a problem that had become all too familiar. I would awaken and think that my husband must already be up and walking the dog. My eyes would then fly open, and I'd remember that he was dead, and so was Bosco, who'd died just three months before my husband, Jack. A wave of panic would hit me. The thought: *I can't do this*, pounded its way into my brain. Next I would begin to feel as though I couldn't breathe.

Jack had had a sudden, massive cardiac arrest while jogging. (He'd replaced his daily walks with Bosco with strenuous morning jogs.) I'd given him a Fitbit for his birthday, but he didn't like wearing it. Or carrying his cellphone in his pocket. Maybe his having known what his pulse rate was on that final jog wouldn't have mattered. Maybe help wouldn't have arrived in time, even if he'd been able to call 911. Maybe I still would have flown into a rage and smashed both his cellphone and his Fitbit into not-so-fit bitty bits in the wee hours of the morning, three days after his service. My poor daughter, who'd temporarily moved back home, found me sobbing uncontrollably in her father's basement workshop, smashing even the smallest pieces into dust. (Normally she sleeps like a log, and her bedroom was on the second floor. It is perhaps a universal truth of motherhood that we will worry about our children's happiness to the ends of the earth, yet are ashamed to cause them to worry about *our* happiness.)

After an agonizing minute or two passed, I managed to steel myself. I told myself that I was in Cawker City, with my dearest friends. And I assured myself it would be okay. That I could get out of bed. That I could appreciate the day. That I just needed another minute or two to collect myself—from wherever the pieces of my heart and soul had gone in search of Jack and Bosco while I slept.

"I needed that nice shower," Abby said to someone in the kitchen.

"I hope you're not all achy from sleeping in the minivan." (Kate's voice.)

"Not at all."

"Are you sure?" Kate asked. "I know we used to biff the butter...." (That's undoubtedly a misquote, but the Pocket Steno app wasn't running because my iPad was recharging, and that's what I remember thinking she'd replied as I nodded out once again.)

I snapped awake as Abby bolted into the room. Abby scanned our surroundings, frantic. "Have you seen Red, Leslie?"

"No. He isn't with you?" I jumped out of bed.

"No!" Abby was starting to cry. "Somebody opened the car door and stole him!"

"Jane must have him with her," Kate said, following Abby into the room.

"Didn't she sleep here?" I felt her side of the bed. The lumps that I'd assumed were Jane were just two pillows under the cover. "The sheets are cold on her side."

"Oh, dear," Kate said. "I heard her leaving last night, around midnight. She said she wasn't tired yet, and that she was going to stare at the ball of twine and see if that could put her to sleep. I just assumed she'd returned and both of you were still asleep."

I squeezed past the two of them, entered the kitchen, and looked out the front window. There were no cars, and no sign of Jane or Red. Kate and Abby followed me.

"The car's parked on the road behind the inn," Abby told me, "where it's quieter."

"Jane must have taken Red for a walk while you were still in the shower," Kate said.

"No way. She'd *know* I would panic. She'd have told one of us she was taking Red on a walk." Abby grabbed her cellphone with shaky hands. "I'm calling nine-one-one."

"Red probably *is* with Jane," I said, but moments later, Abby cried into the phone, "Somebody stole my dog last night!"

I very much understood her immediate panic, but with Jane also missing, it seemed so logical to me that they were together. "She had four large glasses of lousy wine last night. She might be hungover and didn't feel up to talking."

My statement gave Abby pause, but then she resumed speaking into the phone, expanding about our location, as well as the now-empty car's location.

Within a minute or two, with Abby still talking to the dispatcher, someone knocked loudly. Closest to the front window, I pulled back the curtain. "It's a police officer."

"That was incredibly fast!" Kate said, opening the door.

"Never mind," Abby said into the phone. "The police are already here." She stashed her cellphone in her pocket and raced to the door. "Thank you so much for coming. I've been worried sick."

The officer scrunched up his eyebrows as if puzzled. "I'm a one-man police force, I'm afraid. It's a small town."

"You're very efficient," Abby replied. "And we'll all help you search."

"There must be a misunderstanding. I'm Officer Roberts. Someone called in a complaint of vagrancy this morning."

"Because I was sleeping in my car?" Abby asked. "Is there a law against that?"

"Not for an overnight stay, no. But that doesn't extend to sleeping on public property."

"I wasn't *on* public property," Abby said, already impatient and growing more so by the moment. "I was in my *car*. Well, Kate Ryan's car. But did you find my dog yet?"

"Your dog?"

"Yes! My dog! That's what I was calling about. Someone took him out of my car. Kate's car, I mean. They must have been watching me, because it happened while I was in here...using the facilities."

"We're hoping he's with our friend, Jane Henderson, who isn't here right now," I explained.

"Yes, I am," Jane called from somewhere outside, behind the officer.

"She said she had an upset stomach and needed air," he explained, stepping aside. Kate and I promptly poked our heads out the doorway. Jane was leaning against the side of the house, her features wan.

"I'm feeling better now," she said, giving us a wave.

"I found her passed out on top of the ball of twine," Officer Roberts explained.

"It's highly therapeutic," Jane said. "Sleeping on a round object, I mean. My back hasn't felt this good in years."

"Is Red with you?" Abby called to Jane.

"Maybe he's sniffing around in the back yard."

"He's *not* out back, Jane! I already checked!"

"She'd frightened off a family of four just as I arrived," the officer continued, ignoring Abby and Jane's conversation.

"Not intentionally," Jane grumbled.

"They were afraid you were *dead*," he grumbled back at her. He faced me and waggled his thumb in Jane's direction. "I should give her a citation for loitering...if not vagrancy, but I already checked with the owner of the inn, and she assured me that you're in town only the one night."

"Thank you, Officer," I said. "We're leaving within the hour."

"Not until we find Red," Abby snapped.

"I'm so sorry, Abby. I didn't forget about Red. I just meant—"

"He's been stolen," Abby said to Officer Roberts. "Right from our car. But please don't give me a citation! I'd only left him alone for twenty minutes, and all the windows are rolled down a couple of inches. Plus we're parked in the shade, so it's perfectly comfortable, temperature-wise."

"That's not a problem, but I—"

"Can you help us look?" Abby said. "Put out an APB? I've got a photo of him in my wallet."

"Just give me a general description, ma'am, and I'll take a quick drive through the area." He glanced at his watch.

"I can do *that* myself," Abby said, "but I need *you* to find suspected dog-nappers in the area and to arrest him or her."

"It's probably just a little kid," I said.

"A little kid who knows how to break into locked cars?" she fired back. "It's a juvenile delinquent, in that case!"

"Ma'am, give me the number of your cellphone, and I'll see if I can come up with...Red for you."

She gave him her number, then said, "He's super cute, brownish-red with white patches, perky ears, skinny legs, and weighs twenty-eight pounds. Anyone who sees him would want to own him." Her lip started to quiver. "I don't know what I'll do if we—"

(I was trying to signal the officer about Red's pointy head by mouthing *"He has a pointy head"* to him while forming a cone-shape with my hands. Having said the wrong thing just moments ago, I didn't want to upset Abby again, but it *was* a distinguishing feature.)

"Let's get moving, Boobs," Jane interrupted—ignoring the officer's puzzled double-take at her use of our odd pet-name. "First we'll take a drive through the immediate neighborhood. If that doesn't work, we'll bring up a map of Cawker on our cellphones. We'll each take a quadrant, and knock on every door. With this low of a population, we're likely talking about less than sixty doors apiece."

"Ooh," Abby said. "I'll email all of you a photo of Red, so you can show it to the homeowners, and get them on the lookout. Do you want me to send you Red's photo, too, Officer Roberts?"

"I've been married long enough to know when she and her gal friends get an idea, best to stay out of their way." He reached into his pocket and pulled out a couple of business cards. He gave one to Abby and another to Kate, saying, "I'll talk to the folks in the vicinity of your car. Just call me when you find him."

"Assuming we *do*," Abby whimpered.

He started to head back to his patrol car, parked alongside the ball of twine, but hesitated as he met Jane's gaze. "Could I have a word with you, ma'am, in private?"

Jane tugged on the hem of her blouse and smoothed back one side of her hair. "Um, sure." She was already regaining some color in her face. Her

fairly quick recovery only deepened my concern.
This might be a regular routine she'd gotten into—
getting plastered every night and rallying in the
morning. She stepped toward the officer, and he
gestured for her to follow him to his patrol car.

"I hope he isn't going to give Jane a citation
after all," Kate said.

"He's probably just trying to convince her to get
help," I said.

"For her alcohol addiction?" Kate asked. "Let's
hope so. Sometimes it's easier when advice like that
comes from an outside source. Believe me."

I stared at Kate in surprise, wondering if she
meant she had firsthand knowledge. The concept of
her having once had a drinking problem was
bizarre. Maybe her husband had been a heavy
drinker.

"Jane's fine," Abby said. "We need to get going!
I've still got the keys. I'll drive around to the front."
She trotted out the door.

"Let's start by contacting Patty," I said. "She'd
be the best source of information about the
townspeople, and she said she lives just two blocks
away. Maybe she even took Red for some...altruistic
reason."

"I've got her contact information on my cell,"
Kate said. "Let me grab that."

I made a bathroom pit stop. Thinking that it
could be useful for us to recheck where we'd been
and what we'd seen, I turned on the app. Then I
grabbed both Jane's and my own purses.

By the time I emerged from the house, Kate was
standing on the front porch, talking to Patty on the
phone, and Abby had pulled up to the curb. She
shook her head at us as she listened, letting us
know that Patty didn't know where Red was. Jane
was just returning from her conversation with the
policeman. Kate locked the door behind me while

she thanked Patty and said, "I will," for the second time.

Jane, meanwhile, rolled her eyes as I handed her purse to her. "He's another reformed alcoholic," she told me. "No wonder. I checked some stats about Cawker City last night. Want to know what the crime rate is? Zero. What *else* can a policeman do to pass the time but drink? Other than wrapping twine around the ball."

I must have glared at her, because she immediately looked away. I haven't mastered the art of maintaining a poker face. Or even the art of remembering to *have* one.

Kate was still chatting with Patty. Abby got out of the driver's seat and cried, "Just get in, Kate! Move, move, move, people!"

We rushed to the various car doors. Jane had started to get into the front passenger seat, then changed her mind and headed for the driver's seat. "Abby. I'm driving," she said. "You need to ride shotgun. You'll be the best at spotting your dog."

"I'll get into the way-back seat," Kate said, squeezing past me. "I can watch out the rear window."

"I'll shift over to the driver's side." Scooting across the seat, I added, "This way we have lookouts on both sides, front, and back windows."

Jane started to pull away from the curb while I fastened my seatbelt.

"Wait," I said, as an idea popped into my head.

"What for?" Abby asked, her voice shrill.

Kate, still chatting on the phone with Patty, said, "I'd better let you—"

"Don't hang up." I turned around in my seat. "Ask Patty where Jean Smith lives."

Jane looked at me through the rearview mirror. "You think Eugena Crowder took him?"

"Possibly. She was staring at him pretty hard yesterday," I said. "Her second book was dreadful...just scattered scenes. You could never tell what decade it was, let alone what year. Kind of like that book about the elephant we read."

"*Modoc*. I liked that book," Abby said. (She always managed to read books about animals in time for our second-Saturdays' meetings.)

"At any rate, that got me thinking. It's a little strange that she's wearing a denim hat like she wore in her childhood. Maybe she's become doddery in her old age. That could explain why she plagiarized her latest book...and so perhaps Eugena Crowder thought that *Abby's* Red was *her* Red."

"Oh, my gosh, Leslie," Abby cried, "that actually makes sense!"

(I tried not to put too much weight on the adverb she used. Although it *did* imply that my making sense was a stunning happenstance.)

To no one's surprise, it was a short drive to Jean/Eugena's house. Kate remained on the phone with Patty the whole while. "Well, it looks like we're here, so I'd better let you go," Kate said pleasantly. She finally managed to hang up by the time Abby—who'd bolted out of the car ahead of us— was knocking on the door.

With Kate extricating herself from the deepest part of the minivan, Jane and I followed Abby. My emotions were in a jumble. I was excited at the possibility of speaking to an idol of mine. At the same time, I didn't want to discover that the author was now struggling with dementia or had become nasty and embittered. Plus, I wondered how Abby would feel if it was indeed her personal hero who'd nabbed her dog.

"Nobody's home," Abby said, stamping her foot in frustration. She looked at Jane. "I'm going to look in all of her windows, even if that's illegal."

"I don't have a problem with that," Jane said, "as long as you don't—"

While Jane was speaking, Abby yanked open the screen door, turned the knob and pushed open the door. "It's unlocked," she said and went inside.

"—let yourself in uninvited!" Jane shouted. "Abby! Get back here!"

"Eugena?" Abby called. "Red? Come! Come here, boy."

I brushed past Jane. "I'll go get her."

Abby was just then rounding the corner into the kitchen—judging by the gold-and-yellow linoleum in its entranceway. This front room was being used as a home office. The large black desk had a computer screen—a shoebox serving as its stand—with the screen's connector cord dangling from the front, as if hastily unplugged from a laptop computer. A row of books in the bookcase next to the kitchen doorway caught my eye. It was at least a dozen versions of *A Dog Named Red*, translated into different languages.

"This *is* Eugena Crowder's home!" I cried, talking to myself in my excitement.

"I don't care!" Jane snarled at me through the screen door. "You're trespassing! Without sufficient cause! Drag Abby out of there!"

Kate had followed us as far as the porch and put her hand on Jane's arm. "Jane?" she said gently. "Considering you narrowly missed getting a police citation, wouldn't it be best for you to stay in the car?"

I turned and strode into the kitchen. To my surprise, Abby was now examining the contents of Eugena's refrigerator. "Abby, we have to—"

"Look at that," Abby said, pointing at a mustard-colored ceramic bowl in the corner. "I'm not seeing any kind of pet food, but she put a bowl of water out. You were right. She took Red."

"She *might* have, but *we* are *definitely* trespassing in her house. We need to get out of here."

"But maybe if we—"

I grabbed her arm. "Jane already committed an infraction. Let's leave and call the officer."

She yanked her arm free and led the way out the door. Kate was waiting on the porch. Jane was now standing by the car glaring at us with arms akimbo. Kate promptly gave Abby a big hug. After automatically locking the knob, I closed the door behind us. I felt a guilt pang for reacting with frustration—not compassion—to Abby's turmoil.

"You poor dear," Kate said. "We'll find Red."

"Eugena Crowder is my idol." Abby spoke through wracking sobs. "My idol stole my Red!"

"On the bright side," I said as Kate started gently ushering her down the step, "we know that Eugena would never harm him."

Abby caught her breath. "Oh! That's true!"

"She put water out for him and everything," I added. By "everything," however, I meant: *Snatching her computer and some belongings, then stashing him in her car and hitting the highway.* In my mind's eye, I envisioned Abby's sweet little dog in the front seat of a large old sedan from the late 'eighties, driven by Eugena—a little old lady with a big denim hat. And a terrible case of dementia.

In her haste to keep Abby away from the house, Jane all but shoved her into the passenger seat and shut the door. "Kate?" I asked as we got into the car, too, "Can you call Patty again? You need to ask her what kind of car Eugena—Jean Smith drives."

"Oh. Okay."

"*If* she knows," I added.

After Kate carried out my request, she said into the phone, "Are you sure about that, Patty?" She paused and thanked her, and after exchanging pleasantries, hung up and said, "Jean Smith doesn't own a car."

"Really?"

"She had her driver's license revoked due to poor vision."

"Huh," Jane said. "No car, yet she's in eastern Kansas, in a tiny little town. The proverbial middle-of-nowhere. You've got to wonder how she got out here. And why."

"She must use taxis and car services," Kate said.

"The important thing is that she couldn't have gotten very far out of town," I said. "Unless she already hired a car."

"Who cares if she's in a dump truck or a tractor trailer?" Abby said through her sobs. "The important thing is that we find her and my dog!"

We decided to head back to the main road in and out of town, Route 24, where the Ball of Twine Inn was located. Essentially on a whim, I told Jane to turn east. She did so, and within a hundred yards, we spotted Eugena Crowder, wearing her denim hat. She had her thumb out, trying to hitchhike. On one side of her was a black carry-on suitcase with a thick, bright purple string of yarn tied to on its handle.

On her other side was Abby's dog, Red, tethered to a makeshift leash, made from twine.

Chapter 6
A Dog Named Red

Once again, Abby barely waited for our car to come to a full stop before she threw open her door and hopped out. She raced over to Eugena/Jean/the woman who'd glared at us yesterday, and swept Red into her arms. "Oh, my poor baby! I was so worried about you!"

While the three of us approached, Red happily licked Abby's face, clearly excited to see her. At the same time, though, Eugena was keeping a tight grip on the twine leash she'd tied onto Red's collar.

"This is Abigail Preston's dog," Jane said. "You had no right to take him away."

"I had no choice! He was left alone in a car!" the elderly woman declared. "It was getting hot out! He could have died!"

"*I* was sleeping in the car, too," Abby said. "It wasn't hot. All of the windows were partway down. He had a water bowl on the floor. And I'd merely gone inside our rental cottage so I could pee."

"You were gone for longer than that would have taken," Eugena said, "even for someone my age, and I'm eighty-one!" She wrapped a coil of twine leash around her wrist and stepped closer to Red.

"I took a quick shower, too."

"I waited at the car with Red. When I put him down in the shade, he started trembling and trying to scramble up into my arms."

"He always does that. People think he needs to be comforted. They reward him with treats and cuddling. He's got a regular racket going."

The woman lifted her chin defiantly. I had to admit that I was starting to like her. Though I knew it was foolish, I could picture myself in another thirty years, grabbing a dog out of a hot car and giving the owner hell. (Hopefully not while hitchhiking out of town with the dog, however.)

"I waited so long for his owner to return, I got afraid he'd been left to his own fate. So I took him home with me. You should have *seen* how much water the poor little feller guzzled! Any sane person could only conclude his owner was negligent."

"He always drinks a lot of water when he goes to someone else's house. He's planning ahead for marking new territory. Plus, it makes people think he must be hungry as well as thirsty."

"So you decided to leave town with someone else's dog?" Jane asked pointedly.

"You betcha," she answered, narrowing her eyes as she stared into Jane's. "He has a callous owner. Red deserves better than that. He saved my life once! It was only right that I saved his."

Eugena/Jean stepped closer to Abby and Red, and wrapped another loop of twine around her wrist. As she did so, her determination softened into a bewildered look that was all too familiar; my dad had Alzheimer's and passed away five years ago. He'd been seventy-two, twenty years older than I was now.

"This isn't *your* dog, Eugena," I told her gently. "Even though this one is also named 'Red,' Abby merely named him after your dog."

She peered into my eyes and gave me a sad smile. "You know who I am. Yes, I am Eugena Crowder. And I'm well aware that this isn't the same dog that saved my life. I'm not quite *that* senile." She gazed lovingly at Red, still clutched tightly in

Abby's arms. "This dog is a dead ringer for my beloved companion. And I heard one of you call him 'Red' yesterday. Today, when I saw him trapped in the car, I looked into his eyes." She pursed her lips and again, raised her chin in defiance as she peered into Jane's steely eyes. "It's not such a stretch to think that a dog's soul can be reborn."

"Oh, Eugena!" Abby gushed, "I read your entire book out loud to Red...a couple of pages a day. But he's truly my dog, not yours. He's my lifelong companion. When he dies, I'll have a hole in my heart. And I'll get myself another dog, but I won't read 'A Dog Named Red' to him or her, because that was for *this* dog...for this 'Red' alone."

"Goodness me." Eugena sighed. After a few moments of silence, she unwrapped the twine from her wrist. She pressed the knotted handle of the leash into Abby's hand. "You're worthy of Red. You really do love him, don't you? I'm so sorry. I must have frightened you horribly." She gave Abby, still holding Red, a hug. Abby started crying while smiling with relief.

"You sure did. But all is well, now," Abby said. "No bad feelings or anything. You're my idol. Ask my friends if you don't believe me."

Abby proceeded to introduce each of us to Eugena.

"It's true that Abby idolizes you, Ms. Crowder," Kate said afterward. "She says that a lot. It was all we could do to stop her from stalking you yesterday."

"Why would you want to stalk *me*?" she asked Abby.

"When we were at the ball of twine, you walked past us, and Leslie here—" pointing at me with her chin— "thought she'd recognized you from a photograph."

She shifted her gaze to me. "It's remarkable that you found a recent-enough photograph to recognize me. I'm something of a recluse, you know. After my follow-up book was an utter disaster, I felt like I could never again show my face."

My confusion must have registered on my features. I didn't know if she meant the disastrous sales of *A Summer Not Forgotten,* or the plagiarism charges of book three. Eugena reached out and gently patted my arm with her age-spotted hand. "You needn't fear embarrassing me, my dear. I've freely admitted I was guilty of plagiarism. It was inexcusable. I wasn't in my right head at the time. I plagiarized someone's horrid first draft who had hired me to suggest revisions, then refused to pay me, claiming that my advice was baloney. I was in such a state of panic over my deteriorating career and...terrible family matters that I rewrote the draft to the best of my ability."

I nodded. In her shoes, I'd change my name and live like a hermit, too. And quite possibly move to Cawker City, Kansas, where I'd happily help Patty with the ball of twine for the rest of my days. Maybe she didn't have Alzheimer's after all.

"I look back on myself and remember that moment—the specific moment when I decided I had to start working from that dreadful writer's file, instead of starting anew, with my own vision. I'll regret that decision for the rest of my life. At the time, I believed literally that I either get the manuscript finished and published, or I was going to die. Meanwhile, of course, the author took my feedback after all and made her book publishable."

Kate pressed Eugena's hands between hers. "You shouldn't treat yourself so harshly, Ms. Crowder. We all make terrible mistakes. We have to learn to forgive ourselves, and to move on."

"It sounds to me like she plagiarized *your* ideas for her novel," Abby said.

"That isn't plagiarism," Jane said. "You can't copyright an idea, so if, for example, Ms. Crowder wrote on someone's manuscript, 'You should tell the story when Scout is still a little girl, rather than an adult who realizes her lawyer dad is a bigot,' it is not plagiarism when the author does precisely that."

"Gee," I muttered. "That scenario sounds familiar."

"The writer was in breach of contract, though," Jane continued, "and was legally required to pay for Ms. Crowder's services." She shifted her gaze to Eugena. "I hope that your settlement took that into account."

"Jane's a lawyer," I explained. "We're a book club."

"Do tell," Eugena replied, arching her brow. She studied Jane's features for a long moment, then glanced at the rest of us. My heart leapt. Her surprised, appraising gaze told me that she was thinking: *Aha. I've found fellow book lovers, who are kind to my darling revenant Red! I'm no longer alone!*

"Do you want to hold Red for a minute?" Abby asked Eugena.

"Yes, I would. Thank you." The expression on her face the moment she clutched Red to her chest could only be described as sheer bliss.

"We're heading to Branson," I told Eugena (a non sequitur born from my shameful eagerness to brag about my child to a writer I admired), "where my daughter is performing in a revue, then to the Laura Ingalls Wilder Museum."

"How delightful," Eugena said with a warm smile. "What a lovely, lovely thing to do with one's friends."

Abby reached for her dog, and Eugena gently returned him to her arms. "*This* dog named Red needs to get out of the sun," Abby said. "Would you consider coming back to the Ball of Twine Inn with us? I'd love to get to know more about you. We promised the owner we'd check out by noon."

"By all means, I'd be happy to accept a ride back into town, and maybe to a bus stop, if you have time." Eugena chuckled. "Traveling with your dog reminds me of my new book. It's called '*On the Road with Red.*'"

"You've written a sequel?" Abby and I cried simultaneously.

Kate beamed with delight. "This is wonderful news! I can't wait to read it!"

Jane impatiently ushered us back into the car. Abby deserted her front seat in favor of sitting next to Eugena, who sat between the two of us with Red on her lap. Kate sat in the front passenger seat. As we were buckling up, Eugena said, "I've only just now completed the manuscript for the sequel. I'd be honored if any of you would be willing to read it and give me feedback."

"Oh, my God," Abby cried, grabbing Eugena's arm with both hands. "That would be amazing. I'd *love* to read it. It would be the greatest honor of my life." (She'd come a long way from wanting the officer to arrest the thief of her dog.)

"I would, too," I said, but with hesitation. *What if the sequel wasn't any good? Would I look Eugena Crowder in the eyes and say, 'This needs more work,' as if she was one of my Composition 101 students?* "But *A Dog Named Red* was a classic that's going to be extremely hard to live up to."

"That's true, Leslie. But, you see, I've already been told that I won't get many copies printed and won't make much royalties from this book."

"Why not?" Abby asked.

"It's been too long between the first *Red* and the second one. New readers have moved on. Meaning, really, their parents have moved on. I'm a full generation removed now from the original readers. It would be the grandmothers giving the book to their grandkids."

"That's *us,*" Abby said.

Actually, none of us had grandchildren, but I could sense that Abby was eager to say anything that hinted of commonality with Eugena, even if that meant implying we were Eugena's octogenarian contemporaries.

"You ladies might be my best hope for this manuscript's survival," Eugena said, her lip quivering. She pulled off her hat. Instantly, her features seemed much less dowdy. She had snow-white hair in a stylish shoulder-length cut. If she had been wearing elegant clothing instead of her plain smock and Birkenstock sandals, she'd blend right in with the businesspeople on a Manhattan sidewalk. Furthermore, it was all but impossible to believe she was eighty-one.

"What do you mean?" Jane asked. "What's happening?"

"You'll think I'm just a crazy old lady."

"Meh," Jane said with a shrug. "I'm almost old, and I'm already crazy. Although Leslie, here, seems to think I'm drinking myself into an early grave."

(I decided to adopt Susan's tactic and bit both lips to keep my mouth shut.)

"You're not crazy or almost old," Kate declared. "And we are not about to let you drink yourself into a grave."

Jane gave no reply.

"So much depends on the public's opinion of my sequel," Eugena said, in a delayed answer to Jane's question.

"Is the dog in the sequel actually Red, Junior?" Jane asked.

"Are you familiar with the ending of the first book?" Eugena asked, not unpleasantly. Considering the book's famous ending, though, that was a loaded question. The valiant, mortally wounded Red leads the twelve-year-old girl, M.J. (short for her self-proclaimed nickname "Mean Jean"), to a copse of trees, where she finds a female dog that has just given birth to four puppies. The runt of the litter has red fur.

"I'm afraid not," Jane said. "I don't have children, and I'm a cat lover."

"The collective world of children's literature made the assumption that I would indeed be writing a sequel about Red, Junior," Eugena said. "And who could blame them? *A Dog Named Red* was turned into a Disney movie. And the whole story was true. Every word of it. Except for one little thing."

"Red never sired puppies?" Jane guessed.

"Not to my knowledge." She placed a gentle kiss on the top of the contemporary Red's pointy head. "Although, for the first time, I have serious doubts. *Could* this darling animal be from Red's lineage? Is *that* why we're so drawn to each other?"

I almost teared up, it was such a Hallmark moment—this woman with such pleasant features, striking snow-white hair, a lilting speaking voice, with an adorable dog on her lap, looking up at her with such devotion.

"The story was so sad, the puppies were the only thing that made the ending of the book endurable," Kate said. "My kids and I would cry buckets as we read the story, and my husband was battling tears when he saw the movie."

"Yes, and I was an impressionable first-time author, though a journalist by trade. Changing the truth was not an easy compromise for me. Here I'd revealed what was then the most painful moment of my life. I could still smell the smoke from Papa's rifle. And my poor Red, who'd sacrificed his own life to save me from the cougar! I picked him up and cradled him. Our eyes met, and, just like I wrote in the book, I whispered, 'No more M.J. No more *Mean Jean.*' He died in my arms."

There was a pause, in which I was battling a lump in throat. I doubted I was alone in being feeling emotional.

"'Red chose me,'" Abby blurted out, weeping openly, a hand held over her heart as though she was reciting the pledge of allegiance, rather than the opening line of *Red, a Dog*. "He was a scrawny, scruffy thing. But then, so was I. Maybe we chose each other.'" She put her arms around Eugena. "Red didn't die in vain. And now you've finally given the world what we want. The happy story of you being *On the Road with Red*."

Eugena closed her eyes, clearly touched. A moment later, though, she said, "Oh, the world has moved on." Eugena's her voice was carefree, yet there was sadness in her eyes. "I missed my chance. Now I'm on the road alone. Or I *would* be alone, if you wonderful women and Red hadn't come along. I don't have a home anymore." Eugena lifted her chin. "My money-grubbing husband forced me out of my home in Missouri. I'd been renting a little place here in Kansas, but it's time to move on. I plan to relocate to Branson."

"This is such a coincidence," Abby declared. "That's where we're going, too." (I kept to myself the thought that I'd told Eugena we were going to Branson a couple of minutes ago.) "Were you planning on getting there by hitchhiking?"

"Oh, I don't know." From beneath the neckline of her light blue blouse, she pulled out a pretty little silver cross on a silver chain. "I asked the good Lord to provide, and He answered my prayers." She gave us all a positively beatific smile.

Jane let out a bark of laughter that sounded derisive. "Speaking only for myself, I'm not the answer to anyone's prayers. My big gift to mankind is that I help to end marriages, while getting my clients their fair share." She narrowed her eyes at Abby in the rearview mirror. "Although sometimes *friends* worry that they'd be *presumptuous* to hire me, so I can't even take pride in helping people I care about."

Abby's divorce three years ago had been nasty. She could likely give Eugena's tale of the money-grubbing ex-husband a run for the money. Kate and Susan were now our only married members.

I blurted out, "I would have hired you if my husband had wanted to divorce me instead of dying." (*What a stupid remark!* Abby was already embarrassed at not hiring Jane three years ago, and Jane was reeling so badly from her own divorce that she was drinking way too much. I have no idea why those words popped out of my mouth. But there they were on the voice-to-text.)

Abby grabbed one of Red's front paws; he was still seated on Eugena's lap, and she made him pat his paw as if tapping his foot impatiently. "The divorce made me realize I prefer the company of a male *dog* to a man who *is* a dog."

Jane pulled in front of the Ball of Twine Inn and turned off the engine.

"Do you have any children?" Kate asked Eugena, her voice perky.

"I had a son," Eugena said quietly. "He was an officer. He died in the line of duty. A robbery at a liquor store in Philadelphia...the city of brotherly love."

Both Jane and Kate had rotated in their seats and were watching Eugena with matching sad expressions. "Oh, my gosh, Eugena," Kate cried. "I'm so sorry I brought up the subject."

"Don't be sorry. It's a common question to ask. I loved my son with all of my heart, and I still miss him. You just learn how to carry the pain and go on."

"Even so, I'm so very sorry. That's every mother's greatest fear."

"Yes, it was. He was my only child. And, these days, I can't even begin to tell you how much I wish he were here today. Given his occupation, he could have protected me."

"From what?" Jane and I asked in tandem.

She grimaced, her face pale. "I think my agent is stealing from me."

Chapter 7
A Bad Day at the Office

"What makes you suspect that?" Jane asked.

"A couple of years ago, she brokered a deal for a new, fully illustrated edition of *A Dog named Red*, and the royalties were significantly lower than they should have been. My editor assured me it was my right to examine their records. So I tried to get my lawyer to examine my contracts and get a bookkeeper to look at the records. He refused. He said I was just being paranoid...that I was in great hands with Natalie, my agent, and he wasn't comfortable going behind *her* back. I, of course, told him that I wasn't asking him to go behind Natalie's back. My agent's job is to represent *my* best interests, in exchange for fifteen percent of my earnings. And *his* job is to make sure both my agent and my publisher are giving me every cent owed to me. So he said, 'I'll get right on that,' and hung up. I haven't heard a word since."

"To my mind," Jane said, "that sounds like you're being patronized, but not necessarily stolen from."

"That's what I thought, too. Except *then* I found out Natalie and my lawyer are engaged to be married."

Jane raised her eyebrows. "If you feel like that poses a conflict of interest for you, you might want to consider switching attorneys."

"That's what I *tried* to do, but he's been ignoring my calls. Then just yesterday, I discovered that Natalie received an illicit payment for offering my publisher an exclusive deal instead of giving other publishers the chance to bid for *On the Road with Red*."

"Yikes," Jane said. "How did you find out?"

"My editor's assistant told me over the phone."

"You need a new agent and a new lawyer," Abby said.

"I trusted Natalie. I loved her like the daughter I never had. And she stabbed me in the back!"

"Oh, dear," Kate said. "Is this a major loss for you, financially? I don't know anything about how publishing works. But don't you make the same money from one publisher as another? Don't they pay you a percentage of the sales on each book you sell?"

"Most books don't earn as much in royalties as their advances. Furthermore, publishing houses are financially motivated to put their budgets into advertising, promotion, and expensive covers of those books that have received the largest advances. It's a self-fulfilling prophecy. Unless Rachel Jones, the editor's assistant, lied to me, Natalie sold me down the river! I tried to call Rachel on Friday to verify, but she's left the company."

"Was she fired for telling you about your agent getting a kickback?" Abby asked.

"It sure looks that way to me," Eugena said. "There's nobody in New York I can trust. I haven't felt so deserted since Papa shot Red when I was a kid. That's why I want to get back to my home state of Missouri. I intentionally isolated myself here in Kansas so I could write my book in peace and quiet. Now I need to be near my people once again...readers and book lovers...and to be surrounded by my old haunts. I'm slowly losing my mind." She gestured to the heavens. "For heaven's sake, I actually tried to hitchhike with someone else's dog!"

The four of us book-clubbers exchanged glances. We didn't need to put our righteous anger into words.

"I'm pretty sure we're all in favor of taking Eugena to Branson with us," I said.

"Absolutely," Kate and Abby said, just as Jane was saying, "Yes, we are." Jane continued, "We'll help you pack up whatever additional belongings you'd like to bring and put them in the back."

"That's so sweet," Eugena said. "Thank you."

Her eyes misted. She returned her hat to her head. She looked so tiny and fragile. She could be my mother—kind and generous, but also sharp-tongued occasionally. My thoughts flashed to *The End of Life Book Club*. Author Will Schwalbe's mom had changed over the years and became more fearful. Now I realized where that was coming from—how much my mother, too, hated to rely on others for transportation as her eyes failed her with macular degeneration. Yet here was a literary hero of mine, hitchhiking and reliving her past by traveling with a look-alike dog. I made a mental note to text Susan about that. (In actuality, I forgot anyway. I need to make mental notes on Post-Its that I stick to my forehead.)

We finally got out of the car. Jane and I hung back as Kate and Abby went inside the inn. "Are

Sell your books at sellbackyourBook.com!

Go to sellbackyourBook.com and get an instant price quote. We even pay the shipping - see what your old books are worth today!

000323135714

you sure she's on the up and up?" Jane asked me. "That she's really Eugena Crowder?"

"That's definitely her. I Googled her last night and saw her photos."

Jane nodded, but her brow was still knitted. "Are we sure she's telling the truth about her agent, though?"

"Absolutely. Although that's based on the truthfulness of this now-absent employee. She might have wanted to spark a malicious rumor and get back at her employer for firing her."

"Maybe." Jane grimaced. "I hate people who prey on others' weaknesses. After being accused of plagiarism, Eugena would have felt like she was at her publisher's mercy. Meanwhile, her big-city lawyer and agent could be having a field day at her expense."

"Let's put Susan on the job. She can call the publishing house tomorrow. Maybe she can get Rachel Jones' contact information. She loves doing research."

"Good idea, Les. Let's go for it."

Jane and I FaceTimed Susan, shared Eugena's story, and asked if she could look into Rachel Jones. Susan promptly pointed out that she'd first have to discover which house was currently publishing Eugena Crowder's books and that she'd get right on it. Susan seemed to be energized by the assignment. Jane, too, seemed a little happier as we entered our little bungalow and packed up our things, while Eugena happily examined the cluttered house. This was, she explained, her first time in the inn, and she'd always been curious about its insides. While we all chattered away, I realized that this was the happiest I'd been since my husband passed away. Not only was I surrounded by my dear friends, but I was doing something meaningful in helping a literary legend to regain her bearings.

We drove to Eugena's house. Jane busied herself with checking her email, and Kate called the officer and Patty Parker to tell them we'd found Red. While Abby helped Eugena pack, I nosily scanned Eugena's bookshelf to get a feel for her reading tastes. I was delighted to see Wallace Stegner's *Crossing to Safety* and Richard Russo's *Straight Man*—two astonishingly wonderful book-club reads from years past. (I took a photo of *Straight Man* and texted Susan: *Remember how hard we laughed about Russo's observations about academia?!!*) Otherwise, Eugena's shelves consisted of different editions of her own works, Funk & Wagnalls Encyclopedia, a dictionary, a couple of nonfiction books about dogs, US history and geography books, and several Regency romances by Georgette Heyer. (I mulled recommending one of Heyer's novels for our annual "classic" book. One year we chose Henry James' *Portrait of a Lady*, and after a week's worth of reading and barely getting through the first tenth of the book, I shamefully rearranged my vacation in order to be out of town for that month's book club.)

Abby and Eugena emerged from the bedroom and headed for a coat closet. Abby was carrying a tote bag.

"Sorry I've been so unhelpful," I said to Eugena. "I have a terrible habit of being drawn to the titles on people's bookshelves."

"It's not a problem," she replied, grabbing a pair of red rubber boots and a yellow poncho. "We're already done."

"Are you sure that's all you need to bring for now?" I asked.

Eugena flashed a genuine smile for the first time. Her teeth were slightly crooked and stained, but with her face lit up, she was positively radiant, and once again looked to be in her sixties. "You know, Leslie, I think I'm just fine. I already paid my rent for the month, so I've got three full weeks. My husband and I used to live in Springfield, Missouri, just a short drive from Branson. If I decide to stay in Branson, I can always hire movers to pack up my things and ship them."

"Or we can take care of that for you on our return trip. You can count on us Boobs," Abby said with reverence in her voice. "That's our nickname, and we've sworn to always stick together." (*Not unlike an ill-fitting bra*, I mused to myself.) "We're making you an unofficial member."

Her last remark took me aback a little. I took our group membership seriously, and we'd had no discussion of making Eugena an honorary Boob.

We waited as Eugena locked the door behind us. Abby put the tote, boots, and jacket in the back of the van, announced that it was her turn to drive, and took the keys from Jane. We backed onto the road and headed off.

"This is going to be so much fun!" Abby declared.

"Tonight we're meeting up with Leslie's daughter and fiancé," Kate said.

"Kurt *isn't* her fiancé," I hastened to correct. "They've been together since their freshman year in college. They graduated from CU, in Boulder, our hometown. They met when they were in theater together."

"They fell in love when they starred as the Baron and Maria in 'The Sound of Music,'" Abby explained.

"How sweet," Eugena said. "Which one played Maria?"

I chuckled to be polite. I don't react well to jokes about my children, unless I'm the one making them. (In which case my *children* don't react well.) "Alicia made a wonderful Maria," I said.

"She's amazingly talented," Kate said. "So is Kurt, but we all have such a special bond with

Alicia. She's been in our book club for several years."

"The Boulder Dinner Theater got too small for her," Abby said. She met my gaze in the rearview mirror. "I think that's fair to say, right, Leslie?"

"Oh, absolutely. I'm partial, but that's my right as her mother."

"Branson is considered the Christian Las Vegas," Eugena said. "It's the most frequently visited city in America. So that's a wonderful place for your daughter to get on stage. I think they have some twenty-thousand visitors a week in Branson."

"Well, like me, Alicia is something of a lazy Christian. My husband is—" I froze at my misuse of the verb tense. Once again, I felt the air sucked right out of my lungs, even though he'd been gone for ten months now. "Jack was a devout Catholic, but I never converted, so the kids weren't too good about attending church regularly after they became adults."

"They *will*, though, once they marry and have kids of their own," Eugena said kindly.

"I don't know that my son is especially eager to get married. He's pretty independent and strong-willed. As for Alicia, that's the elephant in the room. She wants to get married. Kurt has permanent cold feet, in my opinion."

"Kurt's a wonderful young man," Kate said.

"Oh, absolutely." Kurt was definitely a wonderful person, and they were a great match. It's just that I hated the fact that he was an actor, too. *One* of them needed a steady job.

"We're going to the Dixie Stampede tonight," Kate told Eugena, "and we have an extra ticket. Our book-club leader broke her leg a couple of days ago and couldn't come."

"If you have a spare ticket anyway, that would be wonderful. Thank you!"

"We also have plenty of room at the condo we've rented," Kate said.

"They agreed to let me add Red at the last minute," Abby interjected. (She'd paid a tidy sum for that privilege.)

"Thank you for the offer, but I truly prefer staying in a private hotel room, and I'm a Marriott club member, so I get priority booking." She rifled through her large handbag and produced some sort of plastic ID card. "I'll just need someone's help calling them to make the reservation."

"I'll do that," Abby immediately said.

"Don't you have a cellphone?" Jane asked Eugena.

"Yes, but I have tremors in my hands. Between that and my macular degeneration, it's all but impossible for me to use those keypads that are on phones these days."

"You poor dear!" Abby cried. "Feel free to consider me your eyes and hands. In addition to your biggest fan."

"But not while you're driving," I couldn't stop myself from saying, "for the sake of all of our safety."

"Thanks for the Public Service Address," Abby grumbled.

"You women are my angels!" Eugena declared, which made us all smile.

"We're meeting Alicia and her boyfriend at the Dixie Stampede preview show tonight. They have the night off from their own show, which only happens once a week. Although she—"

My cellphone rang, and I stopped and glanced at the screen. "Oh, it's Alicia!"

"She must have sensed we were talking about her," Abby said.

"If so, she's calling to yell at me. She hates it when I talk about her." I answered the phone, saying, "Hi, sweetie! We're just a couple of hours outside of Missouri."

"Oh, good. I can't wait to see you."

"Hi, Alicia," Jane cried, closely followed by Kate and Abby. I held out the phone.

"That was everybody."

"Say hi to everybody." Her voice sounded a little sad.

"Is everything okay?"

"Sure. It's great. I'm just feeling like maybe I made a mistake."

My heart was instantly in my throat. I needed Alicia and her brother to be feeling good about themselves these days. At least until I could regain my footing. "By moving to Branson, you mean?"

"That and...everything. Kurt and I have passed our sixth anniversary since we started dating. Maybe he's never going to believe that we can succeed when his parents couldn't. Or maybe it's that he's so hesitant to make decisions. Unlike me. But I shouldn't be getting into all that on the phone."

"Okay. I'll be there in just a few hours. We'll meet you at Dolly Parton's Stampede."

"Right. I can't wait!" I heard a noise, and Alicia said, "Kurt just got home. He says hi. Love you, Mom."

"Love you, too." I pressed the off button, then wondered if I'd remembered to press the red handset icon first.

"She knows we're meeting them at the Dixie Stampede in time for the preshow, right?" Kate asked. "I hear it's delightful."

I ignored the question. Kate's casual use of the plural *them* had set my teeth on edge. Kurt's inability to make a decision was hurting my daughter. And I had no way to ease her pain.

Chapter 8
Not Just Whistling Dixie

Never having been to Branson before, the experience of driving along gorgeous, lush mountain scenery marred only by a jillion billboards struck me as uniquely American. My thought pattern led me to picturing the cartoon image of a road crew constructing this highway in its otherwise bucolic setting, closely followed by a signage crew erecting billboards that read: "Coming Soon: All Sorts of Expensive, Exciting Stuff!" That thought brought to mind another book-club selection I'd enjoyed about an author with a particularly peripatetic lifestyle—Tom Robbins' autobiography *Tibetan Peach Pie*. I once again grabbed my phone to text Susan.

I'd missed a text from her, in which she wrote: *Speaking of dogs, which nobody was...* That was a line from Richard Russo in *Straight Man*, which made me laugh. To respond in kind, I took a photo of the billboards and texted a favorite line from Robbins, regarding the funeral of a circus-midway performer known as Lobster Boy: *I hope they at least thought to embalm him in melted butter.*

We quickly got settled into our condo, with Red already ensconced on his dog bed in front of the TV—Abby turning on her recording of "Animal Planet" for his viewing pleasure. Eugena kept herself amused as we rushed about. She assured us that she didn't mind waiting until after the show to check herself into the Marriott, so we drove to the theater that Dolly Parton had purchased for the show she'd created. The theater was a large, self-consciously Southern building, giving the impression of a large-scale replica of Tara from *Gone with the Wind*. There was an enormous parking lot, and some twenty handicapped-only spaces. That struck me as bizarre. Especially when I noticed a handicapped space for an entire bus.

"Does Branson have an inordinately high percentage of elderly tourists?" I asked Eugena (having assumed there was no reason for a high percentage of athletes with leg injuries).

"They also have lots of family activities here," Jane interjected. "Let's not forget about that fake Tyrannosaurus Rex we spotted on the way through town."

"That was *fake*?!" I joked.

Eugena chuckled a little. "A lot of families with youngsters come here. But it's also a nice vacation spot for my particular demographic...your slice of Americana: Square dancing, hootenannies, barbeques, apple pies."

Kate found a parking space, and we joined a line that snaked around the building from the parking lot in back. As we turned the corner, I could see that we were entering the stables for the horses in the show. I'd owned a horse as a teenager and still adored them. The aroma was decidedly barn-like, however. I could also see that, not counting Eugena, who was still clad in khakis and a blue blouse, we were overdressed; we'd all changed into casual-looking dresses. I hoped when they called this show "participatory," they didn't mean that we were going to feed the horses or clean their stalls.

"Have you noticed how many people are wearing T-shirts?" Jane asked me in a half-whisper.

"As in: every single person in line, except for us? No, I hadn't noticed."

She chuckled.

"Not to mention how thin they make me feel. I wonder what kind of food they'll be serving."

"Mostly meat," Kate said. "I checked the menu while I was ordering the tickets." After sneezing twice, she said, "Oh, dear. My allergies are starting to flare up. I'm sorry, but I need to go around the barn."

Eugena, too, rubbed at her eyes. "I'm allergic, too. I'll come with you." They left the line. I smiled to myself, suspecting that Eugena was simply being kind—feigning her own allergies rather than force Kate to wait for us alone. Abby stared after them with a pitiful expression that reminded me of Red's sorrowful look when we'd left him at the condo.

"I hope they aren't going to be sneezing and miserable throughout the Dixie Stampede," she said.

"I'm sure they won't. It's probably just hay fever." A stunning white horse caught in a stall in front of us caught my eye. "Wow," I said.

Abby turned and looked at the horse. "Isn't he beautiful?" she exclaimed. "He looks like the horse a prince would ride to whisk Snow White away with."

"Or the horse that Lady Godiva would ride," I said. As we continued to slowly pass the stalls in our line of T-shirted ticket-holders, I realized every single one of these horses was a gorgeous, healthy-looking animal.

"I'm surprised Eugena asked for help with her hotel reservations," Jane said. "Her hands were steady the whole time we were in the condo. And she certainly doesn't seem to have trouble with her vision. I saw the spine of a paperback in her purse. It wasn't an enlarged-font size."

"So you're thinking you're Sherlock Holmes and trying to catch a con artist?" Abby snapped. She directed the question to me, rather than to Jane—the more formidable foe in an argument; Jane and I *did* tend to take the same side in disagreements.

"She could be exaggerating her minor ailments," I said with a shrug.

"Well, *my* rule of thumb is to put my trust in Red's reactions. He doesn't warm to anyone who isn't a good person. And Red loves her. I have complete faith in my dog's opinion about people."

"Not to nitpick, but if the world's worst con artist had been handling bacon, Red would lick his fingers."

"That's not true," Abby said, looking me straight in the eye. "He can always tell who is kindhearted and who is cold hearted."

Provided they aren't handling bacon. "I suspect that even hardened criminals can be kindhearted and loving toward animals."

"There they are now," Jane said, pointing. Kate waved at us.

As we exited the barn, Eugena and Abby rejoined us. "You're not going to believe this," Eugena promptly declared. "I complained at the ticket counter that my allergies were so bad in the barn that my eyes might swell up. So they gave me coupons for *four* free specialty drinks. I'm a teetotaler, but I thought all of *you* deserve a little something for putting up with me so graciously."

"Eugena, darling," Jane said, her face lighting up, "you're my new best friend."

I grimaced. Just last night she'd passed out on top of a ball of twine! The *last* thing she needed was a free drink.

"I have plenty of friends, but I could *desperately* use you as my new lawyer," Eugena replied. "My people in New York act as if they're driven by the scent of money. I simply *must* have a lawyer I can trust implicitly."

"But you said earlier they thought it was so long between your dog books that you shouldn't get your hopes up," Jane said.

Eugena pursed her lips and nodded. "You picked up on that, too. It's interesting, isn't it? They tell me not to get greedy and expect to earn much money. Meanwhile, *they're* talking about the rights for this and that, and who deserves which slice of the pie that *I* baked!"

"Hmm." Jane raised an eyebrow.

"It's the movie rights that earned the real money for me on my first book. My agent and lawyer are working on a movie script for *On the Road with Red* but won't even tell me who is writing it, which makes me suspect *Natalie* is. She told me she writes screenplays in her spare time. Furthermore, Natalie said something about an interactive-digital version of my book. When you're my age, people assume everything is so far over your head that nothing registers."

"You said your manuscript is finished, right?" I asked.

"Yes, but quite frankly, I'm not ready to send it in, which drives Natalie nuts. She kept flying into Kansas to check up on me. She claimed she simply wants to be more than a voice on the telephone, but it felt like she wanted to keep an eye on me and my book. I'd tell her flat out that all I really needed was to hire a new *assistant*, which I couldn't warrant with my agent acting like she needed to hold my hand."

"What would you need your assistant to do for you?" Abby asked. She had an unmistakable eagerness in her voice, and at once, I envisioned Abby moving to Cawker City, increasing the population on their welcome sign. Worse, our book club would be *minus* one member.

Not missing the implication, Eugena had a definite sparkle in her eye. "Set up my appointments, organize my fan mail, manage my social media, keep track of my sales, keep track of the business side of things for me. If you want the job, Abby, I'll hire you right here and now."

"I want the job," Abby said.

"Splendid! You're hired!"

Abby released a jubilant cry. I had to bite back my own cry of *what about me?!* I didn't want to have a missing Boob! (So to speak.) Plus, well, I wanted Eugena to notice me, too. I so badly wanted a book sale of my own. I yearned for a mentor in the publishing world.

"Would I go on the road with you and...Red?" Abby asked.

"Yes. You could be my driver."

"There's a Beatles' tune about that," I muttered.

"I move around a lot, searching for stories," Eugena continued. "I went to Cawker City to finish writing *On the Road with Red* in peace and quiet. But before then, I was in some not-so-nice sections of St. Louis. You see, the heart of fiction is conflict. I seek it out." Eugena's face lit up and she gestured with both hands as she talked. "If nothing bad ever happened to me, how could I write what I know? It would be as boring as your average Christmas letter."

"I would love to travel to dangerous places! So would my Red!"

Which your friend Leslie would hate *you to do.* Furthermore, not to nitpick, but I was willing to bet my life savings that Abby, with leash in hand, had never once said to Red, "You want to go to some dangerous places with me today, *don't* you, you good doggie you." I turned to face Jane, hoping *she'd* be the one to throw a wet blanket on Abby. (Adding a pinch of cowardice to my envy of a dear friend's good fortune. Next maybe I'd get the urge to snatch someone's wallet during my descent into despicableness.) She said nothing.

"Fabulous!" Eugena declared. "One of my two biggest worries is resolved." We were getting close to the theater entrance. Maybe it would be chaotic inside, and we could end this conversation before Abby decided to ditch her book club and explore the darkest side of Branson she and her new employer could find. Eugena shifted her focus onto Jane. "Jane, I'm going to cut to the chase. My lawyer is trying to take advantage of me. While I was in the theater, he called me. He said we needed to have a serious conversation, that I'm getting the wrong idea about him and Natalie."

"I'm not following," Jane said.

"He *then* said that my book was shaping up nicely. He never should have seen a copy! I caught Natalie in the act of printing a copy without my permission during her last visit. She promised me she was going to read it herself, then shred it. Unless I get suitable legal representation in a hurry, my book is going to be coming out prematurely with me as just a cowriter, and my agent as the other cowriter."

Jane tried to ask another question, but Eugena lifted both palms. "Natalie had suggested we do that more than once—team up as cowriters. I'm worried that's the *real* reason she's visited me three times now...so she can claim she was co-writing my book. With the plagiarism suit already clinging to me like an albatross, she can badger me into conceding to whatever terms the publisher wants. *Or* into letting her get away with lying about her contributions to my book."

"I'm a divorce attorney, Eugena. It sounds to me like you—"

"I'd pay your regular client fees. I could just use you to put pressure on my lawyer to stay on the up-and-up. Tell him that I've hired you to investigate and ensure that the manuscript is entirely the work of my own hand."

"But I can't, in fact, testify to that. We only just met. You might well have co-written with your assistant."

"Trust me, I *didn't*. There are software programs now that can identify an author's writing style. They'll prove that I wrote every word. But even if I *had* allowed her to co-write *On the Road with Red*, this isn't the first time I raised these concerns. When I first chose Natalie as my agent, I asked to have a contract clause stating that she was not to claim writing, editing, or creative content for any of my works."

Jane widened her eyes. "Do you have the written contract with you?"

"Yes. It's in my suitcase. Are you willing to help me?"

Jane nodded. "Looks like you've not only got yourself a new assistant, but a new lawyer!"

I exchanged glances with Kate, hoping to find camaraderie as the two unchosen members of team Eugena, but Kate was smiling ear to ear, clearly thrilled for them. I felt farther from the inner circle of friendship than ever.

Chapter 9
A Veritable Stampede

Moments later, my mood did a one-eighty; Alicia and Kurt were waiting for us in the lobby. "Alicia, you made it!" I cried, doing my internal happy dance. I doubt that my daughter has ever realized how much it gladdens my heart to see her. It certainly never really hit *me* that my mother was excited to see me until I'd had Ian—my first-born—and experienced the depth of the maternal bond firsthand.

"Hi, Mom," she said, giving me a long hug. She turned into a better hugger after her dad passed away. Unfortunately, that's because she worries about me more. With Jane, Abby, and Kate also delighted to see Alicia (plus Kurt) again, we formed a happy-huggers' traffic island in the stream of people heading toward the pre-show entrance. Eugena, though, had graciously stepped aside.

Kurt's and my gazes met, and we hugged. He looked as handsome as ever; perhaps even more so just because he radiated such happiness and love for my daughter. "It's so great that you could both be here tonight," I told him after our embrace ended.

"Oh, my pleasure...Leslie." He had that slight hesitation in calling me by my first name, even though I'd asked him to do so years ago. "How was your drive?"

"Really interesting," I said with a big grin. "We picked up a hitchhiker."

Just then, Alicia had returned her attention to me. "You're kidding," she said.

"No, I'm the hitchhiker," Eugena said, stepping beside me.

Alicia looked at Eugena as if waiting for the punchline—probably expecting her to explain that she was Kate's mother or aunt, whom we'd picked up in Kansas.

"Eugena, this is my daughter, Alicia O'Kane, who's the actress and singer we're here to see on stage. Alicia, this is Eugena Crowder, the writer."

As I'd eagerly anticipated, Alicia's eyes flew wide. "*You're* Eugena Crowder? The author of *A Dog Named Red*?"

Eugena gave her a warm smile. "Yes, I am. You've obviously read my book. I hope you enjoyed it."

"I *loved* it, Ms. Crowder. I've read it cover to cover five times!" (That was true. She was an avid reader. Furthermore, her insights about books were always well-worth hearing. I've mentioned to her that she'd make an outstanding professor of literature. {That turned into an argument. She instantly decided I was *really* saying that she wouldn't make it in show-business. Parenting makes almost every other endeavor a breeze.})

"I'm flattered," Eugena told Alicia.

"I didn't know you were going to be here, or I'd have brought my book for you to sign."

"*None* of us knew I'd be coming here," she replied. "Not even me."

"My parents are saving seats for us at the preshow," Kurt said. "It's a wonderful cowboy juggling act."

"He juggles cowboys?" I asked. (*Author's note*: While reviewing this manuscript, my book clubbers have sometimes asked me to please delete a remark or two that they had made, but I refused. My penance was to include the recorded statements of mine that *I* wanted to ax. This is one.)

Kurt chuckled. (Like Alicia, he's a good actor and kind-hearted.) He ushered us toward a row of seats, which were positioned at wooden counters, overlooking a square stage below us. Kurt's parents sat with seven empty seats between them, indicated as reserved with napkins on the seatbacks. I'd met Emily, Kurt's mother, and her husband, George, when they came to Boulder to attend Kurt's graduation from CU and during two other visits. Emily and George gave me quick hugs, and we exchanged a few lines of polite chitchat. Alicia then took my arm.

"I'll introduce you to Steve, Kurt's dad," Alicia said.

"Great," I replied. It was high time we met, though I was still worried by her text earlier today. Nothing in this world could make me want to hook up with my daughter's significant-other's father. A fight between couples would make holiday gatherings pure hell.

In truth, Kurt's dad sounded like an amazing human being and was an attentive parent; it wasn't his fault we hadn't crossed paths. Steve Winston, had been in a third-world country, providing pro-bono dentistry during Kurt's graduation. Prior to that, my husband and I had been out of town during a couple of his visits. Once I had sent Jack to a family get-together alone, perhaps because I was busy or ill, or was in an antisocial mood. (I'm an introvert.)

The man at the end of the empty chairs rose and smiled as Alicia and I made our way down the small aisle. *Whoa!* He was really attractive in my very favorite way—not with movie-star looks but with an incredible smile, sexy laugh lines, and a boyish glee in his expression. He also had a great, trim body. "Steve Winston, this is my mom, Leslie O'Kane."

"I'm so glad we finally have the chance to meet," he said, shaking my hand.

"Me, too."

"Please, have a seat." He pulled the clunky, tall wooden seat a little closer to his. "These chairs are so packed in here that they're difficult to move."

"So you're Kurt's dad," I said, feeling too flustered to think of anything interesting to say.

"And you're Alicia's mom. I'm honored to meet the person who did such a fine job raising Alicia.

"Thank you. Kurt's also wonderful, and he always speaks so highly of you. You look like an older, more-distinguished version of him."

"I'm glad to hear that." Steve once again flashed his wonderful smile. Maybe his perfect teeth had inspired his choice in careers. "I'm looking forward to tonight's show. I haven't seen it in ages."

"That's because you were too cheap to take your family and pay for four tickets," a female voice snarled. I turned, startled to see that Emily was now standing behind Alicia's and Kurt's seats, eavesdropping.

Alicia widened her eyes as she looked at me, signaling she was ready to smack Kurt's mom. I gave her a small smile of sympathy. Kurt was frozen in place, staring at the empty chair in front of him as if a complex set of user instructions was written there. He appeared to be deliberately ignoring the waves of annoyance that Alicia was radiating.

"Emily, have you tried the specialty cocktail here?" Jane asked, rising.

"Yes, I'm enjoying one now," Emily said, showing her the signature glass.

"Do you have any idea how to make them? I'm hosting a barbeque in two weeks, and I'd love it to be an authentic Dixie barbeque. Can I pick your brain?" (I felt like hugging her. Jane was smoothing things over—inventing the story about a barbeque as a diversion until Emily cooled down.)

"I'm always really impressed with jugglers," I said to Steve. Abby was still held rapt by Eugena's conversation, but Kate, too, had risen, and had squeezed past Emily in order to stand between Alicia's and Kurt's chairs, forming something of a barrier between Emily and Steve. *My book club rocks!* "I tried a juggler's kit once that had you start by juggling squares of colored cloth, but it didn't help."

Steve grinned. "You're a mom and a professor. You've been juggling your family's schedule for years. That's a much more-impressive feat."

"Not one that brings in an audience, though." I reconsidered. "Come to think of it, when my son, Ian, was three, he climbed to the highest shelf at Target and refused to come down. *That* gathered quite an audience."

As Steve and I continued to chat, I felt more and more comfortable with him. (Aided considerably by the effects of the flavorful vodka cocktail.) As seats filled and the noise volume grew, we had to sit closer together. After a while, the "cowboy juggler" came out to the center of the stage in this small arena-style theater. He launched into a laugh-out-loud routine, pretending he'd forgotten the stagehand's name.

As promised, his performance was fabulous from start to finish. His juggling, lariat handling, and balancing act was skillful, and he had a flawless, easy rapport with the audience, making his every joke feel fresh and spontaneous. My buzz from the alcohol was *also* delightful. I felt so blessed to be sitting between the charming Steve and my brilliant and beautiful daughter and surrounded by my friends. I even managed catch Emily's eye at one point. She'd glanced in Steven's direction, with drawn features. I gave her a wink, and she mustered a smile. She clearly regretted her snarky comment to her ex-husband.

Next, we were all ushered into the main arena. Steve asked if I'd mind if he switched seats and sat next to me, so we could continue our conversation. "Please do," I said, still on cloud nine. Truth be told, I couldn't for the life of me remember what our topic of conversation had been moments ago. Jane, I noticed, had accumulated a starter set of glassware for her nonexistent barbeque. She had to be really snockered by now. She'd helped me by bringing a quick halt to a spat, while *I'd* ignored her potential train-wreck of alcoholism!

Steve chatted with Alicia and Kurt about their seat assignments, and he was soon sitting to my left, with Abby on my right, and Eugena seated once again next to Abby.

The serving staff at this dinner show worked like a well-oiled machine. The emcee—a mustached man in a costume that was possibly a circus ringmaster (or possibly a wild-west mayor; I'm not sure how to tell the difference and, if only out of principle, am unwilling to Google it)—explained that we'd be having a true Dixieland barbeque and would be eating with our hands. I then saw Steve pull out a knife and fork from his jacket pocket. "I came prepared," he said.

"A local's insight."

"You can request plastic-ware," Emily called from her seat directly behind mine. I rotated in my seat. She and George had outdone Steve by bringing what looked like heirloom silver.

"Wow. Did you bring an electric carving knife, too?" I teased.

"No, but I brought toothpicks," George said. He held one out to me, which I accepted, thinking that if olives were on tonight's menu, I'd be all set.

A waiter in cowboy garb gave us bowls of soup in ceramic mugs.

"I can ask for all of us to get silverware," Steve said. "I could tell them that I'm a dentist, and I don't want any of us to break a tooth."

Alicia laughed and leaned forward to talk to Steve. "Whenever we went on family vacations, and my brother or I complained about the food, Mom would always say, 'When in Rome, eat like the Romans.'"

"That's true," I said, turning to Alicia, "but in this case, I have to eat like a northerner with a temporary incisor."

"Oh, that's right," she said. "You're getting an implant in a couple of months, right?"

"Right. This feels like the world's longest dental procedure."

Next thing I knew, our cowgirl waitress strode down the aisle in front of our long, eighteen-inch wide rail (which served as a table), and plopped a chicken onto my large, disposable plate.

"Could I get some silverware?" I asked her.

"No problem, ma'am," she replied, "I'll get you right fixed up in a jiffy."

I thanked her, resisting the temptation to say: "Why, thankee kindly, missy!"

I looked at my chicken and felt Steve's eyes upon me. "They sure expect us to be big eaters, don't they?" I said to him.

"They do indeed. Wait until you get the pork loin and beef brisket, not to mention the potato, corn on the cob, the bread roll, and dessert."

"What? No ribs?" I joked.

"This is really tender," Kurt said to the cowboy waiter, who was indeed placing pork loin and brisket on our plates.

"I thought my friend Kate was kidding about the meal being mostly meat dishes," I said to Steve.

"That's southern hospitality for you. Mounds of delicious food. What are you waiting for? Dig in."

It felt rude to tell a dentist about my dental problem while at a social gathering. Furthermore, Kurt had described the chicken as tender. I smiled at Steve and said, "Will do."

(Most likely, you've already guessed what happened next. Either way, note the next chapter title.)

Chapter 10
Trip to the Dentist

(*Important Author's note*: I have no actual memory of the first couple of minutes of the following conversation. The Pocket Steno was still recording, however. My tooth incident was not pretty and felt as if a six-inch nail had been driven through my gums and into my jaw. As a result, I was terrified of the Novocain injection, so the dentist—my daughter's boyfriend's father—suggested we first use nitrous oxide. Apparently nitrous oxide got the name *laughing gas* because one makes laughably inane remarks under its influence. Remember how I mentioned in Chapter 9 my penance for not editing out my friends' minor misstatements? My frequent response to pleas for deletions was: "Tell that to the Boob in Chapter Ten.")

"Are you still doing okay, Leslie?" Dr. Winston asked.

"Better than okay. I'm Tony-the-Tiger GRRRREAT! I'm singing songs in my head. Want to hear? 'Stevie Baby, can't you find a way to my heart?'" (My words, O.M.G., are being sung to the tune of 'Santa Baby.') "You look handsome. There's no need to keep us apart.'" (*Author's note*: When I first read these lyrics on the voice-to-text recording, I turned off my iPad, buried my face in my hands, and sank to the floor, feeling nauseated. After a minute or two, I convinced myself my blathering couldn't possibly get any worse. I was wrong.)

"Maybe I should turn the N.O. down."

"The nitrous oxide, you mean? That is an N.O. to turning down the N.O., Stevie baby. I haven't felt this good since my last orgasm." (*Author's note*: Shoot me now.) "Since I'm a widow and all, I think I'll bite into a chisel every month and get dentally gassed till all my teeth are broken."

"I doubt you'll find that necessary, Mrs. O'Kane."

"Mrs. O'Kane? Seriously? I thought we were on a first named basis. I'm letting you put my fingers in my mouth! Call me Leslie baby. Whoa. Am I drooling? My saliva is red!"

"I need you to be quiet again."

"Kay kay, but I just have to tell you, I find you sexy and so very nice. And I miss my husband so very much." (*Author's note*: {sob}.)

"This will just take a couple of minutes. No talking."

"I'll bet you're grossed out by my mouth. This is a *terrible* first date."

(Pause of indefinite length; Pocket Steno automatically shuts down when no one is speaking. Or singing mortifying lyrics.)

"Everything looks good now. How are you feeling?"

"I'm Tony-the-Tiger GRRREAT! How are you?"

"I've turned off the Nitrous Oxide."

"*What*? Why? I thought you liked me back! It feels like the left side of my lower lip is as big as a veal cutlet. I need all the friends I can get. I think my book club is going to desert me. They've stuck with me so far, but I have a lot of flaws. More than all of theirs, combined. None of them need the group as much as I do."

"Let's have you take a couple of deep breaths, Leslie."

"I'm going to close my eyes."

Another pause.

I opened my eyes. Steve was sitting back in his chair. "Wow. I was talking in my sleep just now, wasn't I?"

"A little. The bleeding stopped, and the swelling's down. I managed to close the wound with a single stitch. I can take it out for you in a week, or you can see your dentist in Boulder. You won't need an anesthetic for that visit."

"That's too bad. The laughing gas was really relaxing."

"I'm confident I've glued the tooth back in place slightly above the surface of your gums, so that it won't aggravate the injury, yet your stitch can still be removed easily."

"All things being relative, that's great news. Thank you, Dr. Winston." He raised his eyebrow, and I said, "Steve, I mean." My head felt fuzzy. "You barely had any time to eat tonight, did you? I'm so sorry I wrecked your evening."

"You didn't. Besides, I managed to get in several bites of my chicken before we left. I'm not even hungry now."

No doubt he'd lost his appetite after having to witness my profuse bleeding, I thought. *I must have looked like a sloppy vampire.*

"You really shouldn't have been eating without silverware, Leslie. An egg-salad sandwich would have been fine for you to bite into like that. But not a chicken leg."

"That makes me sound like a rabid dog...as if I chased down a chicken at a farm and bit its leg."

Steve chuckled and searched my eyes. Feeling playful from the drugs, I put both hands over my heart and jutted out my lower lip. "Does that mean I'm not being as witty as I think I am?"

He laughed. "On the contrary. You're witty...and charming to boot."

I studied his Paul-Newman blue eyes. D.D.S. Steve Winston was truly handsome—something I truly shouldn't be noticing at this particular moment. Unless he was swept away by my bleeding gums, the feeling was not mutual. The corners of his gorgeous eyes were crinkled with laugh lines.

"I'd have given you my knife and fork from my apartment," he said, "had I known that you had a temporary tooth in place."

"You still live in an apartment after all these years?" I asked, hoping I wasn't flirting. Due to the drugs, I had a mere rose-petal grip on my behavior. It was a triumph not to drool.

He nodded. "Kurt's mother got the house. I haven't been motivated to buy a new place. I'm only here in Branson for eight months a year."

"You do all that commendable work giving free dental care."

"Keeps me busy," he replied with a shrug.

"You're a pretty amazing human being."

"So are—" He hesitated. "—all of your friends going to the ghost tour tonight? I know Alicia and Kurt were planning on going."

"I think so. And you're going, too, right?

"That's what I'd planned to do. But you're probably going to want to take a pass, aren't you? I can drop you off at your hotel, rather than at the ghost tour, if you'd like."

The tour was supposed to start at ten p.m. In retrospect, we shouldn't have tried to pack two events into one night, but both Kurt and Alicia had the night off, and we wanted to spend it with them. Furthermore I hadn't planned on injuring myself at the stampede.

"No. I'm fine. And I'd like to let Alicia *see* that I'm fine. Otherwise she might feel guilty about staying at the Stampede show—regardless of the fact that I'd insisted she stay. She and Kurt thought going on the ghost walk tonight would be good exercise. If not a good *exorcise*. Of the ghosts, I mean."

He smiled.

I rolled my eyes. "See? That was witty for a five-year old. Just not for an adult." As long as I kept sticking my foot in my injured and inured mouth, I might as well take advantage of the ability to blame whatever I said on the drugs. "Are you happy about Kurt and Alicia being a couple?"

He paused. "*They're* happy and good together. As a couple. Well-suited. Although I wish Alicia liked living in Branson better. She's pretty intent on going to Broadway. She's got some lofty ambitions."

"She's industrious and talented," I replied, now regretting my question. What if he *didn't* absolutely adore Alicia? I certainly wouldn't want to know that. "As is Kurt."

"To tell you the truth, I wanted Kurt to be a dentist. But he wants to be a lead in a Broadway musical. I'm sure you'd have preferred your daughter to be a teacher, like you."

"Not really. I settled for teaching. I really wanted to be a writer, but for some two decades and counting, I haven't given it my all. Instead, I find ways to shoot myself in the foot...doing a lousy job on the synopses...deserting promising manuscripts at the halfway point. *Anything* to give me an excuse for a rejection, other than that I'm not a good enough writer. So I'm happy that she's giving acting a shot." In for a penny, give a pound. "I *am* concerned, though, that they're *both* actors. I, too, would have preferred Kurt to be a dentist. But I'm impressed that they're supporting themselves."

Steve nodded. "Because it's *Branson*. It's affordable. Just the rent for the same square footage in Brooklyn, let alone Manhattan, would be ten times as much."

"True. But luckily, they're young. They *should* be reaching for the brass ring...while they still have nothing to lose. A few years from now, Alicia can get a job teaching acting, or literature."

He chuckled. "That's precisely the conclusion I drew. Kurt can easily wait a good five years to go to dental school. Which reminds me. Was that really Eugena Crowder at the Dixie Stampede?"

"Yes. You're familiar with her books?"

He nodded. "Through reading her dog book to Kurt and his brother when they were little. Even back then, Kurt would put on plays for us after we read him stories. He changed 'M.J.' to stand for 'Mean Joe,' so he could be a boy." He paused. "I know Eugena's ex-husband."

"You *do*?"

"He's a dentist in Springfield. He said they had a nice enough life, until Disney bought the movie rights for her book. That's when she let success go to her head. Dropped him flat."

I was surprised and a little concerned. She'd been so nice! "To hear Eugena tell it, he cheated her out of her money. Do you know her ex-husband well?"

"No. I met the man at a convention we both attended in St. Louis. We got to discussing peridontry. I'd recognized the name 'Crowder' and mentioned that was the name of the author of one of my son's favorite books. He was pleasant enough about it, but he painted a hideous picture of the woman."

"Could he have just been bitter, maybe, and being wildly inaccurate about throwing around the blame?"

"I suppose that's always possible. But I have to say, I liked the man. I believed him completely."

"Hmm. I like Eugena. And I believe *her*. Maybe they're both telling half truths about the other."

He studied my eyes. "I liked your husband. We talked at length when we went to the football game at C.U. I'm sorry for your loss."

"Thank you."

"To be honest, I would be reaching for the brass ring myself, if the timing was better." I was just about to ask if he meant he'd be auditioning on Broadway, when he continued, "You're still grieving for your husband, and I'm just a dentist who happened to be sitting next to you when you had a dental emergency."

"Don't sell yourself short, Doctor Winston. I don't drop my tooth for every guy I see."

Once again his eyes grew merry, and my heart did a little loop-to-loop that was surely caused by the narcotics. "You stole that line from 'Big Spender' in 'Sweet Charity.'"

"Yes, I did. I'm impressed. Jack would never have picked up on that."

"My son and I are two of those rare men who love musical theater."

"Ah, but how do you feel about ghost tours? Because we need to get going soon."

"Right you are." He offered me his arm, saying, "You might be a little wobbly."

I accepted his offer, joking, "You're too cheap to outfit the dentist chair with an eject button, I see."

He chuckled a little, but I winced and quickly released my grip on his arm. We left the office, and he locked the door. My remark had been stupid, considering Emily had carped to him about being "cheap" so recently. "I assume you've never taken the ghost tour yourself?" I blurted out. "Alicia said *Kurt* hasn't, even though he grew up here."

"Right. Living in Branson is like living next to Disneyland. When friends and family come to visit, you wind up going to the major attractions with them."

"Hence you knew to bring silverware to the Dixie Stampede."

"Yes, but the ghost tour has slipped past our radar."

"Until *I* appeared as a radar blip."

"I wouldn't call you a *blip*. You're more of a *vip*...a Very Important Person."

"Oho. Artfully done, Steve. You not only have a way with mouths, but with words."

He gave me a quizzical look and said, "Thanks."

I was blatantly flirting! I felt my cheeks warm. "Probably not the best of slogans, but it's a compliment."

"Yes, it is. So I won't...look it in the mouth."

He held the door for me, which opened into the parking lot. "Speaking of mouths, am I smiling? With both sides? I can't tell."

"You look beautiful. Your smile looks perfect." He turned and locked the front door to the building.

He seemed to have a case of the nervous babbles, too. Just then, I realized my son's app had been running throughout my dental appointment. I hoped I hadn't said anything embarrassing. If I was smart, the first thing I would do when we got back home was delete that section of the recording without even looking at it.

Chapter 11
We Go on a Ghost Tour

Steve and I walked side by side to his car. I had to fight off a ridiculous urge to take his hand. This wasn't like me. When I'd taken the unfortunate bite of meat, Emily's husband, George, had promptly given me some kind of pain killer that he'd said he carried with him for when his "bad knee acts up." The medication combined with the nitrous oxide was really doing a number on me.

While Steve drove, I stayed silent, trying to decide how I felt about Alicia and probably my book club setting up Steve and me. It was really sweet of them, actually. They were clearly acting out of their love and concern for me.

"You're smiling again," Steve said. "In case you didn't know."

"Oh, good. I'm glad my cheek muscles are working in tandem."

"Penny for your thoughts?"

"I was just thinking that it was nice of Alicia and my book club to arrange this trip."

"Do you think Alicia had a hand in it?" he asked.

"Yes." *Why did he ask me that?* Did Steve know about their matchmaking plans? In any case, I wasn't about to embarrass myself by letting the cat out of the bag. "She had to get an extra night off. So that we could spend an extra day with us. And so did Kurt."

"Oh, right. Sure." He seemed a little confused.

"You've seen their act, haven't you?"

His grin returned. "I have indeed. They do a wonderful routine together. That's why it's so appropriate that...you're here with your friends to see their performance."

"Absolutely." Our babbling seemed weird now. I couldn't figure out in my altered state if I was reading anything right. Did he *know* that my daughter and book club were playing matchmaker with the two of us? Or was I imagining things? It was always possible that things were exactly as they seemed—that Alicia had simply wanted her recently widowed mom to come visit.

Then again, Alicia and I tended to be equally devious. What if she'd put *Kurt* up to plotting with *Susan* to bring us together? That wasn't out of the realm of possibility. In which case, they might have asked Steve if he was interested in dating me. And he might think I had been asked the same question about him.

"*Now* you look worried, Leslie. Just as an FYI."

"Aha. Thanks for telling me." I forced myself to perk up. There was no point in trying to analyze situations with my brain partially incapacitated.

I spotted our destination and pointed. "The place is there at the corner."

We parked and made the short walk to the ghost-tour office. It was a small retail space, with adequate furnishing that looked as if they'd once been used in a schoolroom—an old wooden desk, a couple of dozen chrome and plastic chairs facing the desk, a dry wipe board behind the desk. All that was written on the board was: *Tour begins at 10 p.m.*

Kate, Abby, and Jane were seated together in an otherwise empty row. Eugena wasn't with them.

About twenty tourists were here, some seated, some standing, all but two of them middle-aged. Once again they were all wearing T-shirts. (To be fair, I should mention that my husband often tended to wear tees.) Alicia and Kurt weren't here yet. George and Emily were standing in the back. Steve nodded to them; Emily pointed at her mouth, while asking me silently, "How's your tooth?" I gave them a Cheshire-Cat smile and a thumbs up.

We gave our names to a scruffy-looking mustached man, who was wearing a black, Ghost Tour T-shirt. He gave both of us envelopes and mentioned that we could feel free to tip him after the tour. I resisted the urge to thank him as if I was utterly overjoyed at his suggestion. (I can be a real pill sometimes.)

Steve touched my arm, and pointed with his chin at Emily and said quietly, "I'm going to try to mend some fences. I'll catch up with you during the tour."

"Sounds good."

I headed toward the Boobs, wondering if Eugena had gotten settled into her hotel, and if we had any plans for getting together with her tomorrow. I had another pang of regret that Susan wasn't here. She always knew everybody's precise whereabouts. Jane was on the end of the row of chairs closest to me, and I sat down beside her.

The four of us chatted briefly about my dental procedure and my misfortune at missing the show. "Is Eugena coming?" I then asked.

"No, she checked into the Marriott shortly after you and the dentist left," Kate said.

"The dentist?" I repeated, a little amused.

"Steve, rather," she said with a smile. "He seems like such a nice man."

"Yes, he is." Not wanting to go there, I asked, "Alicia and Kurt are still coming, aren't they? I'm surprised they're not here yet."

"She said she had to run home and put on the type of shoes that *you* wear," Jane replied with a silly grin; she was acting reasonably sober, but was a tad tipsy.

"Did she also describe them as 'ugly'?" I asked.

"Well, yeah, but I was trying to be tactful."

I had to laugh. "She's always giving me a hard time about my sensible shoes. She says I should practice walking in heels." My spirits dipped a little as I thought about my daughter. "Was Alicia in a good mood after the show?"

"Yes. Why?"

"Lately, she's been getting disappointed that Kurt still hasn't popped the question." (*Important informational note* for readers who are not yet parents: Women discuss their children. That is not because they don't value your privacy or want to complain about you. Mothers are only as happy as their least happy child, therefore *your* worst problem—whatever it may be—is *often* on your mother's mind. If you do not wish your mother to share something in particular with her friends, *tell her so*.)

"Really?" Abby said. "You can tell at a glance that he worships her. She hasn't got a thing to worry about."

"His parents had a pretty unhappy marriage, so she thinks he may have a case of permanently cold feet."

"He'll come around," Jane said. "Soon. Kurt's got a great head on his shoulders. He'd never let Alicia down."

"I sure hope not." My stomach fell. I had the horrible thought that the worst possible outcome of this trip would be that Kurt and Alicia would break up, but Steve and I would wind up falling in love. I would have no choice but to break up with Steve, for the sake of our future Thanksgivings with family, if nothing else. I was too old to risk making my daughter unhappy just so I could remarry. I'd had a long, successful marriage with the wonderful memories of many good times. Yet I also remembered how much energy and determination it took to endure bad times. As long as I had my book club, I could be content on my own for the rest of my days.

"Leslie?" Jane said. "Are you okay?"

"Yes. Sorry. I was just worrying about my what-ifs instead of my what-fors."

"What does that mean?"

"I don't know, but it sounded good. I'm projecting. I was thinking about what might happen if Steve and I somehow wound up getting together. I enjoy Thanksgiving too much for us to have two couples in the same families."

"Oh, right." She glanced at Steve, still standing in the back corner of the room. "You'd be dating your daughter's father-in-law."

"*If* they ever get married."

Our ghost guide gave us a preamble just as Alicia and Kurt arrived. She saw me, but simply gave me a little wave, which I returned. The guide, however, stopped mid-sentence and grinned at them. "This is a coincidence. I was at your matinee today."

They both smiled. "I hope you enjoyed it," Alicia said.

"Oh," a female ghost-walk customer told Alicia, "we went to your show last night! You're Alicia O'Kane, aren't you?"

"Yes, I—"

"You were the best one in the show. You're going to have a brilliant career! I was just saying to my husband that we were lucky to catch you at the onset, because you're really going places."

"Thank you," Alicia said, "but I'm truly not the 'best' performer. It's a team effort, and my three costars are all so talented, I'm honored to be on stage with them."

"Oh, sure." The woman craned her neck to catch Kurt's eye. "You were also excellent."

"Actually, I agree with you, ma'am," Kurt said. "I think Alicia's the best performer, too."

"You're talking about the Rockin' Oldies, right?" another woman asked. "My cousin, Gertie? She was here in Branson last month. She told me y'all were so good she went to your show three nights in a row. She was only here for four nights. Said she'd do it again. So I got tickets for Wednesday night. I even asked in advance, just to make sure that wasn't your day off."

"It's not," Alicia said. "In fact this is my mother, along with our book club members from Boulder. They're going to the show on Wednesday, too."

"We should *all* go to see it," a third woman said. "We haven't booked our show tickets for Wednesday yet. I'm just tickled pink to think that there's a celebrity in our midst."

"There are two of us performers here, actually. Kurt's simply amazing."

"Not as amazing as *you* are," Kurt said, gazing into Alicia's eyes. "You're the love of my life."

"And you're the love of *my* life, Kurt." She looked at me, then smiled as if she'd just now gotten a wonderful idea. She shifted her focus back to Kurt. Sounding giddy with glee she asked, "Will you marry me?"

Kurt gaped at her for a moment. "She's kidding," Kurt said, his cheeks turning red. "Let's get on with the ghost tour. We've interrupted the entire flow here."

"I'm *not* kidding, Kurt," Alicia said. "I'm really asking. In front of some of our very favorite people. Kurt Winston, love of my life, will you please do me the honor of being my husband for the rest of your life?"

Kurt looked positively panic-stricken. He stared into Alicia's eyes, his cheeks bright red, and said in a hushed voice, "Darling, this isn't the right time. Okay? Let's talk about this later."

"The right time?" Alicia repeated, her voice more hurt than anything else.

"It's a *ghost* tour, for crying out loud. You're rushing things and putting me in a terrible position!"

"Rushing things?" she repeated, her voice barely above a whisper. "*Rushing* things? After six years of dating? After four years of living together?"

"You're embarrassing me, Alicia. And you're making everybody here uncomfortable."

She took a step back, her eyes flashing. "How thoughtless of me." She still managed to keep her voice low, but the angry tones were unmistakable. "I'm so sorry. I wanted our parents to see us get engaged. But you're right. It's not the right time. It's never going to *be* the right time."

"Yes, it will, darling. Just not *now*."

"I understand. You're unwilling to make the commitment, which is you right."

This was a train wreck. I stood up. "That's a wonderful performance, sweetie." I turned in order to face the biggest portion of the audience. "My daughter and her boyfriend are demonstrating a little skit that they use in their act. As a teaser for what we're in for at Wednesday's show."

"No, they aren't," the woman who'd praised Alicia to the sky said. "The show is 'oldies but goodies.' They go around and chat with folks in the theater."

"My mother is simply trying to help me save face," Alicia said, her voice starting to crack. "But it's too late for that. I won't be in the show on Wednesday, after all. It will be my understudy." Alicia marched toward the door.

"Darling!" Kurt yelled. "Wait!"

She threw open the door and ran around the corner. Kurt grabbed his head, looking positively horrified.

"For heaven's sake, Kurt," Emily cried to her son. "Stop her! Why are you just standing there?"

Kurt looked at Steve. "It's all screwed up. Whatever I do."

"Tell her the plan!" Emily cried, stomping her foot.

"Run after her!" Steve said.

Kurt finally charged out the door.

I, too, didn't know what to do. I looked at the others. Both Kate and Abby had tears in their eyes. "He'll catch up to her," Kate said. "This will be fine."

"I can't go on the tour," I said to the guide. "I'm so sorry we've caused such a disruption."

"Sorry, ma'am," he replied, "but I can't issue refunds until after the tour. We're wasting precious ghost-seeing time."

"This is a whole lot more exciting than hearing about ghosts, if you ask me," a teenaged girl said. She rose and looked at me. "Could I get your phone number, ma'am? Or could I give you mine so's you can tell me what happened next?"

"*No!* I'm sure they'll make a wise decision. Eventually."

The four of us started to leave. "We'll come back for our refunds," Abby said to the guide.

Steve, Emily, and George headed out behind us, although George was clearly reluctant. "We should still go on the tour," he said. "This is between the two of 'em to work out. And, anyway, if you'd asked me, I'd have told you proposing on stage in front of a whole theater of people was a lousy idea."

"What?" I asked in a shriek.

Emily studied my face for a moment, then turned toward my friends. "For heaven's sake," Emily cried. "*Leslie* didn't *know*?"

Chapter 12
Far From the Madding Crowd

"Kurt planned to propose to Alicia? On Wednesday night?" I asked, even though I already knew the answer.

I scanned their faces, with only Emily willing to meet my gaze. To my chagrin, I realized that I was the only person who was hearing about this for the first time.

"Seriously? Just this afternoon, Alicia told me on the phone she was worried about Kurt's cold feet! If only I'd known, I would have advised her to be patient. This never would have happened! But now, everything is a huge mess!"

"Kurt asked us not to tell you," Abby blurted out. "He said that you always tell Alicia everything. That she's your sounding board for everything. He didn't think you could handle a secret."

"Oh, he didn't, did he?" I said, seething.

"Well, don't get mad," she said.

"Too late."

"We figured...what was the harm?" Kate explained. "We'd all be together. Nothing bad was going to happen."

"You should be mad at *them*, not my son," Emily said gesturing at my book club friends. "They're the ones who've known you for years. And poor Kurt was afraid you'd talk Alicia out of it. I advised him to tell you, but he's been in an impossible position, knowing you were grieving for your husband. He didn't know what to do. He already thinks you don't like him because he took your daughter away to Branson. It's a wonderful place to live, if you'd just give it a chance."

"I didn't say it wasn't a nice place to live. I've only just gotten here, and I've spent most of that time in a dentist's chair."

"Well you certainly don't look happy to be here," Emily muttered.

"I'm not! My daughter just drove off in tears! Because your son didn't have the good sense to say 'Yes' to the girl he was planning on proposing to in three days! Who *does* that?!"

"If your daughter didn't get all Marilyn Monroe on him, they'd have worked it out in private."

"What do you mean by using 'Marilyn Monroe' as an adjective?"

"Isn't that a verb?" Kate asked.

"It's a gerund, right?" Jane asked.

"Ask Siri." Abby said.

"Nobody is asking Siri!" I cried. "The next person who asks Siri or Google a question is getting their phone knocked out of their hands!"

"Well, it's much too late at night to call *Susan*," Abby grumbled.

"Leslie," Jane said, "there's no sense in taking your anger out on us."

"Or on my son! He's upset enough as it is," Emily said.

The twenty-or-so people started coming out the door. "You sure y'all don't want to join us?" the guide asked.

"Positive," I snarled at him. As soon as the crowd was out of earshot, I turned to Jane. "But I *am* angry at you! None of this would have happened if you'd just shared what was really going on with my daughter with me."

I heard footsteps. Kurt, panting, was trotting toward us on the sidewalk. He was alone. "Couldn't find her." He put his hands on his knees. "Car's gone. She's not answering her cell, and her phone's off."

"She probably went home to your apartment," Jane said.

Kurt was starting to cry. "I can't think straight. I don't know what I'll do if I've lost her."

"Come on," Steve put his hand on Kurt's back. "I'll drive you to your apartment, and if she's not there, we'll search your neighborhood haunts." He gave me a sympathetic smile. "We'll keep you posted."

"George and I will take our car and help," Emily said.

George grimaced, but I said, "Good idea," glad to avoid Emily's company for a while.

I breathed a sigh of relief when it was just us Boobs.

"It was actually *Susan* who suggested that we shouldn't tell you," Jane said. "We decided she was right. You tell Alicia everything. All of the time. We didn't want to put you in a bad position."

"As opposed to the *good* position you put me in right now?"

"We meant well."

"I'm sure you did. Still. You should have erred on the side of letting me make decisions regarding my own family."

"We intended this whole trip to be kind of a surprise party for you and Alicia," Kate said.

I sighed. "I can see why Kurt didn't want to turn his long-planned proposal into his future wife impulsively proposing to him at a ghost tour."

"She does have a tendency to catastrophize," Kate said. "As charming as that is."

"And *Kurt* has a tendency to be passive and let Alicia grab the reins," I fired back.

"Which is why they're such a great couple," Kate said.

"Yes. They truly are a great couple." Abby said. "Perfect for each other. Can we use Siri now?"

"No! I've decided this is all Siri's fault. Not because that's true, but because I want to blame her."

"Works for me," Jane said with a shrug.

"Somebody needs to find Alicia before she does something nutty and...signs up to work on a cruise ship or something," I said.

"Kurt should have headed straight for their apartment. Immediately," Abby said.

I shook my head. "That's not where she went. I'm sure she drove straight out of Branson without collecting a single thing."

"Maybe she's heading straight back to Boulder," Jane said.

"And drive thirteen hours? I don't think she'd do that, either." I tried to put myself in her shoes. "She'd probably want to head to a friend's house. If she knows anybody who lives an hour or two from here."

"Maybe you should tell Kurt that," Jane suggested.

"I will. First, though, I'm going to call her cell, just in case she'll answer when she sees it's me."

Her phone went straight to her message, which, remarkably she'd already updated. It was now: "The love of my life doesn't love me. My mom's losing her teeth. I'm going off the grid."

I pressed the red phone icon with so much force I was fortunate not to sprain my thumb. I cursed, then said, "Listen to this!" I switched to "speaker" mode and redialed. After replaying the message, nobody spoke. "*Losing my teeth*?" I repeated. "Good Lord, she can be annoying!"

"I don't think you should take that personally," Kate said gently.

"She's referring to me and my teeth! How can I *not* take that personally? She's announcing to everyone who calls her phone that I'm turning into an old hag!"

"There are plenty of young hags with missing teeth," Jane said. (Unhelpfully, I might add.)

"Didn't we read a book about women's teeth?" Abby asked.

"*Sweet Tooth*, by Ian McEwan," I growled, "and it had nothing to do with actual teeth. It was about a young woman hired to spy on a writer and falls in love with him. You just didn't read the book."

Abby glared at me. "That's a bit of a hag-like remark, don't you think?"

"Not under the circumstances!"

Jane mimed zipping her lip, but winked at Abby.

"Don't you think it would be a good idea for you to leave her a message?" Kate asked gently. "About your being worried about her and that Kurt simply wanted to be the one to propose?"

"That would be a good idea, except Alicia doesn't like to listen to her messages," I said. "Or maybe she just won't listen to *mine*. *Hag* that I am."

"*I'll* leave a message," Jane said, pressing buttons on her phone. "Hi, Alicia," she said moments later, her voice sounding suitably concerned. "This is Jane. We're all really worried about you and are so very sorry for what happened. This is all a big misunderstanding, and I feel personally responsible for dragging you to that ghost walk in the first place. Please call me or your mom back when you get this message. Please? We all love you and are worried sick." She shoved her phone into a pocket of her purse. "I hope that helps."

"It might, if she actually listens to it," I replied.

"Wasn't the ghost tour *Susan's* idea?" Abby asked.

"Should we head back to the condo, Leslie," Kate asked, "or is there someplace else you think we should look for Alicia?"

"No, let's go back to the condo."

We got into the car, with Abby behind the wheel. A couple of minutes later, my phone made a noise. "That might be a text," I said, hopeful, in spite of myself that it was Alicia contacting me. After some operator errors, I was able to retrieve my latest message. "Rats. It's from Steve. '*No sign of her at apartment,*'" I read aloud. "I'm going to text him back to ask Kurt to check Alicia's friends who live outside of Branson."

I dedicated myself to writing exactly that in a reply. Pressing the right letters while texting not being within my skill set, I had an impossible time while riding in a car. Not only was I having a hard time keeping my hand steady on the silly-ass keyboard, I was having an even worse time battling my guilt. My behavior toward Kurt had arguably led to this Waterloo. I'd been so proud of my daughter's gifts, yet so unsupportive of her marrying her male equivalent.

"Will Alicia read your *texts*, Leslie?" Abby asked.

"Not if she has her phone off. But you make a good point. I doubt she'll stay off the grid very long. I need to figure out what to say, really briefly."

The others went inside while I insisted on staying put in the car until I'd sent a suitable text.

Was it Mark Twain who once said that he wanted to keep his comments brief, but didn't have enough time to do so? In any case, I sat in Kate's car for a long time. I worked on sentence after sentence, erasing each one. She would *love* being proposed to on stage in front of us and an audience of strangers. She'd be kicking herself endlessly if she found out she'd cost herself that marvelous surprise. Furthermore, Alicia was really intelligent and knew me almost as well as I knew her. If I texted: *Kurt wants to marry you*, she'd put two and two together and figure out Kurt's plan to purpose on Wednesday night.

Alicia's not just my daughter; she's one of my closest friends. But even so, there's a huge arena of things that I'll never talk about to her. One of those things is how keenly aware I am of my own faults. She knows I haven't been as kind to Kurt as I should have been. She knows that I'm not as kind *period* as I wish I was. I know that sometimes she feels the same way about herself. (Although she's wrong.) Ultimately, *that* was the piece of knowledge about my daughter that I decided to access. I texted:

Kurt needs you. Be the first one to forgive the other. Love, Mom

Chapter 13
Jane Versus the Dark Side

Important note to readers: This chapter is told from Abby Preston's point of view. Hoping to keep our Branson road-trip journal going, I gave Abby my iPad while Kate and I took off for a casino in Oklahoma. (That was not nearly as random as it sounds. Abby's narrative explains shortly. And while I'm writing within yet another parenthetical, please allow me to explain that I have honored my promise to Abby not to edit her writing, or even to accept my copy-editor's corrections.)

The next morning, Leslie looked like a total wreck. She has yet to give you her own physical description, but she looks a lot like her daughter, Alicia, just older and less shapely. Plus Leslie doesn't usually wear makeup or put much effort into her clothing. She'd had very little sleep and felt that her only real hope of getting sleep and regaining her equilibrium would be after Alicia had returned to Branson and resolved her and Kurt's misunderstanding. Which was truly not our fault, btw. We could hardly have foreseen the unfortunate series of incidents that led to Alicia proposing in public, and Kurt taking leave of his senses and turning her down. Sorry, Kurt, if you're reading this, but yeesh.)

If Leslie were writing this chapter, she'd go into the exact wording of the conversation that took place at 8:30 the following morning, when Jane informed the three of us that she'd managed to get Alicia to speak with her briefly on the phone around midnight. However, since I'm in charge of this small section of *her* book...throughout which my own shortcomings are delineated at great length...I am going to take the high road, and not repeat the snarky things that *Leslie* said when she learned that Jane had decided on her own to take Alicia at her word...when Alicia had told Jane only that she was at a hotel and was safe, but that she was unwilling to give its name or location for fear her mom would come for her, and she wanted to be alone.

Jane then revealed that she had spent a portion of the night on the phone with Jimmie, the pothead we met at the ball of twine. They'd gotten to know each other during their booze-and-marijuana binge while the rest of us slept. Jane had learned that he and Marcus were computer geeks. They owned quite a bit of hi-tech equipment.

By some means that remains unclear...something about strangulation of signals...math was never my strong suit...Jimmie was able to extract the location of Alicia's cellphone. Leslie was promptly out the door and on her way to try and track down Alicia. Kate insisted on driving her. (Which, believe me, was absolutely essential. Leslie looked like she'd been on an all-night bender and had spent the night face down in a gutter, even though she hadn't taken a sip of alcohol since her tooth got stuck in her chicken. Meanwhile *Jane* looked fine physically, but smelled as if she'd been matching Leslie drink for drink, and gutter for gutter. (However, Leslie was extremely grateful to Jane and told her to give Jimmie her heartfelt thanks.)

Having given Kate instructions to keep us up to date, the two of them took off, and Jane and I went to breakfast, which didn't seem pertinent to this book, although it was the first time I'd eaten grits...only to realize grits are basically cream of wheat, though perhaps its ground-up corn or oatmeal instead of wheat. Afterward, Jane and I decided to check in on Eugena at the Marriott. We called, and Eugena sounded not only wide awake, but positively bouncy at the idea of us all getting together to explore downtown Branson.

We agreed to meet up in the Marriott lobby and took seats in their comfortable sitting area, across from an attractive young couple. The woman was wearing a black pant suit, and Jimmie Choos open-toed espadrilles. The man also wore a black suit, with an open-collar shirt, and black wingtips. They struck me as uptight, him tapping his foot and glowering at his phone; her filing her fingernails and blowing on them.

Jane took one look at them and said, "Are you from New York?"

He didn't bother to look up. "Yes, we are. And *you* are not."

Jane snorted. "It's pretty clear that you have no intention of chatting with me, so I'll introduce myself. I'm Jane Henderson."

He glared at her. "You were right the first time. So why exchange names?"

"Because I want to annoy you."

He grimaced and kept typing along on his iPhone.

"I'm Natalie Price," the woman said to Jane. "I think I've heard your name before. Are you a lawyer?"

"Divorce attorney. Why?"

Her male companion stopped working and stared at Jane. "Oh, crap! You're the bitch who stole my client!"

"You're Eugena Crowder's lawyer?" Jane asked, ignoring his name-calling. Talk about rude! Meaning the man, of course.

"I *was.* Up until she let herself be conned by the likes of you."

Jane shifted her gaze to the woman in the pricey shoes. "And are you her former agent?"

"I'm her *current* agent," Natalie said, sticking her nose in the air.

"She told me yesterday that she'd fired you," Jane pointed out. I (Abby) wasn't there for that conversation. It took place after we'd dropped Eugena off at the hotel. Jane had told us that she wanted to have a brief private meeting with her new client and that she'd take a cab to the ghost tour. Kate and I insisted on waiting for her (Jane) in the hotel lobby, though.

"Well, she didn't. And both of you need to get up and leave right this minute, before we have to call the authorities on you and have you thrown out."

"The authorities of *what*?" Jane asked. "Are there authorities for preventing clients from deciding to fire people who aren't doing their jobs?"

"What is going on here?" I (Abby) asked. "All we did was give Eugena a ride here from Cawker City. Then she *asked* Jane to give her some legal advice."

"You people are sharks, aren't you?" the agent sneered. "You prey on the elderly and want to get your fingers in the pie."

"I don't even understand what you're talking about," I said. "We're the opposite of sharks. We're *readers!* And why would a shark be sticking her fingers in a pie? Actual sharks don't even *have* fingers."

"Eugena hired Abby and me of her own volition," Jane said. "We adore Eugena's writing, and we've been enjoying her companionship."

"Which you suddenly were interested in once she told you about *On the Road with Red*," Natalie said.

"That's not true," Jane said. "We picked her up when she was hitchhiking, after nabbing Abby's dog out of our car. Does that really sound like elderly abuse to you? Because I'll tell you what sounds like elderly abuse to *me*...you taking Eugena's manuscript without her permission and sending it to your boyfriend lawyer!"

"That was on her orders! She sundowns and forgets by the evening what she'd told me to do in the morning. It's quite common with dementia."

"My late father had Alzheimer's," Jane fired back. "I'm well familiar with the symptoms. *Eugena*, on the other hand, seems sharp as a tack to me."

"You're seeing what you want to see. I suppose it gives you false comfort to pretend that *I'm* the bad guy."

"Eugena asked me to read her manuscript," I (Abby) said. "She told me you've been getting kickbacks from her publisher, and you encouraged her to sign with a publisher on an exclusive, which benefitted you, not her, even though *you* work for *her*." (She said this during our amazing heart-to-hearts at Dolly Parton's theater. The show was great, mind you, but Eugena is the most fascinating person I've ever met.)

"I know that's what Eugena believes, but it's total BS," Natalie Price said. (Isn't that a fabulous name for an agent to have? Too bad it's a pseudonym.) "I got the best deal for her I possibly could, considering once you plagiarize, you're a pariah in the publishing world."

"Not when you have a compelling story of redemption," Jane said.

"Hey!" the male lawyer yelled. "You with your nose in a phone!"

After I realized he meant *me*, I looked up. (I'd been asking Siri what the word "pariah" meant. But talk about a pot calling a kettle black! Not that anyone's nose could actually be *in* a phone rather than a book. Unless it was a flip phone and you were holding it sideways.)

"What's your name?"

"Abigail Preston." (Not really. I said my actual name. Leslie let us rename ourselves in this book, and I've always liked the name 'Abby.' I *did* state my full *real* name, though.)

"You're her new assistant," Natalie said snidely. "Where is the manuscript now?"

"In my room. I read it last night," I said. "It's going to be a best seller."

"You need to give it back to her."

"I will, after Leslie reads it."

"Oh, right. The wannabe author." Natalie snorted. (I had told Eugena that Leslie was an author, and because I love to give my friends a helping hand, I asked Eugena to give Leslie a referral to her agent. That must be how Natalie found out who Leslie was.) "I'm sure she has illusions of writing the next blockbuster," Natalie said. (That was a really nasty remark. I was beginning to not like Natalie whatsoever. It made me wonder if I'd made a mistake in wanting Eugena's agent to represent Leslie, but mean, nasty agents would probably be exceptionally good at twisting editors' arms.) "I'm sure she's thinking Eugena's going to take her under her wing and befriend, in return for bringing her to Branson. And you're both secretly hoping she'll want to move to Boulder so you can be BFFs."

My cheeks started warming. Just last night I was trying to convince Eugena to move to Boulder. And like I said above, I'd been certain from the start that Leslie would be eager for Eugena's tutelage and that Eugena would want to help Leslie get published. I had also chatted up Jane to Eugena while I was helping Eugena to pack, as the brilliant lawyer that she is. So when we were at Dolly Parton's theater, I had given Eugena all of our contact information, including their every possible social-media address of theirs, which I typed into Eugena's phone for her, just to make it as easy as possible for Eugena to give their careers a boost. (She had those shaking hands and bad vision, remember.) As excellent teachers, Kate and Susan didn't need Eugena's help, but I gave Eugena their email addresses, too, so she could come speak to their classes in the future. Maybe I was being a little too helpful.

"Face it, Abby. You and your book club friends are taking Eugena for a ride, both literally and figuratively."

"That is totally false. Not counting the word *literally.*" I shook my finger at her. "We are helping the world of literature, and we are helping a talented, aging author regain her footing."

She snorted. "You are as delusional as she is. And also as self-aggrandizing."

Now I was mad. "You're the one who's playing games with herself. You're just attacking me and my friends because we've gotten in the way of your plans for exploiting Eugena to gain fame and fortune."

"For your information, I care deeply for Eugena. I admire the woman greatly. I foolishly thought she valued my friendship with me as much as I valued hers." Natalie looked really upset. She seemed so sincere that I started to feel bad. Meanwhile, her boyfriend had turned a deaf ear. He'd returned to texting on his cellphone. "But she obviously didn't. You can see that for yourself in the email she sent us."

"*What* email?" Jane asked.

"The one she sent me last night. She copied you and Abby."

"She must have sent it to the wrong email address. Did you get the email, Abby?"

"No. I'll double check." I hadn't looked at my emails since yesterday morning. "Nope." That seemed strange. I wondered if maybe I'd gotten all of the email addresses wrong, or hadn't typed them into Eugena's contacts' list after all.

"I'll forward it to you," Natalie said.

"Don't," Jane said. "You're trying to trick us into giving you our email addresses." (That's when I realized Natalie was lying, which made me relieved at not having messed up Eugena's contacts list on her phone after all.)

Natalie gave Jane a dirty look. "No wonder Eugena likes you. You're every bit as paranoid as she is."

"I consider that a compliment." Jane eyed the two of them. "Could I have your attention, sir?"

Eugena's lawyer looked up. (At least, I *think* he did. After my feeling of relief about not mistyping email addresses, a worrisome thought got all of my attention. Last night I hadn't realized that Jane might not have wanted me to tell Eugena to feel free to give her agent the contacts' information I'd typed into her phone. Natalie had gotten one thing right: Jane *is* rather paranoid...and I might have overshared some personal information about Jane last night. Those specialty drinks at Dolly's Dixieland Stampede were pretty strong, and I have a tendency to talk too much when I drink. Although they are really delicious. I recommend them heartily!)

"You two have put Eugena in a bind," Jane said.

"How? What are you talking about?" Natalie shrilled.

"She shouldn't have had an attorney who's in a romantic relationship with her literary agent. It puts her in an uncomfortable spot when she needs professional advice. She can't trust that her interests are at heart when she needs a second opinion about her contracts, etcetera."

"We were aboveboard with our relationship from the very start!"

"Whether or not that's true, Eugena has every right to reconsider the arrangement, which is precisely what she's done."

"Meanwhile," Natalie interrupted, "*now* she's got herself in a cozy little group of strangers who see fit to ingratiate themselves into her life. You have a whole lot of nerve, calling us out for *our* association."

"*You* were the one who suggested she fire her assistant, while you filled in for her so you could conspire to be her co-writer," said I. (Eugena had told me this in private.)

"That's a lie!"

"That came straight from Eugena," I said. "Ask her yourself if you don't believe me." (I was starting to think Leslie shouldn't hire Natalie.)

"Eugena's assistant quit several weeks ago. Eugena said *that* was the reason she wasn't getting farther along in her book. I volunteered to fly in for two four-day weekends to help her finish the book so we could get it in front of her editor in time for the fall catalogs." Her glare kept flitting from me to Jane and back, as she yelled at both of us. "Meanwhile, I'm working with my other writers, being the liaison between her and the editor, *and* I'm acting like Eugena's handmaid, just so *she* fulfills her contractual obligations. Which Chris has vetted to be as much in her favor as any author could possible expect, especially considering her dicey history concerning her last two books." (She patted the arm of the male lawyer, so his name in this book is "Chris." Even though I personally thought his fake name should have been "Blake." He definitely looks more like a "Blake" than a "Chris.")

"And yet Eugena told us she doesn't trust you as far as she can throw you," I said. "She says you've been manipulating her since she first hired you but she was too naïve to know better."

"If she actually said that to you, it only proves that you two planted it in her head." She sized me up and down. "Just who do you think you are, anyway? You're some piss-ant book-club member who thinks she knows more about my job than *I* do! I am not going to sit back and watch you gouge my client so that you can feel important. Eugena Crowder has finally seen fit to write a sequel to her masterpiece, which I've practically pulled out of her, word by word and page by page. You think you're going to swoop in and supplant me while you and your stupid book club are on a ridiculous road trip to Branson? Pull your wash-away-the-gray head out of your ass, lady! That is not going to happen!" (This last couple of sentences was recorded by the app on Leslie's iPad. I had stopped listening because I was watching Eugena walking toward us from the elevator behind Natalie and Chris/Blake. I was so relieved to see her, I wanted to hop up and give her a big hug, but she looked really angry.)

"Natalie!" Eugena said. "How dare you talk to my friends like that!" (I wanted to put a little heart shape here, but I had already read Leslie's forward, and she's a punctuation snob.)

Natalie gaped at her. "You consider these people your *friends*? Why? You're the one who called *me* and said you felt trapped and didn't trust their motives."

"No, I did *not* say that," Eugena said. "I told you that, the more time I spent with them, the more I came to realize that I didn't trust *your* motives."

Natalie stood up and stamped her foot. "That's just not true, Eugena. You said, 'I don't trust *their* motives.' There is zero chance that I heard 'your' when you *clearly* said '*their*.'"

"That can't possibly be true, Natalie. That is *not* the way I feel. It's not how I felt yesterday, and it's absolutely not the way I feel now." (Eugena was so strong and adamant! You couldn't help but admire the way she stood up to the two of them!)

"And yet that's precisely what you said."

"Your ears must have played tricks on you."

I laughed. Eugena was just so witty! Although you likely had to be there to appreciate how she delivered the line. It was kind of like that man who played the Church Lady on "Saturday Night Live."

"You've apparently wasted your trip," I said. (I wished I had Eugena's knack for saying the right thing, with just the right tone of voice.)

"Hardly, Abby. You're obviously star-struck and misguided in your naivety about the publishing industry. Either that or we had it right all along. You're gold diggers, who think you won the lottery when you picked up an elderly woman who turned out to be a Newbery-winning author. Either way, neither Chris nor I are going anywhere until we know that Ms. Crowder's best interests are being met."

Chris crinkled his features. (Which, BTW, is another reason I think I should have renamed him. This is my chapter, after all. And now we've got "Chris Crinkled," which sounds like Santa Claus. But switching names seemed confusing. Bad memory is SUCH a pain! I keep wondering if Ginko Balboa works for memory boosting.) Then Chris sucked in air through his teeth. When Natalie turned to look at him, he said, "Actually, I've got a seat booked for a flight out this afternoon. Client meeting this evening that I can't miss. Should I cancel your seat?"

"*Yes*, Chris. Cancel it. I am not leaving Branson until I have this thing resolved."

"Good," Eugena said. "That clears things up a bit. Chris, you're officially fired, once again, and *this* time, I have plenty of witnesses. Jane Henderson, you are officially my one and only attorney. And, Natalie, you are on probation as my agent for *On the Road with Red.*"

So there, I thought!

"You can't do that, Eugena! I'm already the agent of record! I'm entitled to fifteen percent of every dollar you make from the book, and its subsidiary rights, including movie options, toys, and residuals. I already submitted it to your publisher!"

"As Eugena's attorney," Jane said, "I'll need to examine your contracts."

"We have a verbal agreement," Natalie said, her cheeks bright red.*

"That wasn't wise, Natalie." Jane grinned as she shifted her gaze from Natalie to Chris and back. "Didn't you seek legal advice from a competent attorney?"

*Jane asked me (Abby) to say herein (I'm using legalese herein) that she noticed the discrepancy between what Eugena had said about having their contract in her suitcase and Natalie claiming it was a verbal agreement. She considered it to be in her client's best interest to remain mum about that.

Chapter 14
Meanwhile, Crossing State Lines...

"We're almost there, Leslie," Kate said.

I jolted awake. "I'm so sorry I nodded out. That's risky. It makes the driver all the more prone to falling asleep themselves."

"My mind is too busy chattering for that to happen," Kate said. She sighed. "I haven't been completely honest with you. You were right the other day, Leslie. Alicia told us before she moved to Branson that she thought you and Steve Winston would hit it off. That's a second reason why this trip seemed to be such a blessing...and also why we all agreed to let Kurt keep his adorable plan a secret from you."

The phrase "adorable plan" made me smile in spite of myself. Provided I could free my daughter from the grips of the Shakespearean tragedy she'd imagined for herself, being able to witness the marriage proposal on stage *was* adorable. Although, honest to God, I *would* have been able to keep Kurt's intentions secret but still encourage her to be patient for another month or two; she would *not* have proposed to him last night.

"Well, I have to admit that I doubt if I would have come on this trip if I'd known that in advance. It's strange to think my closest friends were trying to play matchmaker for a long-distance relationship. Let alone with my daughter's future father-in-law."

"That was the only way we could think of to get rid of you."

Kate spoke in an earnest, deadpan tone. Especially considering the source was Kate, of all people, the remark made me laugh heartily.

"Seriously, though, Leslie, if you and Steve Winston are meant to be, it will happen."

Kate was deeply religious, and she knew I was shallowly religious. "So in your opinion we were all playing the part in what was meant to be?"

"With a little help from our friends." She sighed a second time. "Speaking of friends, Jane's in trouble. But she's strong. She can start coming to AA meetings with me."

So yesterday she had indeed spoken from her own firsthand experience. "When did you realize you had a problem?"

Her cheeks reddened a little. "Back when the kids were little. I saw the girls having a tea party one day, mimicking the argument about my drinking I'd had with John the night before. That's when I saw myself through my children's eyes. I called John at work and asked him to come home, and to help me while I found an AA meeting."

"That took such courage."

She shook her head. "John had been urging me to do that for months. He was the one with the courage for both of us."

We pulled into the enormous casino parking lot. There was a row of buses, dropping off what, at a glance, appeared to be groups of Caucasian senior citizens. As Kate pulled into a space, I redirected my attention to the skyscraper hotels that flanked the casino.

"The hotels here are enormous," I said, feeling my blood pressure rise. "We're never going to find her."

"We'll just check the registry of both hotels," Kate said, patting my shoulder.

I tried to muster some confidence as we entered the lobby of the nearest hotel. A young man was typing into a computer at the counter. He welcomed us, and I said, "Hi. I'm Leslie O'Kane. Could you please call Alicia O'Kane's room, and tell her that her mother is in the lobby?"

"Certainly, ma'am." He typed into his computer. After a few seconds, he asked how to spell my last name, and I suggested he try it both with and without the apostrophe. After several more seconds, he said, "Are you sure she's staying in the hotel?"

"She might be in the other hotel, at the other side of the casino," I replied.

"We're both under the same management. Our registries are connected. Maybe she hasn't checked into a room yet."

"Okay. Thank you." Feeling deflated on top of exhausted, Kate and I left. We stood on the sidewalk for a moment, trying to figure out our next step. The desert-like heat felt thoroughly oppressive and seemed to be baking the life out of me. "She probably gave them a fake name and paid in cash. Or else Jimmie and Marcus gave Jane bad information."

"Let's go look for her in the casino," Kate said. I nodded and followed her, suffering from a case of numb brain.

We entered the brightly colored, thickly carpeted, air-conditioned world of the casino. The sudden change in ambience and temperature felt like I'd dragged myself across the finish line of a marathon and promptly stepped inside a disco. It took me a minute to get my bearings.

Mostly to bolster my own spirits, I said, "I have to give Alicia some props for this. There's an I'm-down-and-out appeal in going to a casino after an especially horrific event in your life."

"But let's remember that, even though Kurt loused up, he meant well," Kate said, predictably. "And, on the bright side, this way you and I get to save their relationship. It's almost lucky, really, when you think about it."

I was getting a little annoyed. Cheerful people who never fail to look for the silver lining within the thunder clouds get hit by more lightning bolts than us cynics. "No, it isn't. This is the opposite of lucky. If we hadn't been at the ghost tour last night, it wouldn't have happened."

"That's not true. They'd have still had the same conversation if we'd been someplace else."

"They wouldn't have *been* in the ghost-walk office if it hadn't been for their meeting us there. Alicia pointed out to Kurt at the time that they were 'in front of' us...their favorite people."

"Oh, right. Good point."

We decided to split up in order to search efficiently. The centerline of this enormous room featured enormous pillars to support the ceiling, and we agreed to meet at the farthest pillar on the opposite side. I did a reasonably thorough check on my side. Kate was standing alone at the pillar, talking on her cellphone when I arrived. I heard her say, "Here she is. I'll call you back."

"Were you talking to Jane or Abby?"

"Jane. They're going to go window-shopping with Eugena, then get some lunch. She said they had an unpleasant run-in with her agent and lawyer, and that they'd have to fill us in when we returned."

"Eugena's agent and lawyer traveled to *Branson?*"

"Apparently. They don't want to lose control of the goose laying the golden eggs, in Jane's opinion." She paused. "We weren't talking about you behind your back just now."

"Oh, I know you weren't. Which reminds me. I owe all of you an apology. I didn't mean to be so grouchy this morning about Jane not waking me last night to tell me Alicia's whereabouts. I'll bet if Jane was a mother herself, she'd have realized I'd have insomnia. It was just really upsetting for me to see Alicia so heartbroken, and all over such a bizarre happenstance. Plus I'm really crabby when I'm sleep-deprived."

"I'm pretty sure we all get that. I'm so sorry for our poor decision to keep you out of the loop."

"It's okay. I understand how it all happened, and I'm over it. But...sometimes it still feels like just yesterday when Jack died. The very last thing I wanted to do was cause Alicia pain."

Kate winced. "We should have let you be the mastermind of this trip, or cancel it if you didn't approve. It's just that, well, frankly, you've made no secret about your concern about Kurt's being an actor. He can feel it too, so he's really intimidated by you."

"I can't imagine anybody ever being intimidated by me. I'm a part-time composition teacher at a community college. I'm five-five, too thin, near-sighted...I've got no upper body strength, and like Alicia said in her text, my teeth are falling out."

"You're also the mother of the woman Kurt loves, you have major reservations about him, and you and Alicia are really close."

"Right. That's what Emily tried to tell me last night. I should have realized that long before now."

"Kurt called *Susan*, asking her advice on whether or not she thought he should ask you for

Alicia's hand in marriage. The two of them cooked up this whole plan. He's wanted to propose for nine months now."

"He *has?*"

"*Alicia* was grieving, too. He wanted time to pass. And not to spring the proposal on her as if to force her to cheer up and move on, before she was ready."

"Wise thinking on his part."

She gave me a sad smile, but held her tongue. I had totally underestimated Kurt. Most actors' marriages struck me as doomed by career success or cursed by poverty. Even so, a couple's collective mettle was more important than their marriage-challenging careers. I had no doubts about Alicia's intelligence and character, and I should have known she'd make a wise choice in the man she wanted to be with.

"Enough said." I tried to steel myself. "Let's see if Alicia's in the poker room."

We found her seated at a table, playing with a small pile of chips and surrounded by eight men, including a male dealer. She looked so sad, it broke my heart. I had been such a jerk! All of the pressure I'd unwittingly put on her and Kurt with my inability to embrace their somewhat unwise choices of careers. It was their decision to make! She spotted me as approached. We both teared up when we locked gazes. I could hear Kate sniffling, as well.

"I fold," Alicia said. She stood up. "I lost my entire paycheck. Pretty soon I'll be out of gas money, too."

"Oh, dear," Kate said. She scanned the table. "I played a few hands of poker back when I lived in Kansas. How about if I take over your chips for you?"

"There's practically none left," Alicia said, gesturing at her meager stacks of chips. "Do you really want to play poker?"

She smiled. "Absolutely. It'll be nostalgic for me. But if I lose your gas money, I'll reimburse you."

"No, you won't, Kate. Believe me, I've been doing so badly, I was going to lose my chips on the next hand that was dealt."

"In that case, I'll let my losses or winning be yours."

"You don't have to—"

"I'm taking control of my friend Alicia's chips," Kate interrupted, looking at the dealer. "Is that okay with everyone?"

"Sure thing," the dealer said with a nod.

"No problem," at least three of the gamblers said simultaneously.

"Texas Hold'em, no limit, five or ten dollar ante?" she asked as sat down.

"Ten," the middle-aged portly man next to her barked.

"My name is Kate." She smiled and scanned the men's faces, but nobody spoke. "Could you please deal me in, Ben?" she added after eyeing his name tag.

Alicia and I stood there, both of us unsure if we should leave Kate to her own devices with this group of hardened-looking men.

"How about getting us a table in the bar next door?" Kate told us. "I assume they have coffee. I'll join you in—" she winced as she peeked at her two cards "—a couple of minutes, unfortunately. I can always hope for a good flop." (That sounded like quite the oxymoron to me.)

"Okay, Kate. Good luck," Alicia said with a warm smile.

The moment Alicia and I left the poker room, she burst into tears. I embraced her, wishing I could somehow absorb all of her pain and bear it for her.

After a minute or two, Alicia collected herself. "Let's go get a table, Mom. I'll bet there are women crying here every day," she muttered, drying her eyes. "Nobody will think twice if I look like someone's been gouging my eyes."

"You look better than you think," I replied.

She led the way without comment. Only three of the eight tables were occupied. We took seats in the far corner and both ordered coffee. I chattered at her for a while, but she merely nodded now and then. I, too, fell silent. The waitress served our coffee. Alicia doctored hers with cream and sugar, and took a couple of sips. Despite my exhaustion, I was edgy. I didn't want to say the wrong thing, yet was incapable of figuring out what the right thing to say was. She would snap at me if I told her this would all work out. If I tried to defend that statement, I would risk ruining the happy surprise that she deserved. I toyed with the idea of feigning sleep, but finally decided I wouldn't say a word until she spoke first.

"So was Kurt upset when I ran off?" she asked after I'd slowly sipped half of my cup of coffee.

"That's an understatement. I've never seen any man so devastated as he was," I said. "I'm pretty sure he was just caught off guard when you popped the question. Meanwhile, Steve assured me Kurt talks about you all the time and that he *is* planning on proposing."

She rolled her eyes. "When we're forty?"

"I got the impression that it'll be before the end of the year, actually. He loves you dearly."

"Then why didn't he say *yes*?"

"He wants to get my blessing, for one thing," I replied, thinking my replies were more or less true. "He doesn't want to feel like he's intruding on your grieving period, let alone mine. So he truly meant it when he said that the timing wasn't right."

"Sure, but I'd still have been totally thrilled whenever he proposed to me. Or if he'd simply said, 'Let's do this up right later.' He could have said that, given me a quick kiss, and everybody would have been happy. I just...wanted you and my three other mothers to witness a nice moment in my life. You've all helped shape me into the person I am today. Good and bad."

"It's overwhelmingly good," I assured her.

The right corner of her mouth twitched once. That meant: *you always say stuff like that because you're my mother.* After a brief, doleful silence, she said, "I'm sorry I made you worry. I was just feeling sorry for myself. I always was counting on coming back today. We'll still have plenty of mother-daughter time, since the theater's dark on Mondays. And I'll definitely perform on Tuesday and Wednesday." She added sadly, "Like always."

Once again, I was caught flat-footed. I muttered, "That's great. Thanks."

A tear was running down her cheek. "Kurt and I behaved so badly last night. It's just..." She let her voice trail off. "It makes me think maybe we're not right for each other after all. Maybe we don't know each other as well as we think we do."

"Oh, sweetie. There are always going to be times when you feel like that. I can't even count how many times I've said or done things that shocked me later...things that I'd have sworn on a stack of Bibles that I'd never do. That's all this was. This was Kurt saying something stupid."

"Okay. That makes sense." Her voice had the same absence of emotion as if she was memorizing lines from a script.

I sighed and wished she hadn't sat so far back in her chair that I couldn't reach her hand. "I can tell you're humoring me, Alicia, but it's okay. Let's just give everything some time. If we go over to your hotel right now, you can check out of your room before you have to pay for a second night. I'll pick up the tab."

She shook her head. "I don't want you to pay for my room. It's my responsibility. Things will just be tight for a couple months, is all." She sighed. "I think I deliberately sabotaged myself during poker. I came here with the ridiculous notion that I'd make a fast ten or twenty grand, then head out to Broadway and give it a go on my own." She snorted. "All I could think about was Kurt, though. I'd lost the only thing that really matters in my life, so what difference does money make?" Miserable, she rested her head in her hand, her elbow on the table. "I was such a jerk. I changed my phone message."

"So I heard."

"I mean I changed it a *second* time, omitting the part about you and your tooth." She rolled her eyes. "I can be such a diva sometimes! I *did* call Jane back, though, about an hour ago. That must be how you knew where to find me."

"Through Jane, yes," I said.

"I kept thinking my luck with cards would change." She smiled a little. "Meanwhile, *Kate's* so nice, she is probably insisting the other gamblers take her chips, regardless of who wins."

"I know what you mean." *Yet Kate had recently told me she was recovering alcoholic.* "Apparently she has some tricks up her sleeve. It *is* hard to picture her bluffing, though."

Alicia yawned. She looked half asleep. Heaven knows *I* was.

We got caught up on her brother's life for a while, then talked about television shows and movies, keeping Kurt out of the conversation. After the waitress gave us two or three refills, I asked, "So...are you awake enough to make the hour-long drive?"

She nodded. "I *am* kind of exhausted, but I can make it."

"I'll drive your car," I said. "You and I can keep each other awake, and Kate can drive her van back."

"Sounds good. Thanks, Mom. I just need to give Kurt a call, so he knows I'm on the way. He called me twenty times, but I didn't pick up."

"I suppose you want to be alone when you talk to him. I can go wait in the—"

"You need to wait here for Kate. I'll find a quiet spot and talk to Kurt. Okay?"

"Okay, sweetie," I said. I watched her leave.

Her father died before her wedding day. Most likely, I would walk her down the aisle. I'd be crying my eyes out the whole time.

By the time I drained my third cup of coffee, went to the women's room and returned to the table, neither Alicia nor Kate had arrived. I checked my watch, startled to see that Kate had been gambling for half an hour. It would be such a hoot if she'd won Alicia's money back! I tried to imagine Kate, with a stogie between her teeth, spreading a winning hand on the table and saying, "Read 'em and weep, boys," then snickering as she dragged an enormous pot in front of her.

Alicia approached. The bounce was back in her step as she crossed the room.

"We both apologized," she announced, "and all is well. I told him about our plan to drive back now, but he didn't think it was safe for either you or me to be behind the wheel. Kurt's coming here instead, and we'll be back in Branson tomorrow, in plenty of time for our show."

"That's great, sweetie."

"I feel like I've cheated us both out of our mother-daughter time today, though. This just isn't how I'd planned spending the day."

"That's okay. Nothing about my trip so far has gone like I expected it to... so I'm thinking that means I should just go with the flow." (In truth, of course, I was deeply disappointed to miss this time with my daughter, but that was nothing compared to my relief that she and Kurt had reconciled.)

"Hasn't Kate come back yet?" she asked, scanning the room.

"No. Let's go see what's happening."

"It'd be hilarious if she's actually winning," Alicia said with a chuckle.

"That's just what I'd been thinking."

We entered the poker room. Halfway to the table, Alicia and I stopped in our tracks and stared. Stacks and stacks of chips had shifted positions away from the now ashen-faced men. There was our sweet, soft-spoken Kate, her gentle mannerisms unchanged, but staring at her cards, her lips pursed and her brow furrowed ever so slightly, saying, "Oh, dear. I guess I'll raise you by...oh, gosh. Let's just say...a hundred?"

"I fold," the man on her left growled, slamming down his cards.

"I call, dammit," another man said. He put down an ace and a ten. The three cards from the dealer in the middle of the table were an ace, an eight, and a six, all three in different suites.

"Ooh. Good hand, but I just edged you out," Kate said apologetically, setting her cards face up on the table.

"Three sixes," the dealer said.

"What the hell's going on here," the player who'd folded said, glaring up at Alicia and me. "Is this some kind of scam? Y'all set us up with a young lady to butter us up, then you bring in a card-shark to roast us?"

"No," I said. "We didn't even know she'd ever played poker."

"Yeah, right. They're conmen," the big-bellied man next to her said, his eyes burning with rage. (He not only misjudged us, but got our gender wrong.)

"We've got to get going, Kate," I said. "We're going to be late."

"Oh, I'm so sorry, Moe," Kate said in her gentle voice. "My papa taught me how to play poker when I was little. And my friend Alicia has been having a horrid day. I felt duty-bound to win her money back. I do hope you all understand. Your luck is bound to improve. Moe, you didn't make a mistake with your last hand. You just got unlucky. Again, I'm so sorry." All the while she was speaking, she was stacking her chips and putting them in her tray with, her hands moving as if on fast forward.

She grabbed what looked like a hundred-dollar chip and gave it to the dealer. "Thank you so much, Ben. And I really am sorry for ruining everybody's mood."

We strode out of the poker room. Kate stopped at the first pillar and turned to face Alicia. "I have to run to the restroom." She gave the tray of chips to Alicia. "This is eighteen-hundred and forty-six dollars. Please keep all of it and consider the difference a belated housewarming gift for you and Kurt. I know him well enough to be confident you'll patch things up. I'm sure he just had his own picture in his head for his proposal that didn't include a ghost tour. I'll bet you *anything* he wants to marry you."

"Alicia stared at her chips as if dumbfounded. "It looks like it would be really stupid to bet *against* you."

***

Kate and I were about to enter Branson city limits when my phone rang. I was surprised to see a number that I didn't recognize. I expected the caller to be Abby again. We'd recently ended a phone conversation about our success with Alicia—as well as her telling me how much she disliked Eugena's lawyer and agent. (Abby had explained that Eugena had "gone to a spa," which was why she felt free to give me her honest opinion about them.)

I answered. It was Eugena. Her voice sounded a little tense. "Are you back at the condo with Jane, by any chance?" she asked.

"Almost. We're just about to turn onto the street."

"I'm so embarrassed," Eugena said, "but I need your help. I'm being conned out of an enormous sum of money. I can't afford this. Please come help me. I'll never ask you for another favor for the rest of my life."

Chapter 15
Time-out from Time-Sharing

"What do you mean?" I asked. "Who's trying to swindle you at a *spa*?"

"What's wrong?" Kate asked.

I held up my index finger to signal that I didn't know yet.

"I'm in the women's bathroom of a resort in north Branson. And I'm afraid to come out. I feel like I'm a plump little fish that got thrown into a shark tank."

"So this is a vacation resort? Not a spa?"

"Right. Last night I called a number for discount tickets I got off the internet and agreed to come here this afternoon. I thought it was to give me half-off tickets to shows in Branson. You've all been so helpful and kind to me that I wanted to treat you to a show. And I couldn't afford to pay full price with that terrible deal that my agent and lawyer coerced me into signing."

I held my phone away from my mouth and explained, "Eugena got tricked into attending a sales pitch and needs us to come bail her out."

"Oh, dear. That's terrible!"

"In other words," I said to Eugena, "they're trying to sell you a timeshare."

"Well, yes. They're generous with their pastries, which only made things worse. My digestion doesn't do well when I eat that many sweets, but I just can't resist pastries when they're put in front of me."

For Kate's sake, I recapped: "So you're hiding in the bathroom so you won't buy a timeshare and eat too many doughnuts."

"You should hear these people, Leslie! They just talk so fast. And they pretend to hang on your every word, like you're the most fascinating customer they've ever had. Then they get you to say yes to one thing after another. It's stupid stuff at first. Do you like to save money? Do you like to take vacations in beautiful places? And like that. Next thing you know, there you are, being given a contract to sign for a time-share."

"I understand completely, Eugena." My dander was up. They must have been licking their collective chops at an elderly single woman entering their lair. I searched my purse for a pen and paper. I found the former, and decided to use my pocket calendar as a notepad. "Tell me the address."

"So you'll help me?"

"Absolutely. I'll be right there. Kate and I are already in the car."

"Thank goodness! People walk all over me! It's just so embarrassing. In fact, could you please pick up Jane and bring her, too? I might need legal representation. But...Abby was already so distressed about my agent and lawyer. We had quite an altercation today. I hope this won't get her all worked up again."

"We need to pick up Jane," I said to Kate.

"Will do," Kate replied.

"I feel like such a silly wimp!" Eugena said.

"I can be a wimp, too," I replied. "I'll pretend to be in a hurry, or suffer from a contagious disease to get away from pushy salespeople."

There was a pause. "I don't want you to come here only to have you wind up buying a timeshare yourself."

"No worries. I'm a lot tougher when I'm acting on someone else's behalf than on my own. It always brings out the mama bear in me."

"Still, I hate being such a bother. I really should have just called Jane. But she would have had to take a taxi to get here, too. And it's quite a long distance."

"We'll break you out of there, Eugena. I promise. We're honored to be asked to help you."

Kate pulled into our parking space at the condo and told me she'd get Jane. Meanwhile, Eugena gave me the address, which I jotted down. While Eugena launched into a rather lengthy description of what we needed to tell the guard at the gate of the time-share community, I followed Kate inside, thinking she might need help discouraging Abby from joining us. Kate was filling Jane in, with no sign of Abby or Red. I spotted my iPad on the coffee table and grabbed that. Eugena told me how to find the building and the restroom where she was currently hiding. When I said goodbye, Eugena added, "Hurry, Leslie. Soon they'll send in a female associate after me. She'll talk at me through the stall door and shove contracts at me."

"We've got Jane, and we'll be there soon." I hung up.

"Abby's taking Red on a walk," Jane said, scribbling something on a sheet of paper. "I'm leaving a note that we'll be back soon."

Jane fed the address Eugena had given me into her app, and we headed off. "Poor Eugena," Kate said. "I've been sitting across the table from pushy salesmen before. I really hate to be disagreeable, but the only thing you can do is to say, 'No, thank you,' to their every question."

"Even when they're just asking your name?" I asked, expecting her to reply that this was her one exception.

"*Especially* then. That *really* cuts a conversation short."

I envisioned going up to someone and saying, "Hi, I'm Leslie. What's your name?" and only getting the reply, "No, thank you." That would make *me* turn around and search for someone—*anyone*—else to talk to.

"Oh, I can rip any marketeer to shreds," Jane said. "You two can just wait in the car, if you'd like."

"Actually, I think all three of us should go in," I said. "I've been at these things before. There's strength in numbers."

The resort turned out to be a gated community on the northwest side of town. It had the look of a private golf course in the Missouri foothills. We got past the security guard at the gate by telling him we were going to a timeshare presentation, found the building, and parked in a shady space.

"The Boob Team arrives to save the day," I said as we got out of the car. "We're the Three Musketeers."

"Have you ever read that book?" Kate asked.

"No," Jane and I said.

"I own it on my eReader, though," I added. "I just haven't even tried to start it."

"Should we add it to our list for classics?"

"That's Dumas, right?" Jane asked. "He always makes me feel like a 'Dumb Ass.' And his books are so long."

"True. Let's not add it," Kate said.

Jane opened the door and said, "Ladies?" gesturing for Kate and me to go ahead of her.

Before we could search for the bathroom, we were stopped by an attractive, well-dressed young woman who insisted we fill in the login sheet and show her our driver's licenses.

"No, thank you," Kate said pleasantly.

"I'm not here for a presentation," I explained, "only to pick up a friend who needs transportation.

She felt so badgered by your high-pressure tactics that she's now holed up in the restroom."

"We're just going to go on in," Jane said firmly, "grab our friend, and we'll be out of here before you can fill out the log on our behalf."

"I can't let you through those doors without getting your name and giving you a guest ID card. It's a safety precaution, you see."

"I understand," Kate said. "I'll wait here for Ms. Crowder. Is there a restroom I can use?"

The receptionist's smile faded ever so slightly, recognizing the trap that Kate was setting. "Um...I'm not sure. Let me buzz a manager."

"Okay. As long as he gets here immediately." She leaned over the counter toward the woman and whispered, "I have a really weak bladder." (Kate was looking past the receptionist's shoulder as she spoke.)

"I'll get someone right away."

"She's not kidding about the bladder," I said. "We're talking sixty seconds, tops, then it's a puddle of pee."

The woman nodded, her smile now resembling a grimace. She swept up her phone and dialed, turning her back on us.

"Sheila? Three girlfriends of a guest named Eugena Crowder are here. She's apparently hiding in a restroom. Can you come out?" There was a pause. "I think we need a female associate, though."

I winked at Kate, truly impressed that she'd proven to have a devious aspect to her Miss-Congeniality nature. In addition to being a card shark and a recovering alcoholic. *What an awesome woman!*

As soon as the clerk had returned her attention to us, Jane started eyeing her wristwatch and edging away from Kate, as if her bladder was about to explode any second now.

"An associate will be here momentarily and will escort you to find your friend. Why don't you both have a seat?"

"Oh, dear." Kate touched the sofa. "Has this upholstery been stain-proofed? I would hate to have an accidental...overflow."

"Let me just see if—" She broke off as a woman in a powder-blue pantsuit strode through one of the double doors. "Here's Sheila now."

"Hello," the woman said with an enormous smile that seemed to occupy half of her face. "I understand you want to tour the facilities."

"No, thank you," Kate said, "but I do need to *use* your facilities. I promise to be quick, though."

"My name's Sheila." She held out her hand.

"Leslie O'Kane," I said, shaking her hand.

"Hello, Sheila," Kate said.

"Jane Henderson. I'm Ms. Crowder's personal attorney. I charge by six-minute intervals, and only the first six minutes is free. I've been here for two."

"Do I have it right that you're looking for a guest named Eugena Crowder?"

"Yes, we are," I answered quickly, not wanting to force Kate into a nonsensical "no, thank you."

"Is this your first visit to Branson?"

"No, but thank you for asking," Kate said.

"Right this way. She's apparently indisposed, but we've been checking on her periodically."

"Eugena is merely indisposed to the concept of buying a time share," Jane said.

"I'm sorry to hear that she's making such a large mistake. This is the opportunity of a lifetime."

"Oh, I'm pretty sure she can get the same opportunity every day for the rest of her life simply by returning here."

"These homes will only be available for a short time. Next week, we'll be doubling the price!"

"I see," Jane said with her lawyer's smile. "You'll be making twice the commission next week by selling the very same properties. We're doing you a huge favor, then."

I pushed through the bathroom door. "Eugena?" I called.

"Leslie?" She was in the back-most stall.

"Yes, and Kate and Jane are here with me."

Jane said, "Hello, Eugena," just as Kate was saying, "Hi, Eugena."

"Can we get you anything?" Sheila asked. "An Alka-Seltzer or Imodium AD, perhaps?"

"No, thank you," we all said in unison.

Eugena opened the door. "I'm fine now," she said to Sheila, "but I really need to leave right away with my friends."

"Let me drive all of you around the facilities," Sheila said. "And then I'll take you directly to your car. How does that sound?"

"No, thank you," we said once again in unison.

"You really do look pale and a little under the weather," Sheila cooed. "It's very hot outside, and I'd hate to see you faint and injure yourself, Eugena."

"We'll take it from here," I said, as Kate and Jane flanked her and each took one of her arms.

"I'll get the doors," Sheila said. "I insist. You know, you're walking away from a fabulous investment. We are number one in trade values in the entire *world!* You would be able to rent out the half of the suite you'd be purchasing, and have a free vacation. Wouldn't you want to share an opportunity like that with your friends? With Leslie and Kate?"

"No, thank you," we all said.

"You're all here together, vacationing now. Where are you staying?"

"At a wonderful condo that only costs each of us ten dollars per day," I said. (A slight exaggeration.) "Thank you for holding the door. Have a nice day."

"You, too."

We crossed the parking lot without incident. "Looks like we made it," I said, resisting the Shania Twain music to accompany the lyric. (Ultimately those lyrics hadn't worked out well for her.)

"Yes, we did," Jane said. "I'm a little sorry I wasn't given grounds to intimidate them with legal actions."

Eugena sighed. "Once again, I am eternally indebted to all of you lovely ladies. I just get terrified now by big-ticket salespeople. And I get so nervous when I have to sign a contract that I have to take a Valium." She put a hand to her chest. "My heart is practically beating out of my chest."

"You poor thing," Kate said. "It was no problem. I just wish you'd called sooner. We'd have come right away."

"That's so kind. No wonder you're all such great friends. I wish I had friends like you."

"You do!" Kate declared. "We're all your friends!"

I offered the front seat to Eugena, and we got into the car. After Jane started the engine and pulled out of the space, Eugena said, "As I think I mentioned yesterday, I have plenty of friends. Just not tried-and-true friendships that have stood the test of time. Only Red lasted with me. He died long ago. You all know about my childhood. How I had to rely on myself. I finally met a man I thought I could trust in my ex-husband. But then, when he betrayed me, with my best friend, Jill, I just decided I couldn't handle the pain of opening my heart to anyone ever again. Not after my son died, too." She took a halting breath, fighting back tears. "But then, you wonderful women, with your wonderful little red dog, appeared. It's as if it was an answer to a prayer I didn't even have the courage to make." She covered her face. "I'm just so grateful," she said, tearfully.

I reached around her seatback to pat her upper arm. *Her ex-husband must be lying about her through his ratty little teeth,* I thought. For a minute or so, nobody spoke.

She lifted her chin, as if in defiance of her justifiable emotions. "You...Boobs have been the best thing to happen to me in the last twenty years. There's nothing I can possibly do to repay all that you've done for me."

"That's sweet," I said.

"I mean it. I'm not one to pay someone empty compliments. So..." she met my gaze. "I'm not all that religious, but I'm very spiritual. You wonderful women are either my angels, or my fairy godmothers."

"I rather like the thought of being a good fairy," I said.

Kate signaled and turned into a gas station. "I really do have a weak bladder. "I need to use the bathroom."

"Our poor Tinklebell," Jane said, patting Kate's shoulder.

Chapter 16
Choosing Sides in Dixie

Once again, Eugena insisted on being dropped off at her hotel. She explained that, as an introvert, she'd already felt drained this morning by her agent and lawyer's unexpected arrival, and was then all-but incapacitated by the high-pressure timeshare salesmen. She needed the comfort of solitude to breathe and clear her head.

Back at the condo, we reassured Abby that Eugena was not suffering over her timeshare experience. I then managed to get Kate to tell us about her experiences as she won seven out of eight pots at the casino. (She mentioned "streets" and "rivers" in her description, which launched Abby into a brief tangent about the injustice in the game of "bridge" not having "tunnels.") We were all happy for Alicia and Kurt reuniting and agreed unanimously that Kurt's proposal Wednesday night at the live show would come as a surprise to Alicia.

Kate hadn't been able to listen to Abby's portion of her and my phone conversation, so Jane gave Kate a brief recap of their meeting with Eugena and her former-ish agent and lawyer. "They're just greedy shysters," Abby said. Seated on the Navajo-patterned rug, she gave Red a big hug, who looked up and panted in her face. "*Aren't* they, my little angel," she baby-talked to him.

"Actually," Jane said, "I spoke with Eugena privately after today's confrontation in the lobby. I can't discuss our conversation, of course, but it's fair to say that Eugena told me some things that made her agent sound more rational."

"Personally," Abby said, crossing her arms, "I think Natalie's been changing her story, which is confusing Eugena."

I was focused on Jane's statement. "Eugena definitely fired Natalie's boyfriend, right?" I asked her.

"Right. I wrote up a letter for dissolution of representation for him, which she signed and faxed to his office. He sent me a text that read: 'Good luck. You two deserve each other.'"

"He sounds like a misogynist, if you ask me," Abby grumbled.

"But what does Eugena mean when she told Natalie that she's on probation?" I asked, once again looking at Jane, whom I trusted to give an unbiased assessment.

"I'm not entirely clear on that, because *Eugena* isn't clear. If I were to engage in conjecture, I would say that Eugena hasn't fired Natalie because she realizes that Natalie could well be telling the truth."

"About what?" Abby asked in obvious surprise.

Jane hesitated. "A client can sometimes tell their attorneys about their own state of mind...which makes them uncertain about the instructions that they gave to an employee, for example. Eugena could have admitted, for example, that she could have misspoken about our motives for driving her to Branson."

"Well, *that's* more than a little disturbing," I said.

Abby shook her head. "It's just because Eugena doesn't want to hurt Natalie's feelings. Regardless of how badly Natalie has been trampling all over her."

"Again, I don't feel comfortable discussing this, beyond my personal opinion that Natalie might not be completely in the wrong. Meanwhile, Susan called me back about Rachel Jones, the now-missing assistant editor in Eugena's publishing house. The woman resigned two weeks ago because her husband was relocating to L.A. Eugena had gotten the date of her departure wrong when she was telling us about Rachel yesterday."

"I don't understand," Abby said. "Natalie is obviously lying through her teeth."

I turned to Abby. "Jane is implying that Eugena revealed to her in confidence that she has Alzheimer's." Jane started to speak, but I held up a hand. "Eugena already hinted she was worried about having Alzheimer's when we picked her up, so it really isn't a breach of attorney-client privilege."

"I'd bet anything Red wouldn't like Natalie one bit," Abby said. "She's a con artist, and I hate that she's got poor Eugena in knots." (In book discussions, once Abby decides she likes a particular character, she sticks with that opinion. Maybe that plays a part in her rarely finishing books.)

"Eugena could have been sun-downing during her phone conversation," I snapped. "Ask Siri."

"That's when patients with dementia start deteriorating in the late evening, isn't it?"

"Yes."

"Oh, now I get it," Abby said. "Poor Eugena! I wonder if she ever forgets she'd written something."

My phone buzzed, signaling that I'd gotten a text message. I grabbed it out of my purse. "It's Eugena," I said. "That's a surprise. I thought her hands shook too much to type."

"She probably spoke into her phone instead of typing," Abby said.

"Oh, right." The message read:

Leslie-Hate to be a bother again but any chance you can give me feedback on my book?

I winced. With all of the Alicia turmoil, I'd forgotten all about reading Eugena's manuscript.

"Is she all right?" Abby asked.

"Yes, she just wants my comments on her book. Which I need to read right now."

Using the really awkward, all-thumbs' technique that everyone under age thirty masters with ease, I eventually replied:

Just collecting my thoughts on that now!

(So far, those thoughts were: *Whoops. I need to start reading.*)

Eugena's reply was:

Great! Meet me in my lobby at six.

I cursed and looked at my watch. It was almost three. "We have another dinner show scheduled tonight, right?"

"At seven," Kate said. "Although the tickets say that doors open at six thirty."

"Is that near Eugena's hotel, by any chance?"

"Right across the street," Kate replied.

"Would you mind dropping me off at the Marriott at six? I'll join you at the theater afterward."

"Of course. I'd be happy to."

I sent the message:

See you then.

"I'm going to have to hole myself up in my bedroom and read the manuscript for the next three hours."

"You'll love it," Abby told me. "I read it last night. I put it on the dresser. And by the way, she told me this morning that it was okay to write our comments on the margins. She has another clean copy with her."

"Okay, thanks."

"It's too bad you haven't read it yet. I'm going to her room in an hour. We're going to go over the details for what my new job will be, and she might even let me get started right away. We maybe could have gone there together." She beamed at me. Her voice had a lilt of pride to it.

"That sounds like fun," I said.

She chuckled. "First day on the job!" She swept up Red. "I'm going to take Dogface here for another walk by the lake. Anybody want to come with me?"

Both Kate and Jane said yes. I grabbed the manuscript, rushed to Kate's and my bedroom, and dived right in, feeling that familiar glee at a new adventure, happily swept back into Eugena's life in the rural confines of Missouri in the late fifties. The joy that reading gives me is incalculable. I don't know how I could have even gotten out of bed after my husband's death without books to sustain me. Today, I was no longer a widow with a distraught daughter; I was Jean "M.J." Taylor, now fourteen-years old, determined to hitchhike my way out of my impoverished existence, with Red, Jr. by my side.

Three hours later, I resumed my actual identity, and Kate renewed her offer to drop me off at the hotel. I scrambled to neaten the edges of the now-riffled manuscript, and hurried off to my appointment with its author.

In the lobby of the Branson Marriott, Eugena Crowder was sitting in an overstuffed chair that dwarfed her small, bird-like frame. Her eyes were closed and she was literally nodding out—her head dropping and then raising as she struggled to say awake. She could have been my mother, or anyone's mother, alone and frail. I—along with a huge percentage of children's fiction fans—knew this particular elderly woman was someone who'd led a tough life and whose resolve should never be questioned. She had given the world such a splendid book that touched not only my life, but my children's lives. I admired the woman more than I could say and was indebted to her.

I stood in front of her, unable to decide if I should clear my throat, start talking as if I hadn't noticed she was asleep, or maybe let her sleep for another minute or two. Her head dropped suddenly, and her eyes flew wide. She focused on me then, her brow furrowing and her lips tightening as if I'd breached her personal space. Then she recognized me and smiled.

"Hi, Eugena," I said. "I'm sorry to interrupt your sleep. I'm sure you're exhausted. You've been going through such an ordeal."

"Oh, no, Leslie. It's not a problem. I tend to nod off quite often. I'm just turning into an old bag of bones. I suppose one of these days I'll just drift off to sleep like that and never open my eyes again."

I didn't know quite how to respond, so I simply returned her smile and took a seat on the matching chair beside her.

I glanced down at the manuscript in my hands, wanting to give myself a moment to calm myself before I launched into my critique.

"So did you read it?" she asked. "My latest effort?"

"I did, Eugena. And I'm so honored that you gave me the pleasure of—"

She reached over and touched my knee. "Leslie, my dear, let's please cut straight to the chase. I know you're a big fan of my first book, and I know that you teach a composition course at a community college. Your opinion is more meaningful to me than most. So give me your honest appraisal. Pretend this is the monthly book in your little group, and I was no more important or attached to the manuscript than any member of your club."

"I'll do my best, though that's easier said than done." (I mean, *come on!* This was one of my favorite authors of all-time sitting in front of me. How was I supposed to say to her face that she had written a book that wasn't anything special?) "I enjoyed the book very much, and it's a worthy-enough sequel to one of the best books I've ever read. You kept an excellent focus on Jean and Red's relationship. The dialogue is witty. The story is engaging. Fun characters."

"Yet you didn't like it compared to *A Dog Named Red*."

"Not as much, no. The stakes in this story aren't as high. Her choices aren't as painful. Her story arc isn't as steep. But, let's face it. If you'd managed those feats, you'd have to write virtually the same exact story. Which wouldn't have worked. Instead, you continue the story as it would have unfolded two years later, with Jean having had two more years to learn about herself and her place in this world, while she's leaving her abusive father and carving out a new life for herself, with her trusted canine companion."

"Go on."

"Your readers will love seeing how Jean turned out. We can see how she's gained courage and confidence from the original Red, and you let us know that she's going to be okay as an adult. That she'll build a good life for herself. And, in the meantime, we get the gift of spending more time with the adorable Red. If it's published word for word like this, I'll be delighted to see it on shelves." I held the manuscript out to her, but she merely stared at it.

"Were there things you think I could have improved upon?"

"Not really. And besides, I'm not an editor, so I wouldn't presume to make suggestions to you as if I were knowledgeable enough."

"You're a *reader*, Leslie. What questions did you have as a reader that you wish I'd have answered?"

"None. You tied up everything nicely."

"But...?" she prodded sternly.

"Well, I wished I knew more about why she is so dismissive of her Aunt Margaret. She didn't even give her a *chance* to be a caregiver. Instead, M.J. assumed she'd be indifferent, and set her up to fail."

"Precisely as I intended it."

"But...doesn't that go against what she's telling Red? About when Red should be suspicious of people and when he shouldn't?"

"Jean's doing what we all do. She's saying one thing and yet doing the other."

"Right, but shouldn't *she* realize that herself? Shouldn't she say to Red, 'But I guess I wasn't listening to my own advice when it came to dealing with Aunt Margaret, eh, boy?'"

She glared at me. "Maybe so, but then again, she's talking to a *dog*, so she's allowed to misspeak."

"True," I said with a chuckle, all the while thinking: *But your readers are people, not dogs, and we're the ones who would appreciate that she recognizes her own hypocrisy. Otherwise, why tell us about her contrary advice in the first place?*

"Any *other* observations?" Eugena asked.

"No," I lied, certain that there was no point in mentioning the five other points that I would have gone ahead and brought up for discussion if this was an actual book-club meeting. "I'm truly delighted that you've written the sequel and that it stands up as a worthy continuation of the story."

"I'm delighted that you're delighted. I just wish you were my actual editor. It probably *would* strengthen the story to clue the reader in to Jean's self-awareness."

I shrugged. "I think it would, but it's so minor, and it's just one person's opinion. You could always handwrite the sentence in and see what your editor thinks. Or not."

"But I really mean that. *You* should be my editor, Leslie. You're so very articulate and perceptive."

"Your publisher has been really successful for a long time, and they did a fabulous job on the first *Red.* You didn't have any problems with your editor, did you?"

"Nary a one. But she's retired. My new editor is a twit-head. She's no older than Jean is."

"She's a college graduate, surely."

"Technically she's at least twenty-four, but you should see how young she is!"

"Is she nice? And competent?"

She shrugged. "I'm sure she wouldn't kick a dog. And that she can read and sign her name and get herself to work in New York every day. But do I trust her to make *On the Road with Red* the best book that it can be? Absolutely not! Yet, here *you* are, a professor who teaches writing, an obvious dog lover, an avid reader, an obvious leader...and right away, you're able to find an improvement that I could make. I'm sure you have several more suggestions that you're unwilling to share with me."

"Not really. I loved the book as it is." (I was lying. I truly believed she *would* benefit by my editing the book for her. I just didn't want to hurt her feelings.)

"I want to pay you to edit my manuscript," Eugena said.

I felt uncomfortable. With Jane's implications that Eugena had forgotten that she told her agent she didn't trust us yesterday, trouble could arise too easily. "Let's think on it for a few days."

"I consider myself an excellent judge of character, and I can sense that we're kindred spirits. But if you're not ready to take the leap with me, I'm certainly not going to push."

"We'll talk about this again soon, then," I said pleasantly, wondering all the while if I was nuts to hesitate about accepting a dream job offered on a silver platter. And yet, if there was one thing I'd learned about myself over the half century I'd spent in my own skin, it was to trust my instincts. Right now, those instincts were telling me that if Jane was here now, she'd try to drag me away from Eugena.

On the other hand, Abby was on cloud nine with Eugena hiring her as her assistant. I was happy for her. Furthermore, *I* had been offered the chance to edit one of my favorite author's manuscript! Me! Leslie O'Kane!

What a godsend Eugena was! We'd all gotten a new sense of purpose from her. Jane was taking up a legal cause she actually cared about this time— fighting for the rights of an elderly woman to think for herself and take control of her own career. Abby was thrilled to be Eugena's assistant. Kate was able to drape her loving cape around Eugena's shoulders, her favorite thing to do—helping others to feel valued. And I was brushing shoulders with literary greatness.

I'm going to tell her yes tomorrow night, I told myself.

Chapter 17
An Unfortunate Hypnotic Incident

I left the Marriott and walked over to the dinner show, where tonight we would watch a hypnotist. Kate was pulling into the entrance just as I neared it, so she jokingly rolled down her window and asked if I wanted a lift. Still a little giddy from my soaring hopes at having found a mentor, I took her up on the offer and promptly whined, "Are we there yet?" then rode some fifty feet to a parking space.

Once again, even though we were thirty minutes early for the show, the place was packed, and someone was already speaking into a microphone on stage. A stocky young man in jeans and a T-shirt, his dark hair in a ponytail, was talking about the locations of the bar (along the back wall) and the restrooms (in the far corner). We made our way to an open table right next to the buffet table, feeling fortunate that it had four empty chairs. "Is arriving at places early a character trait of Mid-westerners?" I asked Kate.

"I think it's just a factor of the older demographic that comes here." We both scanned the audience, and she beat me to noting, "Although there are lots of families with children here tonight."

"What's with the guy on the stage?" I asked.

"He's giving us something of a safety demonstration," Jane said. "Not unlike a flight attendant."

He finally left the stage. After several minutes of chattering amongst ourselves, the dinner-theater's "flight attendant" returned and announced that we could go ahead and get in line and help ourselves. We rose as some fifty-plus people rushed in our direction to reach the buffet table, and others rose as well. This could be another version of Dolly Parton's "Dixieland Stampede."

"I'm a little scared," Kate said, as we found ourselves at the front of the seemingly ravenous crowd.

"I'm glad Eugena decided not to come," Abby said. "She's so tiny and frail, I'd be afraid of her getting trampled."

As we spoke, a half-dozen children sprinted in front of us. I was perfectly willing to accommodate line-butting. I had no intention of hijacking anyone's fried chicken, iceberg-wedge salad, mashed potatoes, or, God forbid, gravy. The children, however, were making a race out of piling food on their plates, and there was some spillage and splattering. With my simple sleeveless dress being wash-and-wear, I decided it was best to protect my lips and glued-in tooth. I held my plate high and a mere six inches from my chest to maximize the extension of my elbows. Rows of plastic cups lined up filled with lemonade, iced tea, and water. The girl ahead of me sloshed her lemonade, but none of it hit me. I felt victorious as I headed to my table.

"I'm glad you took my suggestion, Kate," Abby said after we'd returned to our seats. "I figured this would be a really different experience for all of us. I didn't want to book us into another musical revue like Alicia's. This fit the bill nicely."

"So it does," I said.

While we ate and chattered away, Jane kept gazing longingly at something behind me. I soon realized it was the bar. Hoping she was merely eying a handsome bartender, I followed her gaze. A woman was tending the bar; Jane had indeed been staring at the bottles.

The hypnotist went on stage. Her name was Carly. She looked and sounded like a former gym teacher of mine in high school, and she gave a rather dull talk about what hypnotism was and was not. She assured us that volunteers would never do something that they were completely opposed to, such as taking off all their clothes, nor would she ask us to do so.

"That's reassuring," I said. "I don't want to watch anyone take off their clothes, and I certainly don't want to undress on stage."

Abby nodded. "I know what you mean. It's all I can do to convince myself to take off my shoes so that I can take off my jeans. I'd probably fall and hurt myself."

Carly compared hypnosis to having a dream while you're sound asleep, except that you fully experience the dream; if the hypnotist tells you that there is a pink elephant in the room, you see a pink elephant in the room. To demonstrate, she had us close our eyes and hold out our palms. Within a minute or two, she'd persuaded me to believe that I had a heavy book in my right hand. Despite knowing that both of my hands were empty, the muscles in my right arm felt as if I was holding a hard-cover copy of *War and Peace*.

The hypnotist wrapped up her preliminary presentation, stating that children always wanted to volunteer, which was fine, but she also wanted a good number of adults and would accommodate however many people volunteered. She assured us for the second time that sometimes volunteers don't go under, and that they would have more than one opportunity to leave the stage.

"Raise your hand if you'd like to come up on stage and be hypnotized," Carly then said.

"I dare you all to raise your hands," Abby said, raising her own hand.

Neither Kate nor Jane raised their hands.

"Come on, Kate," Abby said. "Raise your hand." She did.

I shook my head. "Sorry. No interest." (In truth, I simply didn't want to leave Jane's side when there was a bar in the immediate vicinity. I intended to be a gadfly regarding Jane's drinking habit from here on out.)

"I'd sooner light my hair on fire," Jane said. "But thanks for asking."

Kate and Abby took seats on the stage, and Carly repeatedly instructed all volunteers not to sit next to anyone they knew. There were roughly thirty volunteers, at least ten of them children. The "flight attendant" set up extra folding chairs on stage, as needed.

Carly told the volunteers to close their eyes and imagine that they were at the beach. She did a nice job of painting the picture with her words. Curious, I, too, shut my eyes from my seat. I could feel and smell the salty ocean breeze. My skin grew hot from the sun on my skin. As she described how parched my throat was, I needed a drink of water. As she described the continuously rising temperature, I felt as if I was having a hot flash. The illusion broke, though, when she described the cloud covering the sun and the temperature dropping. I cooled down, but didn't feel shivery with cold. I opened my eyes and saw Jane watching me with a bemused expression on her face.

"Welcome back. How was your beach vacation?"

"Too crowded."

She pointed at the stage with her chin. "Abby looks close to getting hyperthermia. Kate...not so much."

Indeed, Kate had her arms crossed, but didn't have chattering teeth and a horrid case of the shivers, like poor freezing Abby. Among the three rows of volunteers, the children struck me as playacting and a dozen or so of the adults on stage were every bit as frozen-to-the-bone as Abby. One man seemed to be in a coma-like sleep.

Carly began weeding out the hams and the genial from the deeply hypnotized. She tapped each person and told them to fall asleep. Those who didn't nod out instantly were sent back to their tables in the audience. She told the sound-asleep man to wake up, and he, too, left the stage. She then proceeded to weed out the volunteers as she painted more pictures for them. She had them watching a funny movie, then watching a sad scene, smelling sweet, enticing aromas, followed by repulsive odors.

Abby's reactions were true to her nature and uncensored. She behaved as she might if she was home alone, watching a television show. Kate, however, chose to leave the stage.

"I could really smell the popcorn," Kate told us as she reclaimed her seat, "but the farting thing was a big turnoff for me."

"Did you feel like you were hypnotized?" I asked.

"I'm not sure. On a scale of one to ten, I guess I was a three. It was as if my suspension of disbelief wasn't strong enough to accept that the things she was telling me were happening actually were." She grinned at me. "I learned that phrase, 'suspension of disbelief,' from you in book club, by the way."

Touched that she'd thought to tell me that, I returned her smile. I truly, *truly* love my book club! It occurred to me that I hadn't emailed Susan about any books lately and tried to think if we'd read any books about hypnosis, but none came to mind. Meanwhile, Carly told the volunteers that they'd just won a brand new car in a contest. All they had to do to get the car was to tell her they'd won a car, and she'd give them the keys.

Abby was promptly hopping up and down with glee, and she was the first person to get her keys from Carly. I'd never seen her quite so happy and proud as she started that invisible ignition of hers.

"Abby looks like she's really into it," Kate said, grinning.

I had to chuckle. She was driving the car with such relish. "I wonder what type of car that is that she thinks she's driving."

"She's got to just be playing along, don't you think?" Jane asked.

"No," Kate said, "I think it's exactly like the hypnotist explained. It's like you're sleepwalking and seeing and hearing all that's in your dream. In her dream, Abby is sitting in a car."

"I'll bet anything Red is in the passenger seat," I said. It made me happy to see her beaming like that and waving at everyone as if she was so proud of her new wheels.

The hypnotist approached Abby with the microphone and told her to put her brakes on and get out of the car. Abby mimed doing just that. Charmingly, she hugged herself with delight at her good fortune as she stood in the center of the stage next to Carly.

"That's a pretty wonderful car you've got there," Carly said. "How did you get it?"

"I won it," she replied with a big smile.

"What for?"

"I don't know. You tell me. You're the one that gave me the keys."

The audience laughed.

"That's right. I did. You must have done something really special."

"I don't remember anything," Abby said, her brow furrowed. "I *did* just get a new job."

"Did you now?"

"I sure did. I'm officially a personal assistant for a famous writer...Eugena Crowder! That really just means I'm her new office girl...gofer. Go fer this. Go fer that."

Again she got a laugh.

"You do a lot of mundane office work, I take it," Carly said.

"Oh, no. It's not mundane at all. Though I've only worked for her for two hours." She again got a smattering of laughs. "But today I already did something really sneaky for her."

"You don't have to tell us what you did," Carly quickly replied. "I was just—"

"Good, because if my friends found out, they'd be mad at me." Abby waved at us.

"Uh, oh," Carly said, looking straight at us. "Those are your friends right over at that table, aren't they? The gals you were sitting with?"

"Yes, and *one* of them is a lawyer. And she'd want to *kill* me if she knew I mailed the author's manuscript to a publisher. Eugena was just so scared of her agent taking advantage of her. Her agent's a terrible woman, who's making buckets of money for selling the book. So today *I* sent it to another editor, free of charge."

Jane gasped and grabbed the edge of the table as if to steady herself.

"Oh my God," I muttered.

On stage, Carly said, "Let's get you back in your car, shall we?" She was chuckling, but my impression was that she'd realized at once that her volunteer had spoken too openly. Carly went over to the proud-looking young man a couple of invisible cars away from Abby's and asked him to tell us about his car.

"Is there any chance Abby's kidding?" Kate asked. "That she didn't really send in the manuscript?"

Having been partially hypnotized, Kate had to know the answer better than either of us. Even so, I shook my head. "It's like she's answering questions honestly in her sleep." I asked Jane quietly, "This hasn't put Abby in real trouble, has it?"

"It sure as hell *could*," Jane fired back. "We only just met Eugena. None of us know if we can trust her."

"It sounds like Eugena asked her to send it," Kate said, "and she's now Abby's boss, so how could she possibly get Abby in trouble?"

"We don't know whether or not Eugena asked her to mail the manuscript. Even if she *did*, she might not remember." Jane rose and met my gaze. "I'm going to go get a drink from the bar. But only one."

I gritted my teeth but held back, feeling caught between the proverbial rock and hard place. Meanwhile, the hypnotist had convinced the volunteer that he was Elvis and we'd all come to watch him perform. Shortly afterward, Carly tapped Abby on the forehead and sent her back to our table, telling her she was now wide awake and feeling refreshed. Abby came down from the stage and plopped down beside me.

"Well, that was disappointing," Abby told me. "I thought for sure I'd be hypnotized, but it didn't work one whit on me."

"Are you serious? You don't remember anything?"

"What do you mean? What's to remember?"

"You were convinced you'd won a car, and you were driving throughout the neighborhood, showing off."

"Don't tease me, Leslie."

"I'm totally serious."

She clicked her tongue. "There's no way I'd do something like that!" An instant later, she froze. "Wait. I'm starting to remember something about driving a car."

"You *also* announced to everyone that you'd surreptitiously sent in Eugena's manuscript to a publishing house."

She gaped at me. After a second or two, she grabbed my arm. "Please tell me you're kidding."

"I'm telling the truth. How else would I suddenly know what you did?"

"Oh, holy crap." She rolled her eyes. "Now Jane's going to be all in my face. I was only doing what I felt was right for Eugena's sake."

"She told you to mail it in, right?"

"Essentially. She kept saying she wished she had the guts to send it to this other editor, who was better than the editor her agent had chosen."

"So you sent it for her?" Kate asked.

"Yeah." She shrugged. "I told her afterward she could blame *me* for the mix-up, if the new editor felt she would be stuck in the middle, or if her current editor felt belittled by the whole idea."

She glanced at Kate, who was listening intently, looking miserable.

"So did Eugena talk to anyone in New York about this yet?" I asked.

"Not as far as I know."

"But she *does* know you mailed it?" I asked, mentally crossing my fingers. "And she's okay with that?"

"I don't know. I mean, yes, she knows. It's what she wanted me to do. I overnighted it, but nobody at the publishing house knows about it yet."

"This gives me a bad feeling," Kate said.

"It'll be fine. Eugena was very relieved when I told her."

"And yet you didn't want *us* to know. So obviously you weren't entirely comfortable with the decision."

"That's not true. I simply didn't want to be bragging all the time about my new job...and new employer." Her cheeks were growing pinker as she spoke. Like me, she didn't have the best poker face.

A random memory hit me about my thinking what a wonderful man Steve was last night and my inventing lyrics to "Santa, Baby." "Abby? Isn't nitrous oxide used as a truth serum?"

"I don't need a truth serum. I have nothing to hide! I was just trying to help Eugena. It made no sense for her to keep paying for her agent's mistakes."

Jane returned to the table, a glass of red wine in her hand, and reclaimed her seat. "So nice job with the stripper routine."

"What?" Abby shrieked.

"Just kidding. I'm sure Leslie filled you in."

Abby crossed her arms defiantly and sat back in her seat, glaring at Jane. "And I'm sure you're about to launch into a lecture."

"I *was*, actually, but then I realized *I'm* the one who originally took offense at Eugena's lawyer dating her agent. I'm the one who set us all on this let's-help-Eugena path."

"I'm so glad you realize that," Abby exclaimed. "*Somebody* needs to stand up for the defenseless in our society."

"Oh, Abby, my dear, Eugena is hardly defenseless. She wanted you to send in the manuscript. She's doing precisely what she wants with her new book. And I've decided I agree with her." She lifted her glass. "Hear, hear to capable adults making their own decisions, wise or other-*wise*."

None of us moved a muscle. Jane looked a little surprised that we hadn't reacted to her toast. "Whoops. I forgot. I'm the only one with a glass."

"You're sure Eugena is a 'capable' adult?" I asked.

Jane chugged her wine and set down her glass, but continued to stare at it. "She's every bit as capable of running her own life as I am capable of running mine," she said quietly.

"Oh, Jane," Kate cried. "I've been there myself, and AA works—"

"I'm fine," Jane snapped. "Let's watch the show, shall we?"

Chapter 18
The Young, Old, and Restless

Several minutes after the four of us had returned to the condo, someone began ringing the doorbell repeatedly. My first thought was that this could be Alicia, in hysterics over yet another argument with Kurt. I raced to the door and swung it open. Eugena was standing there on the porch, wearing her denim hat, the portions of her face that I could see looking ghostly white under the porch light. She was still punching the button despite the door being fully opened.

"Eugena. Is everything okay?" (This was a really stupid question in retrospect.)

She put a trembling hand to her chest. "Leslie. I'm so glad you're here."

"We're all here. Come in."

Abby brushed past me and put her arm around Eugena's shoulders as she ushered her inside. "You poor dear! What's happened!"

We were all ignoring Red, who was spinning in circles to get attention.

"I suddenly couldn't remember how to get back to my hotel—or even that I had been *staying* at a hotel. I'd only gone out for a short walk. I've never felt so helpless! I was terrified! Then I remembered I was in Branson with you angels, and that I could trust you to protect me. I found your condo address on my cellphone, thank God, and used Google Maps to find my way. And here you are."

"You're safe here with us, your friends," Kate said.

"Thank you, dear." She gave Kate a big hug.

Jane was peering at Eugena as if skeptical. "Have a seat," Jane said, gesturing at the recliner. "Take a few deep breaths, and settle in."

"I'm so embarrassed," Eugena said as she sat down gingerly. She seemed to be so flummoxed and reluctant to intrude that she didn't want to dent the chair cushions.

"No worries," I said. "It's great to see you, and we'll give you a ride back to the Marriott whenever you like."

"Or you can spend the night here," Abby said. "We have an extra bed."

"No, but thank you. I like my hotel room. I just couldn't *find* it." She removed her hat.

Red had been trying to get her attention, but now grew discouraged and lay on his side next to Eugena's chair.

"I'll accompany you to your room," Abby told her. "I'll even stay with you, if you'd like."

"That's so wonderfully kind of you." She sat back on the recliner, still looking very pale and shaken. She gripped the armrests and blew out a shaky breath. "I'm so sorry. I feel like such a silly old woman."

"Oh," Kate said, patting her forearm and kneeling beside her. "There's nothing silly about you, and you are clearly young at heart."

She snorted. "That may or may not be true, but either way, I'm clearly old at brain." She sighed. "All my adult life, I've been scared of getting Alzheimer's. And I dare say, it seems to have been slowly nibbling at my edges." Her eyes filled with tears.

"You have to understand. My life is my words. My writing. That's all I've got left in this world. And now I'm losing a grip on them. Some terrible criminal took my son from me. As well as my husband. He couldn't recover from the heartbreak, and it tore our marriage apart. That's what led him to cheat on me with my friend."

"Oh, Eugena! You poor thing!" Jane cried. To my surprise, she actually *was* crying. But then, she was also inebriated, so I probably shouldn't have been all that surprised.

"You still write beautifully," Abby said. "I loved *On the Road with Red*. It's every bit as good as the first book."

Perhaps encouraged by hearing his name, Red got up and trotted over to Abby, who patted her thigh. He hopped into her lap and settled down.

"Yes, you can still write with the best of them," I said, thinking that was true-ish.

"That's very kind of you both to say. But the truth is, there are limitations now. I forget words all the time now. I'm living with a ticking time bomb. I'm losing my memories and my entire identity...all that is precious to me. Soon I'll be nothing but a frail old person, perpetually surrounded by strangers. I won't even remember how to type."

"Hopefully, that will never happen," Abby said. "You might not have Alzheimer's, and even if you do, medical science is making wonderful advances. Plus, your books about Red will be your legacy. If worse comes to worst, I'll help you write the next one. You can dictate the story to me, and, if need be, I'll brush it up."

"Oh, no, dear." She shook her head and seemed to be stirred out of her gloom. "That will never be all right by me. In fact, it will be a sign that I've definitely succumbed to dementia."

"Your vocabulary is certainly not diminished at the moment," I pointed out, wanting her to stay positive.

Abby was petting Red, but raised one palm, as if to make an oath. "I hear you, Eugena. I got a little carried away, is all."

"That's why it's so critical to me that *Red on the Road* be the best it can be."

Abby and I exchanged worried glances. Eugena had misstated her own title. Maybe she truly *was* suffering from incipient Alzheimer's.

"I just can't let my agent take control of my book and my career like this. She forced me to send my first draft to the publisher. Now she wants me to send in my second draft before I know that it's ready."

"What do you mean?" I asked. I was getting anxious. *Abby* had just sent in the manuscript, due to Eugena telling her that was what she wanted. "You remember this evening I returned your manuscript to you, right? Was that your second draft, or your first?"

"My second. I read your comments, and they'll make all the difference! I can't wait to get started on your suggestions. But Natalie, my agent, talked to me right after you left the Marriott," she explained. "She thought I should send my manuscript to my editor now, and not take any input from you. I told her 'no' in no uncertain terms. I'm not letting her or anyone in New York see my second draft—or any other draft—until I'm satisfied with every word."

Abby burst into tears. "You already did," Abby said, "you just forgot about it." She hugged Red.

"Forgot *what*? What do you mean?"

"You asked me to send a manuscript to Brandy Carlton, a couple of hours before Leslie arrived this afternoon. So that's what I did."

"I don't believe you! Why would I do something like that? Brandy works at a competitor's publishing house. I'm under contract. I legally can't submit it to anyone else!"

Like Kate, Red got anxious at witnessing disagreements. He dashed to the center of the living room and sat down, watching us while panting heavily.

"That's not what you told me this afternoon," Abby said. "You told me that Brandy and your editor *both* work at Manor House (not its real name). But Brandy was more motivated than your current editor, and your agent was too swayed by her friendship with your editor. I volunteered to send it to Brandy, and you said that was a great idea and thanked me profusely."

Eugena sat staring straight ahead for several seconds, her hands on her thighs, rubbing them as if unconsciously. "Oh, my gosh. That's right." She got that helpless, confused look on her features again. "I remember now. But my contract *isn't* with Manor House."

"No, it isn't," Jane said. "Since Abby only sent it today, she can just call this new editor, Brandy, in the morning and explain there was a mix-up and that your book is under contract with another house."

"Oh. Of course." Eugena breathed a sigh of relief. Red hopped into her lap as if realizing she needed his companionship. She started petting him. "I didn't mean to make a wild accusation, Abby."

"It's all right. I should have asked for your editor's name and publishing house to make sure we were on the same page before I sent it to Brandy."

"You were only just starting your job," I said. "You can't even know what questions to ask right out of the gate."

"Leslie's right. This is my fault entirely," Eugena said. "We'll have to make sure it's morning when I give you any instructions. And you'll have to recheck the following morning, just for sure. You're a true friend, Abby."

"We *all* are," Kate said.

"I'm so grateful," Eugena said. "I need help for the first time in my life. I may have made a mess of things with Natalie and my editor. I might have given them two different versions, with alternate endings."

"We'll help you sort it all out," Abby said. "Plus, you've got the best lawyer around." She grinned at Jane, who merely raised an eyebrow.

Eugena pursed her lips and nodded. "I need to get a good night's sleep. Maybe my brain will feel clearer in the morning."

"Let's get you back to the Marriott and settled in," Kate said. "Both Abby and I will go with you."

"And we'll bring Red," Abby said.

Eugena put her hat back on and made a few more statements of gratitude. She hugged both Jane and me before leaving.

The calmness of just being with Jane in our otherwise empty condo was an unexpected blessing. "In retrospect," I said, "we should have paid a little more attention to the fact that Eugena was stealing Red and hitchhiking when we met her. Now it seems like she's pulled us into her muddle puddle."

"What Natalie and Chris did was questionable at best, blatantly unethical at worst. But not criminal."

"Luckily, like you said, Abby and Eugena can get this resolved tomorrow morning, so nobody will read it before it's retracted."

***

The next day, shortly after the four of us had returned from a nice "country-style" lunch (which, as best I could tell, meant fried entrees, sweet iced tea, pie, and really friendly waitresses), Alicia called and asked if she could pick me up for a stroll downtown. I told her that was a wonderful idea, and

I'd be ready to go whenever she arrived. Inwardly, however, my stomach was doing its something's-wrong-with-my-daughter routine.

I was relieved to find Alicia in a cheerful mood when she arrived. She was immediately hugging our book-clubbers (which sounds better than "hugging our Boobs") as she and they exchanged exclamations about how excited we all were about her performance tomorrow night. She also swept Red into her arms and laughed heartily when he licked her face. She must indeed have sorted things out with Kurt. As long as I could avoid letting the cat out of the bag, we could have a nice, carefree afternoon together.

It occurred to me that Kurt's proposal tomorrow would overshadow everything *else* about her show. We'd be unable to indulge afterward in our typical blow-by-blow conversations about the performance itself. We'd done this for countless live and televised performances throughout the years. She maintained an amazing ability to welcome and take constructive criticism well, and to use or discard my opinions as she saw fit.

We decided to head to Branson Landing and walk along the water. Branson had long, narrow lakes that curved around the city. I asked Alicia if their formations were natural or manmade, but she wasn't in the mood for chitchat and told me she didn't know and to ask Siri. That was the end of that subject. I was starting to reconsider my initial impression of her mood today. Once again, I'd apparently failed to take her acting skills into account.

"Are you nervous that we're going to be there at tomorrow night's performance?" I asked.

"No. It feels like old times. With the book club coming out to cheer me on."

"I'm glad. I don't know how you can perform in public without getting stage fright."

"My stage fright won't be *increased* by your presence tomorrow night. I still get nervous before I go on stage, every single time. I tell myself that it's adrenaline and gives me the extra burst of energy I need to nail my performance."

"That's great."

She glanced at my lips. "So Kurt's dad fixed your tooth, and it doesn't hurt anymore?"

"Yes. It's glued back into place, and it's probably more secure than the original glue job. I'll get my implant next month with my regular dentist."

"Kurt and I think his dad is going to ask you out. Just in case we're right, I wanted to tell you that, no matter what happens between Kurt and me, I'm all for you seeing Steve. He's super nice. He reminds me a little of Daddy, even."

"Me, too." *Which is probably the problem.* But her *no-matter-what-happens* phrase didn't bode well and took priority. I studied her eyes. "So what's wrong, sweetie?"

"Nothing, really. I'm just...worried. Mom, if you knew Kurt as well as I do, you'd know that I'm the one who isn't good enough to deserve *him.* Lately, I can't help but feel that it would be better for him if he found someone else. Somebody who wasn't all...dramatic and demanding. His mom says I'm just like her. Maybe that's why he's attracted to me. And he's so much like his dad. I'd rather not marry him than wind up unhappy, like *they* did."

"Frankly, I think you're more like *me* than Emily. But you can't calculate the odds of your staying together based on your similarities to each other's parents."

"Why not?"

"Because we all have our unique characteristics. And there's an element of luck involved. Both good and bad. Like Eugena's marriage, falling apart when their police-officer son was killed."

"Her son was killed? That's terrible. It's bad enough to lose your child, without losing your marriage, as well."

She slipped into a gloomy silence. Meanwhile, I needed to proceed with caution. I didn't believe for an instant that she would say anything but "Yes" when he proposed. Yet I had to guard myself from annoying her on the one hand versus tipping her off on the other hand.

"Did you have a nice time with Kurt last night?"

"Sure. It was fine."

"Just 'fine'?"

She shrugged. "It's like there's an elephant in the room. Neither of us is bringing up my proposing to him."

"That sounds best to me. Have a little confidence in your relationship and in the nature of life on this planet. Much more often than not, things tend to turn out well in the long run."

She glared at me. "But *in the long run*, we all die. The nature of life on this planet is that we're no *longer* living on this planet. Which means I should be thinking that, no matter whether or not Kurt and I ever get married, I'll die...so who cares?"

"Ack! I was just trying to encourage you, not get into an existential debate."

"You're the one who brought up 'life on this planet.'"

I blew out a puff of air. "Listen carefully, Alicia. Kurt loves you. You love him. You both want to be married to each other. It will happen. That's all I'm trying to say."

She teared up and nodded, then threw her arms around me and gave me a hug. "Thanks, Mom. You always know the right thing to say."

On the thousandth or so try.

Her cellphone alarm went off. "Oh, shoot. I forgot!" Our gazes met. "I'm so sorry, Mom. I've got to head to the theater for a meeting. I can drop you off at the condo first if we hurry."

Which would make her late. "Actually, I'd rather do a little window shopping. I'll catch the shuttle and meet up with the others."

"Are you sure? I don't mind being a few minutes late."

"I'm sure. Go on ahead. I'll see you later."

"Okay. Bye, Mom. You're the best."

"Go be great!"

She laughed. "You used to tell Ian and me that when you dropped us off at elementary school."

"And it worked. You're both great people."

I watched as she trotted away from me, feeling sad at the sight but unable to look away. That was the way parenting worked. She was running off to be her own person, separate from being my child. Exactly as it should be. Which didn't mean that it never hurt.

A young woman about Alicia's age was staring at me as Alicia passed her. When our eyes met, she approached. "Hi. You're Leslie O'Kane, right?"

I hesitated. *How did she know my name?* Her black hair was fashioned in a neat up-do, and she was wearing a plum-colored pant suit with creases so crisply pressed that they could slice through butter. (Which was not to say anyone would ever have reason to do so.) I coughed, laying the groundwork for a hasty departure if this young woman turned out to be another timeshare and/or Bible salesperson.

"Yes, I am," I said, managing a raspy timber to my voice. "Do I know you?"

"Not yet. My name is Mila Cavernacki. I'm a producer for the local show, 'Breakfast with Brittany.' We attended the same hypnotist show last night. I'd like to ask you some questions about Eugena Crowder."

Chapter 19
"Good Morning America?"

Oh, crap! Could Abby's statements under hypnosis be aired on TV? I had to stifle my reaction and knew from that I'd probably failed miserably. "That's nice. Were you planning on doing a piece on last night's show?"

"Maybe. That's one of the big bennies of my job. Our headquarters are in Springfield, which is just an hour away. I can get into any show in Branson I want to attend."

"Lucky you. How did you know my name?"

"Through some research I'm doing regarding an interview on Brittany's show."

My mind was racing. Mila must have seen Abby talking to me when she left the stage. She *had* to have talked to Eugena, who'd given Mila our names and physical descriptions. In any case, I did not want anything about Abby's talking about Eugena's manuscript to hit the airwaves. I decided to stall by barraging her with talk about my daughter's show. "It must be fun to interview people about the Branson shows. For what it's worth, I enjoyed the hypnotist last night. But I'm *really* looking forward to my daughter's show tomorrow night. She's one of the four performers in Rockin' Oldies. I've heard nothing but wonderful things about it."

"So have I. But, right now I'd like to get your comments regarding Eugena Crowder's statements on *Breakfast with Brittany* this morning."

"Eugena was on your *show* this morning?"

She nodded.

I was stunned. Could she be lying to me? "I can't comment. I didn't see it, obviously. I didn't even know the show existed until just now. Let alone that Eugena had gone to Springfield."

"She didn't. They sent *me* down to Branson with a cameraman, since Eugena didn't have a car. We set up an on-screen interview."

"On what topic? Her sequel?"

"Yes. She revealed to us that she's been abused, due to the clamor for her long-awaited sequel to *A Dog Named Red.*"

"*Abused?*"

"In our host Brittany's opinion, yes. She's being treated like a used Kleenex, now that the publishers have gotten the content they wanted."

"Again, Mila, I didn't know Eugena was going to make a public statement on the issue, and I don't know what she said, so—"

"So you're aware that her lawyer and agent have been abusive?"

"Not personally, no. I don't know enough about Eugena's relationship with her agent and lawyer to comment. I didn't hear her statements and didn't know she was going on air."

She started to reach into her blue leather purse. "I'd be happy to let you read the transcripts, or to watch it on my pad. It will just—"

My mind was still racing. Had Mila called Eugena Crowder last night after hearing Abby mention her mailing a manuscript? "How did this on-air interview come about?"

"Well, Ms. Crowder called our show on Sunday evening," she said. "I'm something of a workaholic and jumped right on it."

That was back when we were driving with Eugena to Branson. "Sunday? What time?"

Mila searched my eyes. "Why do you ask?"

"I was with Eugena for a good portion of the evening on Sunday. I can't even figure out when she could have placed the call. Are you sure Eugena called you?"

"We're quite certain it was Ms. Crowder. She told me she's discovered that everyone is trying to take advantage of her. She sees herself as something of a spokesperson for the elderly, who, as she rightly points out, are pushed around and silenced in our society all too easily."

"All I know firsthand about Eugena is that she's under a lot of stress," I said. "She says one thing, and the next morning, forgets all about it. I've only just met Eugena, though, so I'm not the person to ask about her."

Mila cocked her head and stared into my eyes. "It must be very unsettling to suddenly have so much dropped on your lap."

"*My* lap?" I was so confused and anxious, I looked down at my khakis, half expecting to see egg-yolk splatters. "I'm not from around here and don't know anything about the 'Brittany...Breakfast' show. Maybe I'm being overly sensitive or defensive, but I get the feeling you're trying to provoke me into saying something inflammatory."

She spread her arms and smiled. "I'm just trying to get background information for my story, Leslie. We're on the same side."

"There are *sides* to your story?"

"Very much so. It's quite obvious that paid professionals in Eugena's life are now trying to take advantage of her. It's a classic case of elderly abuse, and it's against the law. Her former lawyer and his girlfriend were in cahoots to cheat Eugena out of the royalties she deserved. But you're a good friend of Jane Henderson, Ms. Crowder's new lawyer, right?"

"Yes, I am."

"She'll get to the bottom of this, don't you think?"

I still had the uncomfortable feeling that Mila was coaxing me into saying something unwise. "She's a first-rate attorney. Now, if you'll excuse me, I—"

"Of course, Leslie. Let me give you my card. As the parent of one of our town's favorite celebrities, our viewers will take special interest in hearing how you feel about this travesty of justice."

I chuckled in spite of myself. "My daughter, Alicia, is very talented, and she's certainly *my* very favorite celebrity. But I'm sure Branson citizens have no interest in hearing my opinion on anything whatsoever." I stuffed her card into my pocket.

"Thanks for talking with me, Leslie. And please do give me a call. I'll give your daughter's show a boost."

"Are you telling me you'll publicize my daughter's performance *if* I give you information on my friends' relationships with Eugena?"

"It's not a bribe, Leslie. It's not even quid pro quo. I'm just adding local interest to a Branson story, that's all. A Branson performer's mom comes to town...helps to save an elderly national treasure from being swindled."

I needed to end this conversation and get my hands on a copy of the interview—from someone who wasn't eager to analyze my every facial expression. I reverted to my coughing tactic. "Excuse me. I hope my cough isn't contagious. Last time it turned into pneumonia."

"Meanwhile," Mila pressed, "Eugena says that a group of women, who wouldn't normally give her the time of day, are making like they're her closest friends, now that she's written a sequel to her beloved Newbery book."

Crap! No *wonder* Mila wanted my opinion! Eugena had bad-mouthed my book club. Or was Mila making a last-ditch effort at goading me into fanning the flames? Now I *had* to know what Eugena had said. "Actually, I'd like to look at that interview, after all."

"Certainly. In fact, let me send you a link. What's your email address?"

Now I was going to get swamped with emails from her. Still. I needed a copy in order to share the recording. I gave her my address, and within seconds, my mini-pad beeped.

"Again, Leslie, just call me if you have any questions. My cameraman and I are planning on staying in town. I'd be more than happy to take you to a show this evening, or to meet over a glass of wine. By the way, I'm texting Brittany to do a segment on your daughter's show. Maybe I'll see you there tomorrow night." She grinned at me.

I feigned another coughing fit and waved while rushing away. I ducked into a chain store and headed directly to their restroom. I put in my earbuds and played the broadcast of Eugena's interview, in which Brittany—a generically attractive young woman (blond, blue eyes, small nose, symmetrical features, full lips, nice makeup)—interviewed Eugena from her studio, with Eugena in a split-screen image.

After Brittany praised *A Dog Named Red* to the sky and Eugena thanked her, Brittany said, "Yet here you are in Branson, feeling stranded, and embroiled in a controversy that sounds to me like you're being mistreated by crooks, everywhere you turn."

"It *does* remind me of how Harper Lee and Margaret Mitchell must have felt when everyone wanted to them to write a sequel. The folks in New

York would happily have published their grocery lists," Eugena said.

"But in your case, you actually *have* written a sequel."

"Indeed, I have. It's called, *On the Road with Red*. My book continues my autobiographical story with Red, Junior. It describes how Red helps me to believe in myself, and teaches me how to love."

Brittany grinned. "So there really was a Red, Junior? Just like the Hollywood ending of *A Dog Named Red*?"

"Oh, absolutely. Red's spirit lived on in his son."

"Except he didn't," I grumbled at the screen. Although I could understand completely why Eugena wanted to let this fib continue for the sake of promoting her book. Besides, just because the puppy scene never took place didn't mean she'd never gotten a second dog she'd named "Red."

"I understand that in real life, you're experiencing quite a lot of conflict," Brittany said.

"Yes, although, in a way, I'm my own worst enemy. I get so involved in my writing, I start to feel like that fourteen-year-old girl that I once was, unable to trust anybody—for good reason. Then, when I'm done with writing for the day, I tell myself to be present in the here and now. I find myself trusting absolutely everybody, to act as if nobody could possibly have their own self-interests in mind as they give me unwanted advice to do this or that."

"I can only imagine how confusing that must be for you," Brittany exclaimed. "Having such a creative mind has really put you on an emotional rollercoaster."

"It has indeed. I'm on a financial rollercoaster as well."

"Yes. When we were chatting the other day, you told me a little about that. You've had quite the history with your agent, publisher, lawyer, and assistant, haven't you?"

"Sadly, I sure have," Eugena said.

Brittany waited, but Eugena did not elaborate. After an awkward pause, Brittany read from her notes, "Your agent accepted a bonus for placing you at your current publishing house, didn't she? Which was unethical?"

Still no comment.

"Plus, she was in a romantic relationship with your lawyer, so you haven't received good legal representation. Furthermore, you've since gotten an offer for substantially more money, which you can't accept because you're already under contract."

"*What?*" I cried at the screen.

Eugena pursed her lips. "I've since been advised that I can't talk about any of those frightful situations that you just described. I have people pulling me this way and that. My agent and former lawyer want me to believe one thing. My new lawyer and new assistant want me to believe something else. I don't know what to think! Or who I can believe."

"*Uh, oh,*" I muttered at the screen once more, my heartrate increasing and my breath growing short.

Brittany leaned forward, pausing as if to indicate that she was about to impart jewels of wisdom. "What does your gut tell you?"

Eugena shut her eyes and pursed her lips for a few seconds. Then she sighed and looked up, as if to heaven. "Ah, Brittany. If only I could answer that question." She stared into the camera. "My memories are all fading. My mind has become a deep, dark forest. I am writing this sequel as quickly as I can to preserve the person that I once was. But who I am now? Who will I be tomorrow?" Tears formed in her eyes. She took a ragged breath. "I no longer know, Brittany."

Chapter 20
Return of the Potheads

It was after two p.m. when I got back to the condo. I was reeling. Eugena's last line to the interviewer—*I no longer know*—kept running through my head. I'd forwarded the video clip to my book-club members—except my daughter. Kate had called me within minutes. She sounded sad and said Jane had stayed in the condo, Abby was in complete tears and couldn't speak, and she and Abby were downtown and on their way to the Marriott to see Eugena. Jane hadn't answered her phone when I called.

To my dismay, I was greeted by the smell of marijuana the moment I stepped through the door. I dropped my purse and followed my nose to Jane's bedroom. The door was mostly open, and I let myself in.

Jane, Marcus, and Jimmie were sitting cross-legged on her single bed. They gave me sheepish grins. Marcus promptly lifted his pipe toward me. "Want a hit?" he asked.

I ignored him. "You could get disbarred!" I hollered at Jane.

"Not for marijuana. Not when it's just a first time offense. I only bought a couple of ounces, for my own use."

"Still. It's going to ruin your reputation!"

She made a placating gesture—pressing her palms down as if testing the air's fluffiness. "Les. Chill. My practice is in Boulder, Colorado. And, again, we're talking about a couple of ounces. Period. Nobody is going to care."

"But you only just *got* that citation from passing out on the ball of yarn. *Twine*, I mean. You're…exhibiting a pattern of bad behavior."

Jimmie and Marcus both cracked up. "Bad behavior," Jimmy repeated, nudging Jane. "Go sit in the corner and think about how badly you've misbehaved."

"Yeah," Marcus added. "You're on timeout, young lady."

"Leslie, my dear, you are missing the point. I need the pot to stay away from the booze. I can't just be a cold turkey."

All three of them burst into peals of laughter. "I meant to say *go* cold turkey," she managed to say, having to gasp for breath. "Gobble gobble."

"A frozen Butterball on Thanksgiving," Marcus said.

"Hey." She grabbed at a small roll of flesh on her belly. "I'm not a Butterball. I'm more a Butterstick."

They elbowed one another and continued to laugh helplessly.

Yikes. Talk about not being in on a joke. Although making a rational argument was pointless, I said, "I'm sure the cure for alcoholism is *not* to choose some *other* substance to abuse. You said yourself that if you get arrested a second time, you'll have to answer to the first charge, which was only a warning."

"'*I'm just a drunk who can't say no*,'" she sang to the tune from "Oklahoma!" "'*I need a terrible fix!*'"

"You sure do." I turned on my heel. "You've clearly lost all of your marbles."

I cursed and punched the jamb of the door with the side of my fist as I strode away. I should have known it wasn't going to be easy for her to stop drinking. For all I knew, weaning herself off alcohol by smoking pot *wasn't* a bad idea. I stood still for a moment and imagined her trying to sell that argument to a judge. Nope. It was a terrible idea. Furthermore, I truly needed to consult with my *sober, substance-free*, brilliant friend Jane right now! Susan was laid up back in Boulder. Abby and Kate had apparently decided that they were going to help Eugena through thick and thin. What if Eugena's dementia led her to decide *they* were the bad guys? During my father's final months of battling the disease, he would sporadically become enraged at my mother for no reason. Kate and Abby were virtual strangers to Eugena. We *all* were. We could be falling into a sinkhole!

Needing to calm down, I decided to take a walk around the block. I glanced at Red's bed, wishing he was here; I could so use a dog to cuddle! Instead I grabbed my cellphone and called Susan. She obviously had not checked her email and knew nothing about Eugena Crowder's televised interview. She began the conversation by telling me that her husband had purchased some marijuana patches, and that was making a huge difference in reducing her pain. She was off OxyContin and just taking Ibuprofen.

I'd like to blame her mention of marijuana for my lack of restraint in complaining behind Jane's back about her current behavior. That's a cop out. Even though Jane is one of my very favorite people and I love her dearly, I didn't hesitate to catch Susan up on the goings-on of all of us—from my own slanted perspective. I told Susan that Jane had three drinks last night and was now getting high. I also voiced my concerns about Abby's loose lips around Eugena, which I'd inferred had led to

Eugena passing along to Mila our plans to attend the hypnotist show last night. And, of course, Abby's confession while under hypnosis, leading up to the aforementioned sinkhole.

Susan assured me that I was right to be concerned about Jane breaking state laws. She asked what *I* thought about Eugena's video clip. I answered that it was reasonably in-keeping with the story she'd told us, although Abby had sent the manuscript to a second publisher just yesterday, so it was impossible for her to have gotten an offer from *that* publisher as she'd claimed.

Is she suffering from incipient Alzheimer's? Susan asked me. I didn't know. I thought back to moments with my father, who, unlike Eugena, never once said that he was suffering from Alzheimer's. But I *did* remember a hideous moment when he said, "I can't even talk." My mother patted his arm and said, "It's all right. I'll take care of you."

I told Susan how much I missed her as we said our goodbyes. Speaking with her now had helped me to think a little more clearly. Eugena had said that her mind was in a deep, dark forest. Maybe there were no bad guys in this story. Maybe Natalie was trying hard to represent Eugena to the best of her ability. Perhaps Jane and Abby had simply caught the boyfriend/lawyer on an off day. Heaven knows Alzheimer's is cruel enough not to require any outside assistance in its destruction of people's lives.

When I returned, the condo was vacant. Now I was really worried, and my stomach started to hurt. What if she had gone out for a drive with the potheads, rather than be stuck here with me, and they got pulled over? Jane would get arrested, and *I'd* be to blame. *I* was the sober and straight one. I'd taken out my frustration on her, essentially giving her the boot.

Before I could work my way into a lather composed of guilt and stomach acid, she stepped through the front door. "Sorry about that, chief," she said. "They're on their way back to Springfield. And they assured me they drive slow, like senior citizens, when they're high. No worries."

"Except that *you've* got a baggie of pot poking out of your pocket, which is breaking the state law. What's worse, you've been retained by Eugena Crowder, who needs your help. You took this case mostly because you—like me—know what it's like to have a parent with Alzheimer's. And it's a passion of yours to ensure that the elderly in our society are treated with dignity. Yet here you are, high as a kite." (*Author's note*: There is an excellent excuse for my going straight from: *I wish I wasn't so mean to my dear friend Jane* to: *I'm a know-it-all and refuse to let go of the fact that you screwed up.* Sadly, I don't happen to know what it is.)

Her smile faded completely. "Ouch. Nicely done. I feel like crap."

"I'm so sorry, Jane. I'm a jumble of—"

"No." She plopped onto the sofa. "You got yourself a point there, counselor. I'm going to have to rethink the pot. I've already realized that I've got to stop drinking."

"It's just that Eugena and I need you to be at your best. An hour or so ago, a pushy producer of a local TV show...*Breakfast with Brittany* was trying to get a statement out of me about Eugena. Eugena had gone on the show this morning implying that she's got Alzheimer's, and that her agent and lawyer are cheating her, but that she'd been advised not to talk about it."

Jane furrowed her brow, struggling to follow my words. "Actually, I *told* her specifically *not* to make public statements of any kind. But how for the love of God could she have been on a TV show this morning?"

"Apparently Eugena called their studio Sunday evening. So they sent out Mila—the producer who cornered me—and a cameraman. They set up their equipment so that she could speak on the show from her hotel room. I sent us all a video clip. And I talked on the phone to everyone except you."

"Eugena didn't implicate Abby, did she?"

"No. And she never gave any names. She said that, basically, we were pulling her one way, and Natalie and Chris were pulling her another, and she wasn't capable of judging who was right or wrong."

"Geez! This is a bad time for me to be in Lala Land, all right. I'll have to watch the clip and get my act together...pronto." She tossed the baggie to me. "Hold this for me until we get back to Colorado."

"And wind up getting arrested for possession? My daughter's getting engaged tomorrow! You want me to risk forcing her to raise the funds to bust me out of jail?"

"When you put it that way, it sounds a little selfish of me. I'm sorry, my dear friend." She stood up and gave me a warm hug. (Which I probably didn't deserve.)

"What should I do with the pot?"

"Flush it down the toilet."

"Right away." I went into the bathroom that I was sharing with Kate. I hadn't smoked any pot in thirty years. My gaze fell upon my vanity case. Tomorrow night, I'd be attending a two-hour show, anticipating Kurt popping the question to Alicia. And that a TV station would film it, thanks to me. What if something went wrong? If I'd set up my daughter for a fall? How could I manage to stay calm enough to eat dinner and not get nauseated? My stomach was already in knots. One small toke would calm me down and probably increase my appetite. *Keep the pot! Keep the pot!*

The other part of my brain was crying: *You hypocrite! Flush the pot! Flush the pot!*

Nothing could go *so* hideously wrong that keeping the pot in my vanity case until the day after tomorrow could possibly come back to haunt me. (*Author's note*: I know what you're thinking, and no, this was *not* a case of: *Famous last words*.) I put the small baggy in my vanity case, taking care to hide it under the bottom insert. Then I flushed the toilet. Even if Jane realized that I might have had second thoughts, she wasn't going to discover my hiding spot easily.

By the time I returned to the living room, Jane appeared to be fast asleep on the sofa. As I tiptoed past her she said, "I'm just taking a quick nap. Sleeping it off. I'll figure out where to start with the televised interview once I wake up."

"Sounds good."

"I gotta get sober. And clean. Just worked too hard to lose it now."

"That's so true."

"I miss my husband, Les. I don't know how to live without him."

"Divorce is miserable. One day at a time. Just like Kate said. And we'll all be there to help."

"Unless Abby stays in Branson with Eugena. And Red."

"You don't think that's what she'll do, though. Do you?"

She didn't answer, and a moment later, she started breathing through her mouth, having fallen asleep.

***

An hour later, Jane arose, watched the video, and promptly called Eugena. To our surprise, we learned that Abby had already made an appointment for Eugena to test for Alzheimer's the next day. Eugena invited Jane to come to the appointment in case her legal expertise was needed.

A few minutes later, Abby and Kate returned. Although Abby's eyes were a bit puffy, she was smiling. "Thank you so much for sending that video, Leslie." She sighed happily. "We've worked everything out. Eugena's asked me to help her through this difficult phase in her life, come what may. I finally feel like I've found my life's calling. I think I was meant to be here, to assist the author of *A Dog Named Red.*"

"I think you're right," Kate said.

We all took seats in the living room.

"As it turns out," Abby began, "Eugena's wealthy. Although her creepy husband did indeed kick her out of her house and home. Literally. He *kicked* her and threw her out the front door. She doesn't like to talk about her having lots of money with just anybody, because she would question whether some new friend likes her for herself, or for her money." She paused and flashed a huge smile. "She's decided she wants to partner with me in starting an international charity organization to help stray dogs find homes."

"That's a wonderful idea," I said hesitantly, "but it makes me nervous." I looked at Jane. "What would happen if Eugena *does* have dementia? And she hires Abby for this major charity foundation, and someone in her family objects?"

"She doesn't *have* any family," Abby said. "You were there when she told us she considers *us* her family."

"But that was yesterday," I argued. "What if, tomorrow, she forgets she ever had a conversation with you about you helping her launch this charity? And she accuses you of taking advantage of her? Besides which, there could be some distant cousin someplace who thinks he's entitled to Eugena's fortune."

"Leslie's right," Jane said. "We're going to have to proceed with extreme caution."

"Some of this might get resolved with Eugena's medical appointment tomorrow morning," Abby began.

My phone rang, interrupting the conversation. I glanced at the screen. "It's Kurt's dad...Steve." My heart took a little leap. That was not good. Also not good was that everyone was now smiling at me as if I'd just announced that I'd won the lottery. I pivoted, walked toward the nearest door, and answered, "Hello," with an undeniable lilt in my voice. I went ahead and opened the door, only to realize it was the coat closet.

"Hi, Leslie. How's everything going?"

"Fine. Other than the fact that I'm staring into an empty closet like a total nimrod."

"Why?"

"Oh, because I announced to everyone it was you, and we're all silly romantics at heart...and that made me nervous."

He chuckled. "That's good news for me. The romantic part, I mean."

"Well, I guess it balances out the nimrod part." I finally turned around again. They were all still grinning at me. My cheeks felt red hot. "Instead of locking myself in the closet, I'm currently walking into the bedroom and shutting the door so I can get some privacy." I shut the bedroom door and leaned back against it. "So. Now I feel like I've babbled away every last drop of my dignity. And I suppose you're just calling me to ask how my tooth is doing."

"No, I wanted to know if you happened to be free this afternoon to go grab a cup of tea or coffee or glass of wine with me. Or an in-between meal, even. Can you?"

"Um...sure. Thanks."

"Wonderful. I know what street you're on. Tell me the house number."

"Three-sixteen B as in Boyfriend." (Oh, dear God. Why did I add the suffix "*friend*?" If I wanted to make a fool of myself, couldn't I have simply swallowed my tongue?)

"I know right where that is. I'll pick you up at three-thirty."

I glanced at the clock on my nightstand. It was three fifteen. "Great. See you then."

"I'm glad you kept your end of the conversation behind closed doors. It's become endearingly personal," he teased.

"It has, hasn't it?"

"See you soon." He hung up.

I took a deep breath and returned to the living room.

"Our little girl is ready to see boys again!" Abby promptly declared, clasping her hands together.

We all laughed.

"Okay, stop. This is just—not even a lunch. I'm trying to live in the moment and not overanalyze. So no discussions. No turning a coffee date into an opening chapter of a story about me. Okay? Please?"

"Meh. I don't know." Jane studied my features. "You were right about us all being silly romantics. And I could *really* use a role model right now to show me how to get back into the damned dating scene."

"Me, too," Abby said. "Although I'm probably done with men forever. Red's a great companion. I don't mind being celibate for the rest of my days."

"*I* sure would," Jane said.

"No comment," I said. "Although that makes me worry about my being your role model. I'm not hopping into the sack with Steve on this trip. That would be totally inappropriate under the circumstances."

"You're both adults," Jane said, "and—"

"We're both *parents*, first and foremost. This week is about Alicia and Kurt."

"You're completely correct, Leslie," Kate said, "but I'm still very happy for you."

"I'm willing to act like a mature adult during our group vacation," Abby said. "Fortunately, we're on a short trip."

"It's not short enough for me," Jane said. "I'm trying to get off of alcohol, plus to stop getting high with guys as young as the kids I've never had."

Several minutes later, Steve picked me up. Explaining that he'd decided to give us options for an exotic drink and appetizers, he drove us to an Indian restaurant. The place was located in a strip mall, which made it long and narrow. The mahogany tables and chair and earth-tone palette gave the space an elegant ambience. We sat in a corner booth in the back.

After a brief exchange of pleasantries, which included how great our kids were, Steve said, "It's been challenging, with the divorce, and all. Emily and I managed to stick it out as long as we could, for Kurt and Ted's sake."

"Ted is younger than Kurt, right?"

"He's a senior at Missouri State," he said with a nod. The waiter appeared and we both ordered coconut milk masala tea that he'd recommended, along with some Indian-style cookies.

"This is quite the throwback," I said. "We're having milk and cookies."

"But exotically international ones," Steve said wiggling his eyebrows.

"Is Kurt nervous about tomorrow?"

"Yes. But not so much that he'll back out. How about Alicia?"

"She doesn't know to be nervous."

"You don't think she even suspects that Kurt's planning to propose?"

"I think in her heart of heart she does, but she's bound and determined to keep that thought buried deeply so she won't be totally crushed if he doesn't."

"Ah."

The waiter returned with a plate of what looked like Lorna Doones. Our teas looked a bit like an orange-tinted lattes. He and Steve chatted about the tea and cookies for a few seconds, but I had tuned them out. Unpleasant "what-ifs" regarding tomorrow night started wriggling into my brain.

Moments after the waiter had left us, I said, "Come to think of it, I can't even imagine how horrible everyone would feel if Kurt panics and doesn't propose tomorrow."

Steve lifted one corner of his mouth. "Not going to happen." He took a sip of his coconut-milk tea.

"I hope Alicia doesn't panic and send out her understudy," I said.

Steve squared his shoulder and held my gaze. "Do you think she might?"

"Only if she starts vomiting." Suddenly my stomach started churning. "Dear God. What if she starts vomiting?"

"Does she have a prescription for Beta blockers?" Steve asked.

"I think so." I took a slow, steady breath. "That's a comforting thought. Thanks for asking." I sat back and tried to settle myself down. I took a sip of my tea. The flavor was appealing, tasting of ginger, cinnamon, and honey, along with the coconut.

We chatted about our personal histories, and my angst vanished. Like the tea, the Indian-ish sweets were delicious. I realized that I was enjoying myself immensely. There was a brief pause in our conversation. Steve grimaced and said, "I need to warn you about Eugena Crowder. You know how I mentioned she's the ex of a colleague?"

Eugena was the very last thing I wanted to talk about at the moment. My mind flashed to the amateurish painting of "The Scream" with the ball of twine rolling toward the screamer. I was envisioning myself in that role—a self-portrait. "I remember. And I'm sure he had nothing nice to say about her."

"He didn't. I called Bob last night, to see what he had to say about her now, after some time had passed. He told me she's a narcissist and to warn you to steer clear."

I grew annoyed, in spite of myself. We were already taking care of all things Eugena-related. Steve barely knew me, had never met Eugena, had told me that he barely knew Dr. Dentist Crowder, yet he felt he need to protect me, or enlighten me, or something.

"I'll take that under advisement."

He cocked an eyebrow. "Meaning it's none of my business?"

"Meaning I'm already sufficiently skeptical about Eugena Crowder. My friend Abby is taking her to a clinic to help determine if she's suffering from Alzheimer's."

"That's a start."

"Are you trying to protect me? From deciding to befriend someone you think I shouldn't?"

He grinned. "Am I coming off too macho for your average dentist?"

I laughed.

"I admit that I want to fix things that are broken. Fill the cavities. Repair crowns. Promote flossing. But...that's not really what's happening here, Leslie."

"But what if it *is*? It's not like you've had any chance to witness what Eugena's and...Bob's marriage was actually like, right? You hadn't even met the woman before attending the stampede show the other night."

"That's true."

"And you told me that you knew Bob from attending a convention together. Not that you'd worked together and knew him well."

"Also true. But what reason would he have to badmouth the woman to me?"

"Maybe he came to detest her when the marriage crumbled, and he can't help but vent whenever her name is mentioned. They might have blamed each other for their son's death. Maybe one of them was pushing for him to become a police officer, while the other was completely against it."

Steve looked puzzled. "Did Eugena tell you her son died?"

"Yes. Bob didn't mention that?"

"No." Steve pulled a business card out of his wallet. "Look, Leslie. Bob and I exchanged a few business cards. I know you don't think you'll want to talk with him. But just in case, you can feel free." He paused. "I jotted down his cellphone number for you, too, which he said you could reach him at any time."

"Okay. Thanks." I couldn't muster a smile.

"Are you annoyed at me because I'm bringing you possible bad news regarding someone you admire, or do you really think I'm in the wrong for being curious enough to call my friend who knew her really well?"

"It's probably a combination. It feels like the stuff that used to irk me about my late husband. Plus, I don't *want* to discover that Eugena is ruthlessly ambitious. And I'm questioning your motives for asking me to...have milk and cookies again."

"This is the first time I asked you out."

"I meant that my self-confidence is *sagging* again."

"But if you think about it, that's misplaced. If I didn't care about you, I'd never have called her ex-husband. So it shows that I *do* care about you, and that I'm interested in getting to know you better."

"It also proves that I'm hypersensitive. I think it's all too soon for me. I just don't want to be putting myself through a full self-examination right now."

He sighed, then he peered into my eyes with his lovely blue eyes. "Before you leave town, let's try to find time for a walk. Or a cup of coffee."

"We'll see. Let's talk tomorrow. And see how well the proposal comes off."

From then on, our conversation felt self-conscious. The mood had been ruined. The thought hit me that if we hadn't met Eugena, our road trip would have gone very differently.

Chapter 21
Then We Fall to Pieces

When I arrived at the condo, Eugena was there, sitting in the living room and drinking tea with Jane, Abby, and Kate. They were sharing a laugh. Kate was even drying her eyes from laughing so hard.

I had an irrational pang that I was becoming distanced from the book club. "What funny story did I miss?" I asked.

"We were just sharing dog stories," Kate said. "Abby was telling us about how Red managed to get out of his collar, and she'd gone three blocks, dragging the empty collar attached to the leash before she noticed."

"And I'd waved to no less than four of my neighbors by that time...me thinking how perfectly behaved Red was by not tugging on the leash. My neighbors all thinking I'd lost my gourd and was taking a leash for a walk."

I chuckled, though Abby had told me that story before. I took a seat at the end of the sofa, adjacent to Eugena in the corner, and set my purse on the arm.

"We should talk about the upcoming shows we're attending," Abby said.

"Shows?" Kate asked.

"I thought we were just going to Alicia's show tomorrow," I said. "That's the last one we scheduled."

"I decided to treat Eugena to another show."

"Which is completely unnecessary," Eugena said. "*I'm* the one who should be treating all of you. I truly don't want to impose."

"You *aren't*," Abby said. "Since you insisted on paying me for a couple of hours yesterday, this is how I want to spend my money. There's a show featuring dogs that do tricks. It's not in town until Thursday, and I know we reserved that date for celebrating with the newly engaged couple, but—"

"Wait," I said. "We were planning on celebrating with Alicia and Kurt? Really?"

Abby's cheeks reddened.

Jane was grimacing.

"It was nothing official," Kate said. "Just a small gathering, if that should happen to be convenient."

I'd have been more inclined to accept that and drop the matter, if only Kate hadn't been looking past my shoulder.

"What restaurant is it scheduled for?" I asked Jane.

"Some burger joint. It's where Kurt took Alicia for dinner after their excellent tryouts."

I held my tongue. I hadn't realized they'd established a special-to-them eatery in Branson.

"We could always skip going to the Ingalls Wilder museum on Friday," Kate said. "Susan was the one who most wanted to go there."

"Or you guys can go ahead to see the museum, and Eugena and I could fly back to Denver at a later date," Abby said.

"We discussed that possibility in private this morning," Eugena interjected.

"Eugena's thinking she'll rent a room in my house for a while," Abby added.

Jane, Kate, and I exchanged glances. "That's nice," Jane said, also sounding surprised.

"How was your date?" Abby asked. Before I could answer she turned to Eugena. "Leslie was out with Steve, the dentist, just now."

"Yes, so you said," Eugena said with a tight smile. "I'm not all that forgetful yet."

"It was really nice," I answered, a little put off by Eugena's snippy response to Abby. "Thanks. He's a great guy, and we enjoy each other's company. But it's long distance, so that makes it low risk."

"You don't think you'll be joining Alicia as the second member of the Boobs who'll be Skyping from Branson?" Kate asked.

"Not much chance of that, no. I love living in Boulder. I wouldn't want to uproot myself and move here. Plus, I'm still really turned off by the notion of dating my future son-in-law's father."

"But those detractions become manageable if you fall head over heels," Kate replied. "Which could happen."

"It could. But in that case I'd hope that he would be willing to move to Boulder."

"My ex-brother-in-law is a dentist," Jane said. "It's not easy to pick up and relocate a practice."

"I'm sure it isn't." I felt uncomfortable with this turn in the conversation and stood up, intending to get myself a glass of water and allow my absence to encourage a change in subjects. In my haste, I knocked my purse to the floor, scattering its contents.

"Oh, dear," Kate said, rising to help me.

"It's okay. I've got it."

I scooped up my iPad first, the only thing of monetary value. But three of my pens had also skittered away. To my horror, I realized that Dr. Robert Crowder's business card had fallen right in front of Eugena's feet, with the lettering facing her. She snatched it up before I could reach it myself.

Staring at it, she drew in a sharp breath and rose, her cheeks bright red, her face essentially morphing into a mask of hateful fury. "Where did you get this!"

"From Steve. He's a former assoc—"

"You're spying on me!"

"*Spying* on you? Of course not!"

"Yet you're carrying around my ex-husband's contact information! You must be checking into my background!"

"No, I'm not. Steve knows him from their professional relationship, and he gave me his name and contact information. But I haven't used it and don't intend to."

"Then why did you take it from him?"

"It was just easier that way, Eugena...to take the card, stash it in my purse, and change topics. Which is precisely what I did."

"Don't play coy with me! You're not looking for a dentist in Springfield! You got this card because you don't trust me, despite all the gratitude and kindness I've shown you!" She shook her fist, crumpling the card in the process. "My former husband detests me. He spread hideous, completely bogus rumors about me. All because I didn't want to share my book earnings with him. Which he didn't deserve, and didn't need. He's had a highly successful practice and doesn't want to ever retire."

"Come to think of it, he must be getting pretty old," Abby said, another of her out-of-the-blue comments.

"He's only sixty-eight," Eugena said. "He's younger than I am."

"I'm sorry I didn't mention right away that I had his contact information," I said. "But, it didn't seem relevant, since I wasn't using it. Dr. *Winston* has concerns about you, due to knowing only your ex-husband. But *I* don't share those concerns."

Eugena sat back in the chair, looking only slightly mollified. "Right. Well, I'm sorry if I overreacted.

"I didn't know you were having such serious problems with him," I said. (A white lie.) (Well, depending on what color you assign to untruths that are designed primarily to get yourself out of trouble. A yellow lie, I suppose.)

"I don't like to complain." Eugena lifted her chin. "Worrying about the past serves no purpose. But here the bastard is, once again, his specter rising to haunt me yet again."

"Leslie didn't mean to hurt you," Kate said.

"I realize that. But I'm going to need to calm down. The sight of that man's name or face just instantly fills me with rage. He treated me so horribly. He was abusive. A wife beater. That's probably why our son grew up to be so reckless."

"By joining the police force, you mean?" I asked, confused.

"Yes. He had to witness so many ugly scenes between his father and me. He grew up so damaged."

"I had no idea."

"Of course you didn't. You had no way of knowing. But even now that you *do*, if you were to call Robert and chat with him, you'd discover that he's one hell of a persuader. He'll have you convinced inside five minutes that he's the kindly neighborhood dentist, lovingly taking care of children's teeth, not a nasty bone in his body. And that *I'm* the worst person who ever lived."

"Oh, none of us could ever feel that unkindly toward you," Kate said.

"Never," Abby said, shaking her head emphatically. "You were the answer to my dream. I've never been happier!"

Eugena rose. "I'm going to walk back to my hotel."

"I'll drive you," Kate said.

"No, I want to walk."

"But you keep getting lost," Kate said.

"I'm thinking clearly now. I won't get lost."

"I'll walk with you, just in case." Abby rose.

Eugena fired a glare at Abby, but then her features softened. "Thank you dear. If you insist."

The two of them left. Kate, Jane, and I stayed put. My emotions were a jumble. Originally I truly had no intention of contacting Dr. Crowder. Now I *did*. But maybe I should resist that reaction. Maybe I too would have gotten as upset if someone had dropped my abusive ex-husband's business card. But, what if Steve was right about Dr. Crowder? If Eugena had just now realized she'd been caught in the act, she would *definitely* accuse me of being the one in the wrong.

"Did you see that look Eugena gave Abby?" I asked. "Just for an instant?"

Jane nodded. "It looked like she wanted to strangle her. Do you still have the number for her ex?"

"Unfortunately she took the card with her." I hesitated, unsure if I'd upset Kate by admitting that I *now* had serious doubts about Eugena. "It really bugged me that she immediately put me on the defensive."

Kate arched an eyebrow. "You're going to call Steve and get the contact information again?"

"Yes. Do you think I shouldn't?"

"It seems wrong to me," Kate said.

"I want to trust Eugena. I really do. But let's face it. She's got Abby wrapped around her finger."

"I heard that," Abby snarled, flinging open the door. Her face was red and she was glaring at me as if she wanted to rip my head off.

Startled, I could only babble, "You're back so soon."

"Eugena insisted that she really needed to be alone. And I can see why, now that I realize how you really feel about her. You hurt my hero's feelings! What's wrong with you?"

"Abby, there's nothing 'wrong' with me. I'm simply worried that there's something wrong with *Eugena.* And I don't mean Alzheimer's. We've known the woman for all of *three* days now. We're going on very little information. She could be presenting a false front to us for her own benefit."

"It's obvious to her *and* me that you're green with jealousy that she offered *me* the job as her assistant! Not *you.*"

The remark stung. In all the years we'd known each other, Abby had never said anything so harsh to me. "That's not true, Abby. (Well, not *completely* true.) But even if it were, it would still be prudent to check into her background a little before we throw ourselves on swords for her."

"She's asking us for *friendship,* not to die for her! She's a lonely, elderly woman who's being scammed by a greedy agent and lawyer! You threw her under the bus at the first speck of difficulty!"

"And by a speck of difficulty, you mean Kurt's dad telling me that her ex-husband is dead certain she's conning us? Or that she became belligerent toward me just because I had his phone number?"

"Anybody would have gotten upset at suddenly discovering that a so-called *friend* was secretly keeping contact information for the person who'd beaten her repeatedly!"

"That's a good point, Abby. But it's also a valid point that we barely know Eugena, and her ex *could* be telling the truth about her. We won't know one way or another unless we hear his side of the story."

"She'll never forgive you if you betray her like that!"

"Betray her? By talking to her ex on the phone?"

"Yes! What if he's been tracking her all this time? What if you contacting him leads him directly to her hotel room?"

"That's not going to happen." (*Author's note*: In truth, my thought at this moment was: if the man was truly dangerous, he already got all the information he would need to find Eugena when Steve first called him.)

"You can't guarantee that," Abby countered. "In fact, the more I think about it, the likelier it seems that you've put Eugena's life in jeopardy."

"I have not! I haven't even contacted the man! Who's probably perfectly sane, and quite possibly never laid a hand on her in the first place."

"*Red* trusts her. I trust her. I thought I could trust *you*, but obviously I can't."

"Oh, Abby," Kate cried, "let's all please just take a step back and use our indoor voices."

"I for one am not going to take any chances. I'll protect her myself. I'm going to move in with her at the Marriott."

"Did she *ask* you to do that?" Jane asked.

"No. She would never be so presumptuous."

"Don't you think you should at least call her and ask if she wants to share her room with you?" Kate asked gently.

"Do you want us to keep Red here?" Jane asked. "Does the Marriott take dogs?"

"You see what a mess you've made?" Abby snapped at me.

"Apparently so. But all I did was accept a business card from Steve. If the card had landed on the floor with the back side up, none of this would have happened."

"Yeah, but...then you decided to call her horrible, brutal ex-husband, even though our friend who needs our help is terrified of him." She was starting to cry.

"Since you feel this strongly about it, Abby, I won't call him."

"And if Eugena's scared and needs us to take her to an airport or bus station, I'll drive her there," Kate interjected.

And I'll stay out of sight, hiding my head in shame. I'd never seen Abby react like this. The closest was years ago in book club when we unwisely chose to read *The Art of Racing in the Rain*, which was written from the dog's point of view, with the fascinating premise that dogs experience their first lives on earth and then become human beings in their next lives. Unlike the rest of us, Jane had been utterly unimpressed by the book and said that it was ridiculous anthropomorphizing that a dog could have the intelligence of a human being. (Those were fighting words where Abby is concerned.)

"I *really* think we need to speak to Eugena's agent, though," I said. "She's known and worked with Eugena since long before we came onto the scene. We need to at least listen to her opinion on whether or not her ex-husband is dangerous, and so forth, before we write off Steve's concerns about her."

Abby's jaw dropped. "No, Leslie! We are not going to talk to Eugena's arch enemy!"

"Fine. Then I'll speak with her on my own."

"You're absolutely intent on stabbing the dear woman in the back!"

"We know *she's* not posing a physical threat to Eugena. They're staying at the same hotel, for heaven's sake. And with Eugena talking in the interview about how we're telling her one thing and Natalie's telling her something else, maybe we're simply sitting on opposite sides of the very same sinking boat. I've never even met Natalie, so she and I will start out with a clean slate."

"Let's just not contact anybody whatsoever concerning Eugena, okay?" Kate pleaded. "This is our vacation. We're here to celebrate Alicia and Kurt's engagement. Remember?"

"But if *you'll* remember, I didn't even *know* that's why we came here! You all were perfectly willing to be accomplices in keeping that secret from me. Now I'm getting flak for wanting to make sure we're not the ones getting taken for a ride!" (*Author's note*: I was being bitchy by dragging this back up.) (*Kate's reviewer's note*: Leslie was perfectly justified. I was wrong not to defend her sensible desire to gather more information. As she noted in Chapter 1, I truly hate conflict.)

Abby threw her hands in the air. "I can't even talk to you, right now! I'm taking Red for a walk!" She stormed out the door.

"She'll calm down," Jane said. "Furthermore, you're right. Eugena could be a complete nutcase. But if that turns out to be the case, Abby's going to be devastated."

"Exactly," I said.

"You're keeping your promise to Abby, though, aren't you?" Kate asked.

"I guess so. I certainly don't want to break a promise. But I believe talking to Natalie is the right thing to do."

"I'm going to see if I can catch up with Abby," Kate said. "But Jane's right. Abby will calm down." Kate left.

"What do you think I should do, Jane?" I asked.

"I think you should call Natalie and ask if she'll meet with *both* of us and try to come to an understanding. What's the worst that could happen?"

"Eugena could spot us talking and accuse the two of us of consorting with the enemy at her expense. Then she could tell Abby about our supposed betrayal, which could get *her* so mad at us she could end our friendship and quit the book club. Then Eugena could try to get you disbarred by accusing you of violating a confidence, or something."

"She's given me permission to talk with all parties involved in her contracts."

"In other words, you're unlikely to be disbarred, but everything else could happen."

Jane drummed her fingers on the armrest for a moment. "Yes. Eugena appears to have some signs of Alzheimer's. Paranoia being one of them."

"Do you think so? In spite of what you said last night...about her being able to take care of herself?"

Jane winced. "I got a bit intoxicated. So, yes, in spite of that, I think she has Alzheimer's. In its early stages, symptoms of the disease can come and go, one day to the next. She's told us we're her knights in shining armor. She's been battered. She sees one of her knights with a tie to her batterer. It makes sense that she'd have a wild reaction. And, conversely, she has nothing to gain by pretending to be addled. Or to lie to us, or play games."

"Maybe not, but I don't see how this ex husband would have anything to gain by badmouthing her to a colleague of his. Especially when you consider that Steve's odds of ever actually meeting Eugena were really remote."

"In my line of work, I deal with more than a few wife-batterers. They tend to be the *most* likely to badmouth their spouses, and with the most vehemence."

I nodded, chastened. I'd given a similar argument to Steve. Poor Eugena. She deserved all of Kate's and Abby's kindness. And Jane's expertise.

She rose. "Do you want to call Natalie to try to set up an appointment, or should I?"

"I'll call."

She retrieved the number from her phone and wrote it down for me.

As she handed me the slip of paper, I said, "You know, Jane, I think it's best if I meet with Natalie alone."

"I disagree. If, God forbid, this leads to a civil suit between Natalie and Eugena, you could wind up having to testify. For that matter, Eugena and her ex could get into dispute, and you could find yourself embroiled in the fray. It's always best to have a counselor with you when you speak, especially when you'll have my services for free."

"Yeah, but Eugena's already mad at me. If she finds out about my talking to her literary agent ex-parte, it'll just validate her anger. If she sees *both* of us with Natalie, it'll feel like we're all ganging up on her. Let me feel this out over the phone. Chances are it'll go fine." I swept up my cellphone and entered Natalie's phone number.

"Hello? This is Natalie Price."

"Hi. This is Leslie O'Kane, Eugena's friend. It seems that my friends Jane and Abby got off on the wrong foot with you the other day, and I'd love to meet you and see if we can all reach a common understanding."

She snorted. "I knew you'd call me."

Okay, that wasn't all that promising of an opening remark. "Pardon?"

"You want to kiss up to me and give me your latest manuscript. Even though, all the while, you and your gang of thieves are trying to insinuate yourself into a usurious relationship with my client."

"No, that's not at all why I called. I'm just a couple of miles away, and I'm a big believer in face-to-face conversations. I believe we can join forces."

From the corner of my eye, I could tell how intently Jane was studying my features. I winked at her.

"Can we meet someplace for coffee or a glass of—" I remembered too late that Jane wanted to come—"milk? My treat, of course."

"*Milk?* Are you from a *farm* in Colorado? I'm *working.* This isn't a lark for me, Leslie. But, fine. I'll meet you at six p.m. sharp at the Starbucks in the Marriott."

"I was hoping we could...meet someplace in between. At a diner or coffee shop. Or I could pick you up. How about—"

"How about you take it or leave it? Would that work for you?"

"Six o'clock. I'll meet you there." I hung up, then grinned at Jane. "Done!" I was using my best easy-breezy tone, but it felt like all of my saliva had dried. "Piece of cake."

"What flavor?"

"Hmm?"

"Is that a Lying-lemon cake?"

"No. She just sounds a bit...bitchy."

"I'm coming with you."

"Fine." (I now suspected I could use all the help I could get.) "But it's in the Marriott Starbucks. Does that have a separate entrance from the hotel, do you know?"

Jane rolled her eyes. "It's just a kiosk, right in the middle of the lobby."

Chapter 22
Agent Orange

I sighed. My ever-communicative gut was all but shouting at me. Would a wife-abuser really go to the lengths of telling a fellow dentist an hour's drive away that a female acquaintance could call him "any time" merely to badmouth his former victim? Meanwhile, would a literary agent conclude with no corroboration whatsoever that her occasionally unreliable client was being conned by a *book club*?

"Okay," I said to Jane, "this just isn't going smoothly. I'm going to have to go back on my word to Abby. I'm getting Steve to give me the number again, then I'm calling Bob Crowder."

"You probably shouldn't tell me about that. It could be construed as my not acting in my client's best interests."

"In that case, I'm just going to call a dentist for advice after I possibly injured a tooth...by biting a bullet. I'll be sure not to tell you what he says." I pondered that statement for a moment. If I was being honest with myself, I would need to discuss the conversation with somebody. Abby was a no go. Susan had never met Eugena and wouldn't feel comfortable giving advice. Kate never wanted to see the bad in anybody and tended to restrict her reactions to: "Oh, dear," and gifts of home-baked muffins. With a marriage proposal coming tomorrow night, burdening Alicia was out of the question. Jane was my only feasible ally. "And speaking of teeth, what should I do if he convinces me his ex-wife is lying through hers?"

Jane looked thoughtful for a moment. "Then you'll have to tell me, and I'll have to have a serious conversation with my client."

"Okay." I grabbed my phone and checked the time. Four-twenty. I left the condo, intent on finding a private spot along the lake. I chatted with Steve for several minutes, and true to the weakness in character that I've already revealed (and never mind that I'm currently writing all of this down and publishing it—so I'm probably on Santa's, the Dalai Lama's, and Jesus's lists of incorrigible gossips), I shamelessly talked about Abby's reaction to Eugena's anger at spotting the business card.

Feeling much better after our conversation, I sat down on a bench near an unoccupied boat launch and dialed. A male, surprisingly youthful voice answered who was indeed Bob Crowder. I introduced myself and explained that I was a friend of Stephen Winston's, and he said, "Oh, yes. You're the lady who is my ex-wife's latest patsy."

I paused. *That* was an inauspicious start to our conversation.

"I should apologize for being so blunt, Leslie. I was the biggest patsy on the planet, where Eugena's concerned."

"Well, she's said a few things that are a tad...confusing. Yet she seems to be such a sweet little old lady."

"She's the opposite of sweet. She's more like...toxic waste. She knows that the surest way to make someone like you is to ask them to do you a favor. Furthermore, she's not even that old. As the song goes, she's no lady, she's my ex-wife."

I decided to start with his least subjective assertion. "How old *is* she?"

"Sixty eight."

"She claims she's eighty one!"

"That's just a ruse she started when she first sent *A Dog Named Red* to a publishing house twenty years ago, claiming it was her memoir in order to increase its sales. She doesn't even *like* dogs. That's the real reason she didn't want to write a sequel. She knew she'd have to be around a dog again."

"I...don't think I'm following. You mean, once she got to be an *adult*, she didn't like being around dogs?"

"I mean, she grew up without any pets in the house. She was the only child of a wealthy family in Poughkeepsie and went to boarding school in Switzerland. Her last name was Taylor, and she went by her middle name, Sarah. To help ensure nobody would recognize her, when she was ready to submit her manuscript to publishers, she went by her actual first name—Eugena—and stuck with her married name, even though we were already divorced by then."

I had to give myself a moment to let his statements sink in. "I'm...stunned."

"Everyone always is, when they learn the truth. Ironically the only real thing about her is her white hair."

"So...how did you two meet?"

"She was my dental patient. She'd gotten something stuck between her teeth without realizing it. At the movies. Popcorn and soda are a dentist's best friends."

"Ah."

"Anyway, as you can imagine, she can be utterly charming when she wants to be. My first marriage fell apart after the death of my son, and I—"

"Wait. This isn't the son who was a police office and was shot in a robbery, is it?"

'Yes," he said, his voice harsh for the first time. "That's the lie of hers that really sticks in my craw. When she uses my son's death before the two of us even met to gain people's sympathy. It makes me want to wring her damned neck."

"I can imagine," I said. My thoughts were reeling. Was there any chance that *he* was the one who was telling the lies? Why *would* he? What did he possibly have to gain?

"No offense, Leslie, but you probably *can't*. I was married to Sarah...I mean, to Jeanie for twelve years. Things started falling apart after two. But I kept trying to hang on, believing her when she told me it was all my fault. The least little thing could cause her to erupt. I was always walking on eggshells around her. Whenever I brought up the subject of separating, she'd claim she needed me. And I *did* seem to be her only friend in the world. But she'd berate my salary, my profession, everything about me. She'd inherited plenty of money, then she earned a small fortune from *Red*. Nothing was ever good enough for her. She makes herself miserable, but it's never her fault. She uses everyone for her own gain, yet sincerely believes the world is out to get her. When things are good, they should have been better. When they're bad, it's proof that she's being cheated. The woman is a narcissist. With absolutely no conscience."

I tried to picture him as a wife-beater, telling me these lies about his former wife. It just didn't fit. I couldn't imagine that he'd lie about his own son's death. "So she's wealthy, due to an inheritance?"

"Yes. The woman's living proof that money doesn't buy happiness. As for me, I have my practice. I have my friends. My life's just fine, now that I've sworn to stay the hell away from her."

"This is a lot to wrap my head around."

"You probably don't want to believe me. Depending on how deeply she has her hooks in you."

"I just befriended her a few days ago. I love her book so much. My children loved it. I read it to them every night." I had to ask an awful question. "She *did* really write that book, though, didn't she?"

"She did. Just with a whole lot of help from an amazing editor at her publishing house, who has since passed away. Of course, if she hadn't ever written that book, Jeanie wouldn't be able to get away with half of the B.S. she's now pulling on people. And it was actually my *mother's* story. *Mom* was the actual M.J. in the book."

"In a way, she stole your mother's story to gain fame, and your son's death to keep it."

"Precisely. So you can probably see why I'm more than a little testy when the subject of my ex-wife comes up."

I cursed to myself. If he was telling me the complete truth, we'd let ourselves get into such a mess! "My friend Abby is trying to work as her personal assistant. And my friend Jane is her attorney now. Abby worships the ground Eugena walks on."

There was a pause. "Can I send you the newspaper notice from our wedding day, Leslie? That might at least begin to convince your friends that she's lying about her age and that Sarah...Jeanie isn't who she claims to be."

"By all means. You could text it to me at this number. It couldn't hurt."

"Once Jeanie perceives she's been wronged by someone, she'll bury you. The least little thing will set her off. Whatever you do, don't let her know we had this conversation."

"I won't."

"My advice is to head home after your vacation and don't let her know your address."

"I don't know what to say."

"Say that you'll verify my statements on the internet, take a look at the wedding notice and its photo, and get away from her. And...if you can help it, don't make me testify against her."

"*Testify against her*?" I repeated.

"She can become violent. Later, once she regains her head, she'll claim it was self-defense. I'm just...throwing out worst-case scenarios, Leslie. If push comes to shove, I'll testify, but I truly don't want to ever see that woman again."

***

At six p.m. on the nose, Jane and I entered the Marriott. I was so anxious, my knees were shaking. The combination of my uneasiness at the news from Bob Crowder, Natalie's snarkiness over the phone, and this upcoming conversation was making my heart pound so fast that I felt a little short of breath.

Although I was armed with a copy of the wedding notice, taken twenty-five years ago when a forty-something version of Eugena Sarah Taylor was marrying the dashing, forty-something DDS Robert Joseph Crowder, I had told Jane only that I was eighty-percent convinced that Eugena had duped us. Jane had once told me that the memories of both parties in a divorce were permanently colored. None of us can ever truly see things from a partner's point of view, and our emotions change our perceptions. The upshot for me was that Robert could be right, and we were being duped by Eugena. But, despite everything, that still went against my instincts. She seemed so nice. And I loved her book so much, I loved *her* for writing it.

Natalie wasn't here yet, so we ordered—decaf chai tea for me and black coffee for Jane—and we settled into the Marriott's comfy lounge chairs. Now that I looked, this was the same exact spot where I'd met with Eugena to discuss her manuscript. I don't know how I missed the Starbucks enclosure a few steps away; it had just failed to register.

"You seem nervous," Jane remarked.

"I am. I feel like I should have stayed in the condo, with a pillow over my face until it was time to get ready for Alicia's performance tomorrow."

"One way or another, we'll handle this. And it will be so precious to see our Alicia get engaged." Jane shifted her gaze toward the elevators. "Here comes Natalie now."

A thirty-something woman was striding toward the baristas, her features set into a borderline grimace. She was wearing a Home-Depot orange pants suit. I rose. "I'm going to introduce myself."

"She's dressed like a traffic cone," Jane said. "Orange really *is* the new black, I guess."

"I'd like to pay for her coffee," I said to the barista then smiled at Natalie. "Natalie? Hi. I'm Leslie. It's nice to meet you."

She made an "mmm" noise. That fell short of "nice to meet you, too," but I wasn't surprised, just disappointed that she seemed to wear her indignation with every bit as little subtleness as her pants suit.

"What can I get you, miss?" the barista asked. His skin was a lovely mocha shade, and he was very handsome.

"Are you still treating?" she asked me.

"I am."

"In that case I'll have a venti soy hazelnut vanilla cinnamon white mocha with extra white mocha and caramel."

"I...don't even see that on the menu."

She smirked at me. "It's on their secret menu."

I paid while she was awaiting its creation. (I've paid less for a lobster dinner.)

I told her that we'd see her in a moment and went back to my seat. The "we" must have caught her interest, for she widened her eyes and looked over at the chairs, clicking her tongue at the sight of Jane. I loved the little tilt of the paper coffee cup that Jane gave her. Jane was in her element. She had been handling people with attitudes since before Natalie knew what the word meant.

"We'll have to keep this quick," Natalie said, trailing me by a half minute or so. "I'm not looking for a new BFF, or anything. And, frankly, I resent the fact you brought your lawyer with no warning."

"I'm *Eugena's* lawyer," Jane said. "Leslie is my friend."

"Fine. What is it you wanted to talk about?"

"Eugena, of course." I wasn't about to tell her I'd spoken with Eugena's ex. "I'm hoping we can be open about how we feel about our respective friendships with her, and what we—"

"I'm Eugena's agent, not her friend. Although we were very friendly before you and your cohorts insinuated yourselves into the picture. I am paid to always have her best interests at heart."

"Up until she fired you," I replied. "Then put you on probation."

"She didn't mean that. She has an artist's temperament. She likes to fire people to let off steam."

"So you consider yourself Eugena's legal representative of her books?" Jane asked.

"Of course."

"Does *she* consider you her agent?"

She smirked. "Absolutely. Not that it's any of your business."

"Then why was she telling us that you were stealing from her?" Jane asked. "And that your romantic relationship with her lawyer left her unable to get an unbiased second opinion on any of your or his decisions?"

Natalie looked shocked. "She didn't actually accuse me of stealing from her, did she?"

"That's precisely what she said. All four of us were there and can verify that," Jane said. (Although, when I checked the text recording later, she actually had said that she merely *thought* her agent was stealing.) (*Jane's reviewer's note:* I am not at liberty to reveal what was told to me in private conversations with Eugena when she had attorney-client privileges.)

After a moment of silence, Natalie shrugged, then sipped her extortionist's-menu drink. "She must have been in one of her moods, is all. She wades into her woe-is-me dungeon in order to find that dramatic voice of hers that infuses her writing and makes it so compelling."

I grinned, wondering if the deadpanned tone was a mockery of the famous quote on her book jackets.

Natalie caught my smile and glared at me. "You should hear what she has to say about *you*, lately."

"I can imagine. She isn't keen on how I was given her ex-husband's phone number."

She rolled her eyes. "Tell me about it. She should take that guy to court for slandering her."

Natalie looked up and stared at someone behind my shoulder. Jane, meanwhile, was wearing her poker-face. I knew at once who it was and was not eager to turn around. I forced myself. Eugena was seething under the brim of her denim hat.

"Hello, Eugena," Natalie said. "This was Leslie's idea, not mine."

Chapter 23
The Proposal

The ensuing twenty-nine hours were awful. Let's just say that Eugena grew so irate, anyone in the immediate vicinity would have thought I had slept with her spouse after draining her bank account. Neither Jane nor I could get a word in during her diatribe. In what probably would have been the middle of said diatribe but became the end, Abby appeared, with her suitcase and Red in tow, and carrying a plastic shopping bag from a pharmacy. (During their arrangements over the phone to have Abby join her, Eugena had claimed to have a migraine.)

Abby flipped out at the sight of us, and once again, made the valid points that she had "begged" me not to do this and I should have warned her. She and Eugena went up the elevator, with Abby's parting words that she would see me tomorrow night at Alicia's show for *Alicia's* sake, and that she was lucky that Eugena had been so generous to allow Red to join them, now that she could no longer trust me to take care of Red.

I was devastated. Kate and Jane were able to shore me up enough not to do anything too crazy. I did, however, borrow the car, having lied about needing to buy Alka-Seltzer. Instead I bought a fifty-dollar bottle of Chateauneuf-du-Pape, hid myself in the bathroom in order to conceal my purchase, and consumed most of the bottle, using my toothbrush glass in lieu of stemware. Then I called Steve and talked for an hour. I don't remember a word of our conversation, and I hadn't turned on my pocket stenographer.

The next morning, I was hungover and spent much of the day on the covered back porch, watching the rain. The skies, my head, and my mood eventually improved.

When we arrived at Alicia's show, Abby was already there. She gave me a hug and asked me not to bring up the subject of Eugena, which I was going to suggest myself. (I had yet to learn the results of the Alzheimer's tests that morning; Jane had been disinvited to attend.)

All of that said (or rather *written*), I enjoyed the first half of the show more than I can say. One of my all-time favorite TV commercials is one in which a man smiles with pride as he listens to his daughter play the cello beautifully. Although the product being touted has long since left my memory banks, the poignant voice-over told us that discovering one's child has found their life's passion was a moment to cherish forever. That, in a nutshell, is how I felt, watching my daughter's performance.

The show was in a compact theater with a small stage. The majority of the seating was auditorium-style, with a wide aisle down the middle, used periodically by the performers with their traveling microphones. (Think: the Tonight Show, with the host doing an audience-questions' skit.) Immediately in front of the stage, however, were the top-tier seats: three rows of chrome, circular tables with four chairs per table. Steve (I later learned) had preplanned the seating so that although the four of us Boobs were at the same table, he had the seat at the adjacent table closest to mine. At the time of ticket purchase by Alicia and Kurt, Steve had anticipated bringing a date, but he gave that ticket to a male family friend. In front of Steve sat Kurt's brother and a friend. George and Emily were at a third table, to the right of us.

At the intermission, Mila, the *Breakfast with Brittany* producer I'd met, came over to our table. She was dressed in dark blue pencil pants and a cute blouse, her dark hair now looking rather windblown. "Hi, Leslie. I heard this was going to be a special show. Eugena Crowder told me all about it."

"Oh?" I said, my stomach instantly in knots. Luckily, at that moment, Steve and I were the only ones in the immediate vicinity; everyone else had chosen to mill around or use the restrooms.

"I'm here with the cameraman. We got permission to record a song and the proposal. Your daughter's even better than I'd imagined. You can't even *believe* the boost our show's coverage will give her career."

"She deserves it," I said, though my head was in a whirl.

"You're so right about her," Mila replied. "It's like watching a young Audrey Hepburn who can sing like Adele."

(Even *I* think that was an oversell.) "Thank you."

"So I was wondering if you could clear up some things for me that Eugena has told us. She seems to hold you in contempt for—"

"Mila, I truly appreciate what you're doing for my daughter. And I'm happy to chat with you tomorrow. But as for tonight, I'm a bundle of nerves. I need time to get my head straight."

"I understand. I'll call you tomorrow."

"Fine. Thanks."

She turned on her two-inch heel and left. The lights flickered. The second act was about to begin.

"What was that about?" Steve asked. "Did I hear her say that Eugena told her about Kurt's surprise?"

I nodded. "It's turned into such a mess." I looked over my shoulder and saw that Abby and Jane were heading back to the table but weren't yet within earshot. "You were right about Eugena, but Abby's so thoroughly under her thumb that I'm lucky she's still speaking to me."

"I'm sorry to hear that. But for now, let's watch our kids get engaged, and be happy for them."

Although Steve's words were both wise and well-intentioned, they brought my husband, Jack, to mind. He should have been sitting beside me, with his arm around my shoulder as we witnessed our daughter's marriage proposal together. My pang was so acute that Steve reached over and gave my arm a squeeze. Our eyes met, and I saw understanding and empathy in his gaze.

After a half dozen songs, flawlessly rendered, with charming and witty mini-skits involving two to all four cast members, Kurt widened his eyes at his fellow male costar. I realized the moment had arrived. They completed their high-spirited version of "Book of Love."

Alicia then delivered a line that had to have been scripted: "That song makes me wonder. They keep asking 'who wrote the book of love.' *Is* there such a thing, Kurt? Have you ever searched online for the book title: 'The Book of Love?'"

Although Kurt pulled a cellphone out of his pocket on cue and turned it on, he said, "No, I haven't. Since our parents are here tonight, let's have one of them look that up for us."

As he came bounding down the steps toward us, Alicia chuckled. "By all means, let's." (If I didn't know that this was hitting Alicia in surprise, I never would have guessed that she was adlibbing.) "They've fed and clothed us, provided roofs over our heads, raised us, and footed the bill for our college degrees. It's high time we put them to work on our behalf."

The audience laughed.

"Ladies and gentlemen," Kurt said, "we have in our midst several extraordinary people who mean the world to Alicia and me. As do our singing cohorts, Nathan and Maddee." (The other duo in the cast took a bow; they were smiling so broadly, Alicia now *had* to know what was coming next. Her gaze darted to mine, but I quickly shifted mine to Kurt's.)

"At this table, Theodore is my awesome younger brother, who always looked up to me...but only because he's shorter. In all other ways, I looked up to *him*. And this guy, Dave, and I have been best friends since grade school. (They raised from their chairs just enough to turn and acknowledge the audience.)

"This handsome man is Andrew, who's been my de facto uncle my whole life. This is my step-father George, and the beautiful woman seated beside him is my darling mother, Emily. She's a brave woman who really had her hands full, bringing me into this world and never once strangling me."

"Oh, Kurt and Teddy are the finest young men in the entire world," Emily said. She gave Kurt a long embrace, eliciting applause from the audience.

"This woman, Kate, was my fourth-grade teacher, and we've kept in touch all these years. For good reason. She is the nicest woman in the world. Ask anybody. I have not yet had the pleasure of getting to know Jane and Abby as well as I'd like, but Alicia considers all three of them her backup moms. Also because *this* lovely lady is Alicia's mother, Leslie. She is the woman in this world I most admire and appreciate. She's responsible for raising the best woman I've ever known and ever will know."

Kate was already sniffling, but showed Kurt her cellphone. "Let's not forget Ian, Alicia's brother," she said with undisguised emotion. "I'm recording this next number for him now."

Kurt beamed and leaned toward Kate's phone. "Hi, Ian!" Kurt hesitated as he looked at the middle-aged couple at Emily and George's table. "I don't know you two. What are your names?"

"Mike."

"Edith. But you can call me Edie."

"Mike and Edith-but-you-can-call-me-Edie, thanks for coming tonight. I'm sure you are credits to the human race."

"Yep," Mike said.

Kurt walked over to Steve. "And this is the *man* I admire most. My dad. I could go on and on about him, but I've already taken so much of your time."

"*I'll* say!" a grumpy woman at a chair directly behind me growled.

Kurt laughed amiably. He and his father exchanged a brief hug. In the process, they deftly swapped the cellphone for a ring-sized box. Instead of Steve typing in search words, he turned on the phone's camera.

"While my father tries to discover who wrote the book of love, this brings to mind the question I've been meaning to ask you, Alicia. For a long time now." He walked toward her.

"A question?" Alicia repeated. She blushed, and my hands flew to my lips simultaneously with Alicia's.

Kurt got down on one knee. "Once upon a time, every love song I sang was painful, because I was alone. Then, one wonderful day, I met you. From that moment on, I knew I'd never be alone again, if I had anything to say about it. Every love song I sing now is for you. Every breath I take fills me with the knowledge that I want to be beside you, forever and always. Please, Alicia. Make my life right. Make all my dreams come true. Be my wife."

Alicia was sobbing so hard, she couldn't speak. Tears streamed down her face, which made me cry as well. I glanced in Steve's direction and saw a tear running down his cheek. I felt such a pang of love for him at that moment—for this man who was crying with happiness at his son marrying my daughter—that I knew he might even be worth my moving from Boulder someday. (In the distant future, that is. No pressure, "Steve.") But, even so, I could imagine Jack smiling down at Alicia and Kurt, too.

"Is that a yes?" Kurt asked.

Alicia managed to nod.

"Is this the ending of the show?" the grumpy woman demanded. "I was expecting a musical number. This is all just you people talking. On and on!"

Alicia started laughing through her tears. "You're the love of my life, too, Kurt," Alicia said. "I can't wait to be your wife."

"Come on, Leslie," Steve said to me. "Let's give them a standing ovation."

"Yay, Kurt," I called, rising to my feet.

"Thanks, Mom."

"Aw!" Edie said to me, leaning over the table so I could hear more easily. "You must be so thrilled to see your daughter getting engaged on stage."

"It's just an act," the old woman yelled. "I bet they do it every single show."

Kurt nodded to the band, and they played the intro for "Going to the Chapel." Kurt started singing and laughingly enticed Alicia to join in. Steve gave my shoulders a squeeze and started singing too. He gave me a wink, and I too started singing along, swaying with the music.

Within seconds, Abby, Kate, and Jane were on their feet, singing about the chapel of love. By the end of the refrain, every member of the audience had risen, and was singing along.

Then I looked behind me and realized that the elderly woman was the exception. She remained in her seat, arms crossed. She caught my gaze and covered her ears. "You people are nuts!" she cried. "I *hate* this song!"

Steve grinned at me.

"We've got to remember to get her name and address," I told him, "so we can invite her to the wedding."

Chapter 24
Harder and Harder to Breathe

"Well, I still can't get Eugena to answer her phone," Abby said the following morning. Last night she'd grabbed her bag and her dog and left Eugena a note inviting her to help us celebrate our book-club member's engagement. "I've tried both her cellphone and her hotel room."

Mila had assured me Alicia's segment would air this morning, so we had gathered around our TV for coffee and bagels to watch *Breakfast with Brittany*. Alicia and Kurt were here, too, as was Steve. Emily and George had declined the invitation, however. Meanwhile, Eugena had failed to return Abby's calls and emails (and texts), and these last-minute calls had failed to get a response.

With a sigh, Abby set her phone on the floor beside her. She looked positively crushed. She was seated atop Red's doggie-bed. Either she was feeling so low she was metaphorically putting herself in the doghouse, or she needed the comfort of feeling as close to Red as possible. He, meanwhile, sat in her lap and every so often craned his neck to lick her face. He was obviously as fully aware as we were that his beloved owner was feeling blue.

"I'm so sorry, Abby," I said for at least the twentieth time. "I truly believed it was important to try to get Natalie's perspective."

"That was more my fault than yours," Jane said. "*I'm* the one who suggested the idea and insisted on coming with you as an attorney."

"Mom," Alicia said, "I think Steve's right about Eugena's ex being the steady, reasonable one, and Eugena being the schemer."

Abby's eyes flashed in anger and she grumbled something under her breath about "wishful thinking."

"In any case, with all my heart, I hope my actions, however well-intentioned they truly were, didn't cost you your dream job with Eugena."

Abby gave me a small smile and nodded, as she stroked Red's soft fur.

Steve, standing behind the sofa, placed his hand on my shoulder and gave it a gentle squeeze. It was nice to know he was supporting me. Earlier this morning, Jane and I had gotten Alicia and Kurt up to speed with our book club's tempest in a teapot, and Steve had been emphatic about his confidence in Bob's truthfulness.

"Here it comes!" I cried as the show returned from the commercial break to a close up of Brittany's smiling face. (This was the third time I'd made that particular announcement, but the first two turned out to be false alarms.)

After some chit-chat with the newsman as they wrapped up a previous segment on the duck race someone had put together in Table Rock Lake (a white duck named "Quacks" was the winner by a beak), Brittany said, "And now we have a real treat for you. A future superstar is creating quite the buzz at the Rockin' Oldies Show in Branson...where love is in the air."

I started holding my breath, my heart racing.

"Superstar?" Alicia said.

"She means you," Kurt said.

"Or you," she replied, but Alicia's face was already on the screen, singing "The Greatest Love" in her lovely, lilting voice.

We all applauded briefly when they cut away. A few moments later, the screen showed Kurt getting down on his knee in front of Alicia, who was sobbing. They showed Kurt's proposal and Alicia's tearful acceptance. Thankfully, they deleted the grumpy woman complaining, and instead cut to the foursome leading the audience in "Going to the Chapel."

The camera returned to a grinning Brittany. With teary eyes, I scanned the room and reveled in how we were all beaming. Kate and Alicia had tears in their eyes, too.

"Yes," Brittany said on the screen, "that's Alicia O'Kane, soon to be Mrs. Alicia Winston, if she takes her husband's, Kurt's, name. Although she probably won't, because she's from Boulder, the homing-station for liberals."

"Ugh," I said, her annoying last phrase spoiling my mood.

Like mine, Brittany's smile faded. She stared into the camera. "All of us at *Breakfast with Brittany* very much wanted to end this story on this happy note of young love. However, Mila, our crackerjack producer, is in Branson right now with a woman who alert fans might remember from Monday's show. Back again for a second appearance is the famous Newbery-Award-winning author, Eugena Crowder."

Instantly, I felt like throwing up.

"Oh, crap!" Abby said. She leapt to her feet, tucking Red under one arm as if he was a rolled-up newspaper.

Mila Cavernicki became the ever-so-concerned face on the screen.

"Mila, you've uncovered quite the story, which we're proud to bring to our viewers first."

"That's right, Brittany."

"It seems as if Alicia's mother is allegedly involved in committing at least two federal crimes. Is that true, Mila?"

"Let's allow the famous author, Eugena Crowder, to speak for herself."

"Yes, indeed," Brittany replied. "Right after this break for our wonderful sponsors." She winked at the camera.

An advertisement for paper towels aired.

"This can't be happening." My heart was racing. I felt dizzy.

"Mom. You're white as a ghost. Put your head between your knees and breathe." Alicia rushed over to me as I complied.

I heard someone open a refrigerator door behind me, and the *ticky-ticky* sounds of Red's claws on the tile floor as he followed. "Abby?" Jane said. "Leslie's just feeling a little faint. She doesn't need an ice bag."

"I know. I'm getting myself some ice cream."

"Ice cream?" Kate said. "Are you stress eating?"

"No. I just want to eat ice cream."

"'Stressed' spelled backwards is 'desserts,'" Kate said.

"And 'bingo' spelled backwards is 'ognib,'" Abby growled. "What's your point?"

"I don't have one," Kate replied. "But could you please grab me a spoon?"

Steve had worked his way around the sofa and was kneeling in front of me. "Just keep taking big breaths." His voice was wonderfully soothing. In spite of myself, however, I was reliving the moment at the hospital when the doctor told me that there was nothing they could do for Jack. My brain had shut down, and I couldn't understand that he was telling me that my husband had died on the operating table.

The room was spinning. Here was a man I found immensely attractive, being kind to me, after we watched my daughter get engaged on television—and I was about to be put into the slammer for committing two crimes. What on earth could Mila be talking about?

"There's marijuana in my makeup kit," I cried from my face-on-knees position. "Flush it down the toilet."

"Okay, Mom."

"No, not you!" I gestured wildly and smacked somebody in the stomach. "I don't want you to go to jail as an abettor!"

"I'll do it," Jane said.

"No, I don't trust you to flush it! Kate or Abby. You can take the ice cream with you."

"Your heart is racing," Steve said. *No wonder he was pressing his index and middle fingers onto my wrist.* "She needs a beta blocker. Does anybody—"

"I've got a prescription," Jane said. "They're nice and mild. The bottle's in my makeup bag. Kate? Can you bring my pills?"

"Is that why women always go to the restroom together?" Kurt asked. "To do drugs?"

"No, it's—"

I stopped and sat up at the sound of Brittany's voice saying, "We're back with our breaking story about the world-famous children's author of 'A Dog Named Red.'" The camera pulled back to show a second screen, with Eugena sitting on a sofa. Mila had perhaps been demoted, because only her elbow could be seen, near Eugena on the couch.

"How are you today, Ms. Crowder?" Brittany asked.

"Call me Jean," Eugena said, to my surprise. "That's what my friends call me."

"How are you today, Jean?" Brittany beamed at her as if she'd just been invited into a wonderful inner circle.

"I'm...improving. Thank you. It's not easy to talk about what's happened to me over the course of the last few days. I've been stabbed in the back, figuratively of course, by a group of women who pretended to befriend me."

Abby gasped. "She can't possibly be lumping me in with the rest of you! She *has* to mean some other group."

"We bumped into one another in Kansas," Eugena's screen image continued, "where they were vacationing. They were in a book club, on their way to visiting Laura Ingalls Wilder's Little House in the Prairie, but they befriended me, *after* they learned who I was, and insisted on bringing me with them to Branson, Missouri."

On the screen Brittany had begun to shake her head and interrupted, "A famous children's book writer—the author of *A Dog Named Red*, who...by the way, many literary critics call the Laura Ingalls of our generation."

Eugena held up a hand as if to modestly wave off the praise. "Because I'm Eugena Crowder, and I've acquired quite a bit of money over the years, they kidnapped me."

My mind filled with expletives.

"When you say 'kidnapped,' what do you mean? They forced you into the car?"

"No, they gave me a piece of candy, not telling me it was from a marijuana dispensary in Boulder. It made me so sleepy, I would have consented to their stuffing me into a rocket ship and blasting me off to the moon."

I slid to the floor next to Steve, not fainting, but in a preemptive measure.

Brittany laughed, then immediately sobered. "I'm sorry. I forgot myself for a moment. Your imagery is just so delightful! It's no wonder you're a writer!"

"Thank you. These four women, led by Leslie O'Kane, packed up my bags for me and threw them into their car before I could even figure out what was happening. Tragically, I'm fighting the battle of my life."

"With these women, you mean?"

"No, with Alzheimer's. Thankfully, I have my lucid days, such as now. But that's especially thanks to my agent, Natalie Price, who wrested me away from the clutches of those evil women. My agent rescued me. She called in a new prescription for my meds—which I now realize the women were deliberately depriving me of."

"She has a medical prescription?" Kate asked.

Abby began to sob. "*Natalie* did this! She poisoned Eugena's mind! And she sabotaged us."

"These are serious allegations you're making," Brittany was saying on the screen. "Bringing someone across state lines who is physically incapable of giving legal consent is a federal offense. These women should be in jail!"

"Is that true?" Kate asked Jane. "Could we be arrested for kidnapping?"

"Yes," Jane replied. "If she can prove that she was incoherent."

"She can't," Kate said. "We can prove she was completely coherent and cognizant the whole time. We have the text recordings."

"I would never be willing to testify against them," Eugena stated. "I find our litigious culture repellant. In my new book, *On the Road with Red*, I shed light on those very issues, when—"

"Hold the phone, Jean," Brittany interrupted. "To get our viewers up to date, Eugena Crowder has written a sequel to one of the world's all-time most beloved books."

I groaned and leaned forward to put my head between my knees again. "This again! Her sequel's second-rate!"

"Yes, that's right. Now that my angel-in-disguise agent rescued my manuscript from their money-grubbing hands."

"Do tell! This story is so engrossing, it should be a book all on its own!"

"You're not the first person who's told me that," Eugena said.

"Kate." Jane was in full throat as an affronted lawyer. "Call her room at the Marriott."

"Will do." She grabbed her phone and pressed some buttons.

I sat up again. *At least Jane was here!*

Eugena cleared her throat. "Getting back to *On the Road with Red*, one of the—"

Brittany interrupted, "Which is sounding like it should be retitled: *On the Road with Women with Blood on Their Hands*."

Eugena gave her a forced-looking smile. "Go on."

"One of the women took it upon herself to mail an earlier draft of my book to a second publishing house. A publisher in direct competition with my own."

"What did she hope to gain by that?"

"Well, they offered more money than my original publisher. So this...*woman*," Eugena disdainfully intoned, "acted as my agent to get fifteen percent of that sum of my hard earned advance and royalties, all for herself."

"How unethical!" Brittany cried. "Please tell me her plan to steal from you won't work!"

"It *won't*. Even though they didn't need to do so, my publisher was so generous that they offered to *match* the competitor's figure. When my wonderful agent got to the bottom of what the women were doing, my publisher did not seek any financial compensation, and decided to let me keep the salary raise, if you will. They felt that *On the Road with Red* was worth every penny, and more!"

"Amazing. Just amazing. I'm sure many of our viewers consider you a hero for enduring this trauma and coming out on the other side."

"I must admit that it's no secret that M.J. as my main character was nicknamed was based on me."

"On Mean Jean," Brittany said with a smile.

"I've always had true grit. Through all of my hardships, being molested, impoverished, beaten, and yet always, always holding onto my core principles as a child of God. I know that I've written an even better book now." She lifted her chin in a gesture I'd seen before and now disgusted me. "I want the women to know that I forgive them."

"You do?"

"Yes, I do. None of us know the inner demons that another person is facing. We know only the surface that others present. That's true for them, and it was true of me. I am a writer. That is who I am. Who I've always been. Writing is what gives me my grit. My strength. And now I'm losing my words. It's terrifying. So I have kept a stiff upper lip. I have hidden the frightened, handicapped writer, who is losing her identity, her soul, to dementia. I've pretended to be as sharp as I could. And those dreadful women *did* show me kindness. One of them even took me to a doctor, upon my request."

"And is *that* how you got the medicine? Wasn't it through your agent?"

Eugena closed her eyes for a moment. "This is where I must humble myself to your TV audience and admit that I don't remember. I don't know if that doctor gave me a prescription or if my agent called it in for me. But, if you don't mind, this has been far too much about me. I want to acknowledge the true hero of my story, my angel agent, Natalie Price."

Pausing, Eugena gave a brave smile into the camera lens.

"She alone has saved me as those women deliberately and maliciously tried to insinuate themselves into my life so they could control her. They were even trying to make it look like I was incompetent and made me sign a proxy."

Brittany put her hand over her heart, her other hand dabbing at her eyes. "Stay tuned. We'll be right back with more of this riveting story, after the break."

Chapter 25
Still a Big Mess

Within thirty minutes, Jane had used her connections to locate and hire a criminal lawyer. My phone rang, interrupting Jane's description of what was likely to occur during our initial appointment that afternoon. I cursed when I saw that it was Kurt's mother, Emily, calling me. She must have seen *Breakfast with Brittany*. I answered, and she said, "This is Emily, your daughter's future mother-in-law."

I was fighting a gag reflex, which was unrelated to my daughter's future mother-in-law. My mind had unwittingly taken me to an old arcade game—Whack-a-Mole—and I was feeling really sympathetic to the moles.

"Hello, Emily."

"How are you? Did you watch that show this morning?"

"Yes, I sure did." I had no idea what to say next. It was all too much to apologize for or explain.

"I'm sorry I couldn't join you. But it was best for all concerned. I'm not fit to be seen before nine a.m. Our phone has been ringing off the hook with friends trying to congratulate me, but we don't want to spoil it for ourselves. We recorded it, and we want to watch it ourselves for the first time with Kurt and Alicia."

Flabbergasted that they were still in the dark, I mumbled, "Alicia and Kurt?" looking at them.

"Yes. Even though I know they watched it with you earlier this morning, we get equal time for equal sides of the family."

I still had no idea how to respond and said nothing.

"But, listen, the reason I called is I just wanted to make certain you've heard about this evening's engagement celebration. Kurt's been in on the planning all along, and I'm afraid he steadfastly refused to let us host a big gala tonight. He felt that Alicia would want her own friends and her brother to come from out of state, so he felt the only way to be fair would be to make it a small gathering. The restaurant he chose isn't up to snuff, but we'll make it up to everyone at the rehearsal dinner."

I was busy deep breathing, feeling light-headed once again, and it took me a moment to realize she'd stopped talking. I'd already heard about the dinner, but it was nice that Emily was cluing me in personally. "I'm sure it will be wonderful. Thanks for doing this."

"It starts at six o'clock."

"Does that mean five-forty-five, Missouri time?"

"Always better to be early than late."

"Okay," I said, holding up my hand to let Alicia—who was watching me and seemed to be crestfallen—to know it wasn't a problem. "Five forty-five it is. Tell me the location."

"It's Walnut Cove Grill," she said. After giving me "you-can't-miss-it" directions (in my experience truer words were often said), I thanked her and said we'd see her there.

Alicia crossed the room and slumped down beside me on the sofa. She put her arms around me and rested her head on my shoulder. "I'm so sorry this is happening to you, Mom. You don't have to go to the party tonight, if you'd rather not."

"I would never want to miss your party." I kissed the top of her head. "Hey, enough sadness, everybody. Jane's already hired an excellent criminal lawyer. And Eugena is just trying to get people talking about her and her book. It's a publicity stunt. That's all. She probably has no intention of actually filing charges against us. At least for the time being, there's nothing to worry about."

"That's one-hundred percent accurate," Jane said. "And guess what? I'm a lawyer. I know these things."

"Well, personally," Abby said, "I think it's a big misunderstanding. Eugena's too good of a person to do this to us just to generate publicity and beef up her book sales. I'll bet it's that Natalie Price who filled Eugena's head with nonsense about us."

"Either way, Abby, we know the truth," Jane said, "and we're the Boobs. We've got one another's backs."

My smile turned sincere. The Boobs were back! Jane was determined to go on the wagon. Although Abby and I disagreed about Eugena's motives, we were once again on the same side. Kate was always on the right side of her friends. We hadn't called Susan yet, but she would also be a source of comfort and a valuable sounding board.

"So here's what I want you to do for me, Alicia," I said. "And you, too, Kurt. I want you both to be the wonderful actors we already know you to be. I want you to go home, get dressed in your favorite clothes, and come to Walnut Cove Grill, at six or so, and pretend that this messy incident this morning never happened."

"Okay, Mom. But aren't Emily and George going to have seen the show by then? They'll be really upset."

"They haven't watched the recording yet. But even if they do, we'll explain that charges haven't been filed, and we're innocent and can prove it." (*Probably.*) "So let's all kick up our heels and have a wonderful time tonight."

The next few hours passed in a blur of un-fun things to describe, let alone experience. Dave, our attorney, was kind enough to charge us a mere $400 for the consultation, and said that with luck, this could come to nothing. We sat in his office for an hour, and exchanged questions and answers; Jane—to our mutual relief—did most of the talking. Alicia had insisted upon joining us and was being stoic, refusing to acknowledge how badly this mess of mine had ruined what should be a celebratory day. Abby's opinions about why Eugena said what she did on live TV wavered considerably from minute to minute. What stayed consistent was that she was inconsolable about losing her dream job, even though Kate tried her best to be the voice of optimism. (Which isn't always effective and non-irritating).

We then pretended to be successful at putting our worries out of our mind, got dressed up, and arrived on time (5:55 pm which meant we were fashionably late for Missourians). We gave Kurt's and Alicia's name to the maître d', who smiled, said, "Yes, our party of twelve," and led the way.

Our reserved room was quite nice—something of a small, enclosed porch, defined by a step down into the space. The view through the windows could have been nicer—the parking lot was all that was visible—but the open windows gave us a pleasant cross-breeze. Our long table was actually six small, square two-tops pushed together, with six chairs on either side. Unsurprisingly, Emily, George, and their guests were already here and seated.

Emily had taken it upon herself to create place cards for us. Jane and I were seated next to each other at one end, facing into the restaurant; Abby and Kate were directly across from us. Next to me was the yet-to-arrive Alicia, with Kurt's also-unfilled seat across from her. Emily was on Kurt's other side, and George on Alicia's. Next came Kurt's brother and best friend, and finally, Steve and the family friend who'd attended last night's performance. Emily whispered in my ear that he was recently divorced—and said that she'd considered putting us together but felt that I'd prefer sitting with Alicia and my book-club friends. She made no mention of Steve and me enjoying each other's company last night and at the Dixie Stampede (although to be fair, she could have simply inferred that he'd had a professional interest in my teeth).

Steve and I waved at each other. He then rolled his eyes and looked (less than kindly) at Emily. The conversation around the table—spearheaded by Emily—was focused on the lovely proposal. I was a nervous wreck. Any second now, the name "Brittany" would be mentioned, which felt much more like waiting for an anvil to drop than the proverbial "other shoe."

Jane's phone buzzed. She gave a double-take at her screen. "That's odd," she told me quietly. "Natalie Price forwarded a file to me."

"It couldn't be a copy of an affidavit...stating that she's going to be a witness against us, could it?" I asked.

"Not bloody likely," Jane muttered. She pressed an icon on her screen, and her eyes widened at whatever had popped up. She started cursing and scrolling through screens.

"What is it? What's wrong?" I asked.

"That bastard!"

"*Which* bastard?"

"John! My ex! He got married! These are photos of his wedding. He looks happy. So does his pretty-little-thing trophy wife."

"How could Natalie have possible found photos of them? And why would she send them to you?"

Jane shot a darting glance at Abby. "My guess is that Abby must have told Eugena about John's and my miserable divorce. And maybe *Eugena* is the actual sender and 'borrowed' Natalie's phone. The bitch figured out how horribly this would mess with my head."

"I'm so sorry, Jane."

She shut off her phone and jammed it into her purse. "It's his prerogative to get remarried, of course. I knew he would. He wanted a younger wife, and now he's got one. He posted the photos on his goddamned Facebook page, where I'm totally *not* one of his friends!"

I glanced over at Kate, hoping to catch her eye. She's so much better than I am at knowing what to say to console people. She was happily chatting with Emily. I was on my own.

This was too soon to assure Jane that she'd meet someone else who would be extremely lucky to have her. (Even though I was certain that was the absolute truth.) Instead, I said, "I'm sure that John was lonely and depressed *prior* to meeting her. That's the way social media works. We don't go around circulating pictures of ourselves with teary eyes and our heads in our hands and captions that read, 'This is me, missing my wife, Jane, whom I was an idiot to divorce.'"

"Yeah. Still. His lonely-and-depressed period of time hasn't lasted nearly long enough." She was getting the jitters, reminding me of how she'd been acting in the restaurant during our drive from Boulder. "Eugena must be a skilled researcher to get hold of these pictures. She didn't know me from Adam until we ran into her. And by 'ran into,' I'm now wishing I meant 'ran over.'"

Kate had broken off her conversation with Emily and now picked up on Jane's and my distress signals. She asked Jane what was wrong, and Jane repeated what she'd told me, almost verbatim. Moments later, Abby also asked Jane what was wrong. This time Jane answered tersely, "Natalie sent me photos of John marrying some girl who looks like she's in her twenties."

"Where did Natalie get the photos?" Abby asked.

"Off Facebook," I said.

"He got married last night," Jane said.

"On a Wednesday?" Abby exclaimed. "Do people get married on Wednesdays now? Is that because summers are so popular?"

We ignored the question.

"Why on earth would Eugena's agent want to make you feel bad?" Kate asked. "What does she have to gain?"

"Maybe she's just a mean person, Kate," I answered. "There are people like that in the world. Which makes me suspect *Eugena* was the one who found those photos and instructed Natalie to send them to you."

"Eugena would never, ever deliberately be mean, Leslie!" Abby insisted. "The only person she's angry at is *you*. This is all a terrible misunderstanding. That's why she hasn't filed a police report."

"As of this *morning*, you mean," I retorted. "For all we know, she may very well have done so by now."

Jane stood up. "I'm going out to the patio to get some air."

Which meant she would have to walk past the bar. And ignore waitresses serving drinks on the patio. I sprang to my feet. "I'll come with you."

"No, stay here. I need some time alone." She rounded the table.

"Jane, wait."

She turned and narrowed her eyes at me. "Don't worry, Les. I'm just getting air, not drunk."

I didn't believe her. Frustrated, I dropped back down in my seat. "She's going to get drunk," I said. "I know it."

"I'll check on her in a couple of minutes," Abby said. "If she's drinking, I'll knock it out of her hand."

"She's likely getting tequila shots," Kate replied. "They have a special going."

Abby rose. "On second thought, I'll go talk to her right now."

Just then, Alicia and Kurt entered the restaurant. All thoughts of Jane left my head as I cried, "Alicia's here!"

"Oh, my gosh," Kate cried, literally hopping with glee. "She looks so lovely!"

I, too, hopped up from my seat, waving at my daughter. She looked radiant, and so did Kurt.

She gave me one of her stunning smiles and ran toward me. She hugged me, saying, "I'm so happy, Mom! It's almost surreal. It's so hard to believe that the man I love loves me, too!"

"Of course he does, sweetie. And you'll have a wonderful lifetime together."

She pulled away to study my features. "So he's finally won you over?"

"Absolutely." It was true. Getting to know his father and seeing the similarities between him and his son had convinced me. I could see Kurt and Alicia surviving life's obstacle course together.

Thinking about obstacle courses brought Jane's struggle back to my mind.

Kate and Abby were still here, waiting to hug Alicia. While Abby *did* hug Alicia, I gestured at her to please go see Jane. By then Kurt was hugging me, and I realized that I needed to be mother of the future bride. Once again, I was not going to be able to keep Jane boosted upon the wagon tonight.

Just then, a threesome entered the restaurant that made my heart stop. It was Eugena, her chin held high as she marched toward us, followed by two uniformed policemen.

"Oh, dear God. We're screwed."

Abby followed my line of sight. "Oh, no! Something terrible must have happened to Eugena!"

"Are they here to arrest you?" Kate asked me.

"Probably. I need a lawyer." I spotted Jane at the far end of the bar. Sure enough, she was drinking shots. Terrified, I returned my vision to the trio, who in my mind's eyes, might as well have been carrying scythes and dressed like angels of death. Eugena's gaze met mine just then. She grabbed an officer's arm.

"Kate, go get Jane! Quickly!" I cried. She dashed away.

The threesome arrived at our table. "That's her, right there," Eugena said, her voice quivering as if in fright as she pointed at Abby, not me.

"Eugena. What's wrong?" Abby asked her. "Did Red escape through a condo window? Are the police here to tell me something's happened to Red?"

"You've got a lot of nerve, talking to me about my dog, after what you and your fellow flunkies did to me!" Eugena snarled.

"It's *my* dog, Officer," Abby said, her cheeks bright red. "She gets confused sometimes. I did *not* steal her dog."

"Nobody says you did, ma'am," the officer replied.

"Four of them were responsible," Eugena said. "The other two are probably trying to flee. They were all in this together."

"What's happening?" Emily gaped at the officers, then turned toward me. "Leslie? Are your friends drug dealers?"

"No! Of course not!"

"That woman is a scam artist," Steve said to the officers, pointing at Eugena. "You can't believe a word she says."

Alicia stepped in front of me, as if to shield me.

Kate and Jane were striding toward us, behind the officers. Jane's gait already looked unsteady.

"What has Ms. Crowder accused us of doing now?" Jane said, her words a little slurred. "Weren't your false accusations on TV bad enough?"

I groaned as I spotted Mila and the cameraman rushing into the restaurant. Mila espied the officers and ushered the cameraman toward us. This felt like a tsunami of garbage suddenly hitting me from all sides. *What could be next? Locusts? Snakes?*

"What's going on, Officer?" Mila asked. "Are you arresting these women due to my exposé on the *Breakfast with Brittany* segment?" She was unable to resist grinning at that possibility. She made a cranking gesture at the cameraman to signal he should film us. He turned on his camera.

"You know very well what you did!" Eugena told Abby before the officer could answer. "You hit me in the face!" (Only then did I notice a bruise on Eugena's cheek.) "Then you tied me up and said you wouldn't untie me until I agreed to give you half of my advance for *On the Road with Red*." She held up her wrists, which were red and chafed.

"That's not true, Officer," Abby cried again. "Not a word of it! She's got dementia. She's confused."

"Abby forced me to write a check to her, then she put it in her purse," Eugena said. "It's probably still there."

"No. That's not true, Officers." She pointed at her purse, which was under the table, next to her chair. "Look for yourself!"

"If it's *not* there, it's only because she already cashed it," Eugena said.

The one officer crossed over to the chair to start looking through Abby's purse.

Alicia continued to shield me. "Alicia, I can handle this," I said. (A ridiculous assertion if there ever was one; I just didn't want my daughter to get caught up in my mess.) "Kurt, Alicia, everybody. Just please take your seats. We'll get this straightened out."

"Abby," Jane said, stepping down and heading toward our table. "Eugena could have stashed a check in your purse when you stayed in her room the other night."

"Shut off the camera, sir," one of the officers said to the cameraman.

"She's faking the dementia, Officers," Jane said slurring her words. "She's played us like fools. She probably sent the photos to me from Natalie. For all we know, she's the one who found them in the first place on Facebook."

"*What* photos?" Mila asked. "Keep filming!"

"Of my ex-husband's wedding yesterday."

"Ma'am, take a step—" an officer started to say to Eugena as she headed toward Jane.

"You're nothing but a skinny, drunken cow," Eugena growled, "who can't accept—"

Just as the second officer was rising with Abby's purse, Jane balled her fist and cocked her arm back. She cracked her elbow into his face, catching him right in the mouth and made a feeble swing at Eugena, which missed. Jane promptly turned around and gasped when she saw that she'd injured the officer.

"That's it!" the officer growled, blood from his lip running down his chin. "You're under arrest!"

"It was an accident," we book-clubbers cried in unison.

"She was aiming at Eugena! Who deliberately egged her on," I said.

"Oh, my God," Jane cried, still staring at the injured officer in abject horror. "I am so, *so* sorry!"

"Tell that to the judge," he said, grabbing his handcuffs. He started reciting her rights as he fastened the cuffs on Jane's wrists.

"This is all my fault," Abby sobbed. "I couldn't see through Eugena like the rest of you did."

"I demand you arrest these women for assaulting me and kidnapping me!" Eugena yelled.

Several of the diners in the main room were now on their feet, watching the scene. Playing to the camera, Eugena looked right into the lens. "This is all professional jealousy. I found success with my books. They think they're writers. They're trying to steal the money I've earned from my work."

Abby grabbed Eugena by the shoulders and started shaking her. "I believed in you! I accused my best friends of being jealous of you! And you lied! You set us up to be arrested!"

"She's giving me shaken-senior syndrome!" Eugena said.

The non-bloodied officer pried Abby away from Eugena and pulled both of her wrists behind her back. "You're under arrest, too!" He put his handcuffs on her and started Mirandizing Abby.

"You don't understand, Officer." Kate pointed at Eugena. "Eugena had her employee send photos of her ex-husband getting married to my friend Jane, knowing she was an alcoholic and that seeing the pictures would set her off. And she told the reporter and cameraman to be here so that they could get the whole thing on television. You're arresting the good guys!"

The officer looked at Eugena. "Your ex-husband married the woman who punched my partner in the mouth?"

"Oh, dear." Kate looked at me. "That came out completely wrong, didn't it?"

"Ma'am," the bloodied officer told Kate, "whatever you were trying to say, do not interfere with police business, or we'll arrest you, too."

"Fine." Kate picked up a paper napkin from the table, dashed over to the nearest window, and stuffed the napkin through the opening. "There. I've littered. Arrest me, too."

"Please don't!" I said. "I'll go get the napkin." I tried to head toward the exit, intending to steer clear of Eugena, but she took a step back. Her heel hit the step, and she tripped. She got her hands back in time to break her fall and wound up sitting on the step.

"She pushed me!" Eugena exclaimed, pointing at me. "I'm eighty-one years old and she pushed me to the floor!"

"No, I didn't! She tripped on the step! And furthermore," I looked straight into the camera lens myself, "this woman's dentist says she's only sixty-eight." I waved at the cameraman. "Can you give the officer an instant replay? Show him that I never touched her?"

"Ma'am, we don't arrest litterers," the uninjured officer told Kate. I'll issue you a ticket if you insist, but—"

"Fine. Issue me a ticket, and I'll rip that up and throw that out the window. Surely *that's* an arrestable offense."

"Look, ma'am, let's be reasonable for a change. You don't—"

Kate grabbed the officer's arm. "I'm interfering with your arrest of my friends. And I won't let go unless you arrest me, too!"

"For Pete's sake! All four of you ladies are under arrest!"

"Thank you, officer. I apologize for grabbing your arm. I know what a difficult job—"

"You should arrest me, too," Alicia said, once again trying to push her way in front of me. "I'd rather go to jail than see my mom behind bars."

"Oh, good grief! No, Alicia. Do *not* insist on getting arrested. *One* of us O'Kanes has to act maturely, and I already blew it."

"We're going...to need somebody...on the outside," Abby sobbed. "Little Red is in the condo, all by himself. He'll be so worried."

"Is 'Red' a small child, ma'am?"

"I'll watch out for Alicia," Kurt interjected, "while you're incarcerated, ma'am... Leslie...Mom."

"Ugh."

"We'll both take care of Red," Alicia said, flashing a stern look at Kurt. "Who's a dog, Officer," she added to the policeman standing next to Abby.

"I'll post bail for you," Steve said. "Don't worry."

"The HMS 'Don't Worry' Ship has already sailed and is heading for an iceberg," I retorted.

"Do you have any more handcuffs?" the officer asked his partner.

"I can go get the plastic ones out of the trunk."

"Are the...plastic ones...reusable?" Abby asked—still sobbing but a conservationist to her very core.

The first officer gestured toward the door with his chin, and the second officer left. "You and you," he said to Kate and me, "lace your fingers behind your necks."

That seemed a little silly, but I obeyed the instruction.

"Thank you for trying to pick up the napkin I dropped, Leslie," Kate said. "It was a misplaced, rebellious gesture."

"You see what I mean, George?" Emily said. "*This* is why I never join any all-women book clubs."

"Why? You're afraid they'll be arrested and wind up on chain gangs?" I snapped.

"Quiet, Leslie," Jane said.

"No," Emily said. "Because unisex groups are more inclined to fall subject to mob mentality. With inter-gender groups, everyone tends to be on their best behavior." She grinned at me—standing there with my hands clasped behind my head—and at least a dozen onlookers watching us as if we were yet another floor show. "That's why I insisted on joining a couples-only bridge club with George."

"How very festive of you," I said.

"Leslie, no more talking," Jane said.

"I'm going to have to call for backup. We can't fit all of them in our car," the officer said.

"You should have thought of that earlier," Eugena admonished. "I *told* you all four of them were going to be here."

"Her whole story is ridiculous," I cried. "Why would *any* of us have told our whereabouts to someone we'd kidnapped? Were we supposedly afraid she might be worried about our staying out too late?"

"Shut up, Leslie," Jane said. "Not one more word!"

I glared at her, but shut my mouth. *You're pretty bossy for someone who just tried to strike a witness in front of the police—and gave an officer a bloody lip in the process!*

Jane glared right back at me. Maybe she could read my mind. She probably knew me well enough to come close to guessing.

(*Jane's Reviewer's Note:*—I was too busy thinking, "*Stop acting like a headstrong dummy, Les,*" to ponder what she was thinking about me.)

Chapter 26
Doing the Jail House Rock

We were taken in two police cars to the police station/courthouse/jail (which they called "a holding cell"). It was a brick building with nicely maintained surroundings that included a lovely little garden that we'd strolled past two days ago, when we were carefree book lovers as opposed to prison inmates. After instructing both Kate and me not to say a single word, Jane had requested to be in the car with Abby. The officer who had not been hit in the face was in the passenger seat, and we hadn't met the officer driving. (Not that we expected a formal introduction, or anything. For one thing, shaking hands while wearing handcuffs would have been problematic.)

The officers helped Kate and me from the car (I assume you can guess which one of us said "Thank you,") and into the building. Instead of taking us through the main entrance, we were led past the aforementioned garden and downhill into the back entrance. The woman behind the receptionist's desk was wearing a police uniform; the Branson police station apparently occupied the walkout-basement level of the courthouse.

Jane and Abby arrived a minute later. Jane was accompanied by the officer with the bloodied lip, and he still looked angry. Abby couldn't stop crying, although she was managing to sob quietly. Jane promptly said, "Boobs, I'm the only one with no chance of being a catch-and-release. Do *not* mistake loyalty for foolishness. Just post your bail and go back to the condo. I'll be fine."

"No way," I retorted. Within seconds, Kate and Abby concurred. "This is all my fault, anyway," I said. "I'm the one who made Eugena so vindictive by talking to her ex and her agent."

"But I'm the one who wouldn't listen when you realized what an awful woman she was!" Abby wailed. "How can someone who writes such good-hearted books be so mean?"

"My wife says that about John Mayer's songs," the officer who was holding onto my right arm remarked.

"For the love of God," Jane cried, stamping her foot. "Leslie and Abby! Stop making statements!"

"You started it," I muttered, not because I was being petty but because I didn't want Jane to martyr herself. I was assuming that her catch-and-release fishing analogy meant that she would be jailed as the only one who'd thrown a punch—and had injured a policeman in the process. Yet we were all from out-of-state and could be considered flight risks. Furthermore, Abby and I were both being charged with assaulting Eugena. Though unfamiliar with the criminal justice system, I considered it a safe bet that Kate's littering and momentarily grasping the officer's arm were not going to be met with the same gravitas.

Jane's angry officer led her to the receptionist/officer, who winced as she looked at his mouth and handed him an icepack. "Geez, Davis. Weren't you simply giving Ms. Crowder a ride home?"

"Yeah. She insisted on identifying the kidnapping suspects we wanted to bring in for questioning." He tilted his head in Jane's direction. "This one clocked me."

"Accidentally," we all added in unison.

"Uppercut?" the female officer asked.

"Elbow," he replied, shaking his head. "They're tourists. They all need to be booked." He glanced back at us. "Except the nice one with Johnson. Unless she absolutely insists on sticking with her friends." (I knew he meant Kate without reading anyone's badge.)

Just then Alicia raced into the building, followed by Kurt and Steve.

"Do any of them have a relative in town?" Officer Receptionist asked Officer Split Lip.

"That would be me," Alicia said. "That's my mom over there, Leslie O'Kane. I'm Alicia O'Kane. I'm a local. I'm in the Rockin' Oldies cast."

Officer Receptionist smiled at her. "I saw you on *Breakfast with Brittany* this morning. Your singing voice is to die for."

"Um, thanks," Alicia said, without enthusiasm.

"And you're her fiancé," Officer Receptionist said, grinning at Kurt. "Your proposal was so romantic!" She returned her attention to Alicia. "So your mom is one of the alleged kidnappers that Crowder lady was talking about. You've had quite the emotional rollercoaster, haven't you?"

"I'm fine. But we're here to attest for my mom's and my friends' good characters. They're not flight risks, and they're in no way guilty of kidnapping Ms. Crowder. We all witnessed what happened tonight, and my mom never touched her."

"They're all outstanding citizens," Kurt said.

"Upstanding," Alicia corrected.

"That, too," he added.

"We'll take this into consideration after they've been booked into custody. That will take a couple of hours at least."

"Sweetie?" I said, "Why don't you all go back to your dinner party?"

"We cancelled it, Mom," Alicia snapped. "Did you really think we'd just all order dinner and celebrate, and check in on you at the jail house after dessert?"

"Well, no, but...almost half of the guests, including Emily and George, barely know us. There's no reason *they* couldn't go ahead and have a nice meal, at least."

"Except it was our *engagement* party, and we're here at the police station!"

"I don't want to argue with you, Alicia, but if you leave now and go back to the restaurant, it's not as if the restaurant will have run out of food."

Alicia merely made a growling noise and turned to face O.R. (Officer Receptionist). "Thank you, officer. We'll wait here."

She spun around, marched past me, and sat down in the far corner without making eye contact. *This is my most embarrassing incident ever,* I thought. Even so, my second thought was: *At least now I have something entertaining to say about myself if I ever have a book-signing.*

Steve's and my gazes locked. "Are you holding up okay?" he asked gently.

I forced a small smile. "I'm giving you a thumbs-up behind my back."

O.R. opened the door into the inner offices of the police station, where I've never actually wanted to go. We formed an officer-felon line. Jane was escorted inside first, followed by Kate (who of course thanked O.R. for holding the door).

Next came the softly crying Abby. "We're not going to be strip searched, are we?" she asked O.R. "I'm at my highest weight ever. I'm a stress-eater. I feel bad enough about my body already."

O.R. gave her a sympathetic smile. "No, you won't. Even if we remand you overnight for arraignment, we'll let you keep your own clothes on."

Skipping ahead a little, my mug shot made me look like a corpse. As the flash went off, my thought was: *At least I'm better dressed than your average felon.* Not to be a whiner, but you really can't see any of my dress.

The photos were just one step toward our individual booking into custody. It was a time-consuming process. We gave our names and social security numbers as an officer typed that information in, along with our charges. (I was charged with assault.) Then came the mug shot, followed by the lengthy process of accounting for each individual item in our purses. (Time-saving tip if you're ever arrested at your home: grab your wallet; leave your purse.) Next came fingerprinting, a pat down by a female officer (a hideous experience, regardless of the patting-person's gender), then they computer-checked for outstanding warrants (nothing about me is outstanding, unless you count my children {pardon my dumb-joke reaction even while writing}), and asked us if we had any medical conditions including allergies. (I asked if it would make any difference if I was allergic to jail {compulsive reaction yada yada}). Then they offered us sandwiches and beverages. I declined food and asked for water.

We were taken to the holding cell; I'd been last to be processed, so the others were sitting there. It was a clean, beige-painted room that smelled of Lysol. (That is: up until I vomited in the toilet, but let's just skip that unfortunate incident.) Not counting the bars on the one wall and the locked door, it wasn't much worse than a dorm room for four. Jane and Abby were seated on the bottom bunk on one side of the room. Kate sat on the other.

"Kate and I already declined bail, because Jane wasn't given the option," Abby said the moment the officer clanged the door shut behind me.

"Are you feeling okay?" Kate asked me. "You look really pale. Is it your stomach?"

"Officer?" I called after the man who'd locked us into this cell in order to protect the outside world from our indecent book club.

He turned. "I'm going to refuse bail, as well. Could you please tell my daughter that I'm sorry to have kept her waiting? And that I'm here for the night and to please go home?"

"Suit yourself," the officer said.

"You really don't have to do this," Jane said. "I'm the idiot alcoholic who hit a policeman in the face."

"And we're the Boobs," I said, "who always have one another's backs. What's your point?" (Then I had to run to the toilet, but again, we're skipping that.)

"They gave us toothpaste and toothbrushes," Kate said upon my return.

"So I noticed."

"The good news is that I'm determined to never have another sip of alcohol as long as I live," Jane said to me.

"I'm glad. That *is* good news." *Despite everything else sucking.*

"Abstaining from alcohol isn't all that awful, most of the time," Kate said. "I am hardly ever tempted anymore. And that's what lets me forgive myself. That and my faith in the Lord."

Jane was an atheist, and she flinched a little, then said, "I have faith in the three of you. I've done nothing to justify your faith in *me* lately, but I appreciate your friendships more than I can say."

I burst into tears. So did Jane and Kate. Abby started crying even harder. Fortunately, our bathroom was stocked with tissues.

My iPad was one of the items in my purse that had been locked away. None of our goings-on since leaving the restaurant were recorded. Suffice it to say that we had a cryfest and beat up on ourselves and defended whichever of us was currently engaged in self-flagellation. Kate deserves the most credit for bringing that messy conversation to a close. She asked Jane if it was okay with her if those of us who believed could say silent prayers for her. She answered that sitting in a jail cell and waiting to be arraigned made prayers not only appropriate, but deeply appreciated.

Kate had us join hands as she led us in saying a lovely prayer, which was deeply personal and truly uplifting. Her words remain written on my heart.

Without pausing to appreciate the irony of how quickly we parted company with the Divine, we then vented at length about Eugena. Kate wisely pointed out that we should have pity for her, because none of us could begin to imagine what it must feel like to believe that you were justified in treating others like this.

Abby noted that the doctor had said Eugena's Alzheimer's test results were "all over the map" and suggested she come back for more tests. I held my tongue to stop myself from blurting out: *That's because she was faking dementia!* Abby, however, asked Jane if it was in any way possible that she truly had Alzheimer's and believed her own accusations against us. Jane's response was to ask Abby if the police found a check in her purse. They had. It was for $20,000. Jane then asked if we could concoct a reasonable scenario in which a woman with short-term memory loss and dementia would secretively slip a large check into someone's purse and, two or so days later, believe that she'd been tied up and harangued until she'd agreed to hand it over. Abby ran a few "what-ifs" past her, but then conceded it was too far-fetched.

"I wonder if a policeman could bring us a book to read," Kate then said. "We could each read a chapter aloud and then discuss it."

Abby, who'd finally stopped crying, said, "I'll never forget the way the father of the blind girl carved the model of their neighborhood for her." (She was referencing a scene in *All the Light We Cannot See*.)

"That's something I'd be interested in knowing," I said.

"How he did it?" Abby asked.

"No, I'd like to know what first comes to mind— or maybe what lessons we learned—regarding some of the books that we've read recently."

"That's a great idea," Kate said. "I learned so much from Laura Ingalls Wilder's books. I'd have to say my most important lesson is to cherish your family. If I had to live in a log cabin with dirt floors and virtually no possessions, I could, as long as my husband and daughters were with me."

"I learned that blind people don't see images," Abby said, "but still have sensual dreams."

"I learned that bear meat is apparently delicious," I said, "that a pig's bladder can be used as an organic beach ball, and that human nature remains the same throughout the centuries."

Jane said, "I learned from Ms. Wilder that if an author sticks his or her manuscript on the shelf, the reading public should be grateful for that author's honest assessment, and should *leave* it there. Ditto for the book that we read a month ago. Which I'd prefer not to name."

"You're talking about *Go Set a Watchman*, right?" Abby asked.

***

At eight a.m., our defense attorney, Dave Haggerman, arrived, and we went through some tedious protocol to allow him to access my iPad so that his assistant could print the text recorded by the software application and present it as evidence at our preliminary hearing.

He informed us that filing a false police report is merely a misdemeanor, which, considering the outrageous wrongs that Eugena had done to us, was really deflating. Given our setting, we were already as deflated as unfilled balloons. (Or pig bladders.) He suggested we sue her in civil court for defamation of character. While we were mulling that idea, I said, "My theory is that she never really expected to get away with convincing a judge and jury that we'd kidnapped her. So *now* she's pretending to have Alzheimer's to escape culpability for what she's done to us."

"Are there any conversations on your iPad that recorded Ms. Crowder admitting to framing you?"

"No, but once we get out of here, I could get her to admit it," I said. "Maybe."

"Then we might have solid evidence that would win a defamation case. You'll need a video recording to prove that it's her speaking, though."

"Let's suppose I get precisely that," I said. "Would the D.A. be persuaded to drop all charges against Jane?"

"Not necessarily," he said with a sigh. He looked at Jane. "You punched an officer of the law in the face. You can be disbarred."

Jane looked ashen.

"But if we can demonstrate just how egregiously Eugena mistreated us, won't the judge and D.A. drop the charges?"

"Perhaps. I'll do my best. Officer Davis is a good man. When he testifies, he might take it easy on you. Even though you loosened his front tooth. And with Crowder's confession that she did all this to you deliberately, we can at least demonstrate that a lot of people would have wanted to give the woman a proper smack down."

***

Some three-plus hours later, the four of us were called in front of the judge. Some ninety seconds later, the D.A. charged Kate, Abby, and me with misdemeanors, and the judge released us on our own recognizance. Jane was charged with assaulting a police officer. The judge set her bond at five-thousand dollars, which our attorney paid. (After she'd written him yet another check.) In our one true stroke of good fortune, the preliminary trial was scheduled to take place on Monday morning; we had no complaints when it came to receiving a speedy trial. The officers returned our purses to us, although Abby's bogus check was retained as possible evidence for a future trial. The four of us emerged together from the inner-workings of the courthouse feeling dazed. I wanted to jokingly start a chorus of "Free at last!" but my numbed state of exhaustion overruled my compulsive humor.

While heading toward the door to the glorious outside world, I stopped short. So did the other Boobs. To my utter delight, Steve was waiting for me in the lobby, holding a lovely bouquet of red roses. He smiled at me. He handed me the bouquet, simply saying, "These are for you," then he gave me a quick kiss, and said, "I've got to get going. I have patients waiting for me."

"Thank you for the roses."

"My pleasure," he said. Then he pivoted and strode out the door.

The book clubbers had witnessed our exchange in silence. I turned to face them, dumbstruck.

"Was that your first kiss?" Abby asked.

"From *him*," I replied. "This has been the weirdest vacation ever." *Next up, I need to borrow Alicia's video camera and cut a hole in my purse.*

An hour or so later, Kurt and Alicia joined us at the condo and brought a faux-leather black purse that was a stage prop. They'd taken it to a costume seamstress, and she'd attached a pocket and elastic straps to hold Alicia's video camera perfectly in place, and fashioned a well-camouflaged opening in one side for the lens.

Meanwhile, we needed to vacate the condo. Kate found us other lodging for three more nights and explained our situation to her husband, as well as to Susan, who had the opportunity to give Jane some encouragement with her upcoming ordeal.

More importantly, Jane called the Marriott and learned that Eugena had checked out, as had her agent. Jane then got ahold of Natalie on her cellphone. She was in New York. She said that Eugena had fired her last night, so she took a Redeye. She had no idea where Eugena had gone, but opined that: "She probably went to hell to check up on how her right-hand man, Satan, was doing."

While the above was going on, Abby had been paying Red lots of attention, which she felt was grossly overdue. (Abby had spoken to Alicia before I'd arrived at the holding cell, and they'd arranged for Alicia to get a key and take Red to their apartment last night.) Yet Abby, too, was eager to help with getting Eugena to reveal her true colors. Upon learning that Eugena had left the Marriott, I asked her to ask Siri about Alzheimer's facilities in Branson.

There was only one, and it was just a short drive away.

I called the facility. A woman with a wonderfully warm speaking voice answered. "Hi," I said. "My name is Leslie O'Kane. I've just now learned that my Aunt Jean checked into your facility yesterday, and I'd like to pay her a quick visit this afternoon."

"You're a good niece," she replied. "You must mean Jean Smith."

I jumped out of my chair and shook my fist in triumph at the others. As calmly as I could I said, "Yes, although I doubt she'll remember she even *has* a niece, the poor thing."

"She was very disoriented yesterday," the woman said. "But we'll hope for the best."

Yes, we will, I thought.

After getting off the phone, I talked strategy with the others. Kurt and Alicia drove me, but stayed in their car. Thirty minutes later, I had signed in to visit Jean Smith, was admitted through the solid metal door to her wing and shown to door 104.

I knocked and mustered a smile.

Chapter 27
Old Friends

Eugena slowly opened the door, managing to keep her features placid as she met my gaze. "Yes? May I help you?" she asked. She was shaking her head continuously as if from palsy, which was a nice visual touch, although not anything I'd seen as symptomatic of Alzheimer's.

"Hello, Eugena." With my purse tucked under one arm, and the shoulder strap adjusted just so, I'd already determined this to be the perfect angle to capture her face. "I *thought* I might find you here."

"Do I know you?" Eugena asked, her face still expressionless, although her head had already stopped shaking.

"I'm your niece, Leslie. May I come in?"

"Certainly."

She stepped back. I waved off the staff member and entered, shutting the door behind me.

"I don't remember even *having* a niece," Eugena said, still maintaining her ruse of amnesia despite the lack of witnesses.

"If you ever *did* have a niece, you probably ate her."

She smirked at me and said, "I can't remember when this happened, but I got lost in the grocery store. The manager, or maybe the butcher, called the police. And they brought me here. That's what the nurse told me happened. Or maybe she's a doctor. Or a maid. But somebody who works here."

"Are you going to file *kidnapping* charges against her? Then will you hold an interview and convince the public at large that you're being abused by a bunch of money grubbers like me?"

"You sound angry. I think you should leave."

"It must be so tedious to have to put on this helpless-little-old-lady act, when you're actually sharp as a tack."

She snorted. "I wish that were true, Elsa."

"My name is Leslie, as you well know. I also know that, back when you were first submitting your manuscript of *A Dog Named Red*, you added thirteen years to your age. You wanted to employ historical aspects in your novel, yet make it sell better by claiming it was a memoir."

"I don't know what you're talking about, young lady!"

"Your ex-husband sent me your wedding announcement in the newspaper, which had your photo, along with the date at that time, and your full names. A simple call to city hall proves who you are, and your actual age. When the police match it to all of my recordings of the times you lied to us, it forms a nice, clear picture of what you're up to."

She paled. "*What* recordings?"

"I recorded almost all of our conversations. My son created a software application. It functions as if it's an automatic stenographer. We'd already matched our voices to our names, so *yours* were recorded as: UIF—Un-Identified Female."

"I don't believe you."

"Fine. Don't. It will be put into evidence at the preliminary hearing on Monday morning. Natalie Price is back in New York, but she told me she'd be happy to return on Monday to testify against you. You'll be paying for her flights, of course, as a part of the penalty for filing a false-report charges that are being brought against you." (I was adlibbing a bit. Or ad-fibbing, if you prefer.)

"You bitch!"

"Now that the gig is up, you can't keep claiming to be the victim of foul play. And, if it's true that there's no such thing as bad publicity, you're going to want to be in the courthouse at ten a.m. The *Breakfast with Brittany* crew will be there, recording everything." (Or not. I doubted live recordings were allowed in a court of law. But maybe *Judge Judy* had brought an end to that policy.)

Eugena was literally shaking with fury. "You wannabe authors have no idea what it takes to succeed in today's market! To capture sales! I worked my fingers to the bone. And for what? So that I can get a column inch in the *New York Times* when I die? So that I can be a one-book wonder? I won the Newbery, for God's sake! But all people want is the next book. To be perpetually entertained by my imaginary, long-lost best friend in life, my stupid dog, Red."

"Did he ever even exist? Other than as your mother-in-law's dog?"

"Sort of. I adopted a mutt for a few months from the pound for research purposes."

Fearing I hadn't angled the lens to show her face, I adjusted my purse.

"Are you recording *this*?" Eugena asked.

"I just want to know why, Eugena," I stated flatly instead of answering. "Why did you sucker us in like this? Why did you paint your agent and lawyer as corrupt?"

"Because they *are*." (That was the great thing about trying to trick a narcissist into talking about herself; it was easy.) "To sell books, Leslie, you need a platform. Otherwise, nobody cares. I fabricated a good background story for how this book came to be. That was going to be all there was to it—the victim of Alzheimer's who wrote a sequel to her best seller, only to be used by her agent and lawyer. When I spotted Red, I realized I'd stumbled upon the perfect fall-guys."

"You accepted help from us, framed us, and had us arrested." I studied her features. "It's despicable."

"Oh, come now, Leslie! You've hardly been abused here! You got to toot your own horn...act like you're saving the day for a big-deal celebrity author. You'll have your day in court. You can tell the world how evil I am, how I took advantage of you all."

"And you won't care either way, because, again, there's no such thing as 'bad publicity.'"

She shrugged. "I have to keep escalating the charges and situations in order to keep the news and social media interested. If I could claim that I'm John F. Kennedy's and Marilyn Monroe's lovechild, I would have done so. That's what it takes to turn a book into a blockbuster these days, Leslie. It's a dog eat dog world."

"We're only cannibalistic when we choose to be. To further your career, you stomped on my friends. They're wonderful women. We'd have been your friends for the rest of your pitiful little life."

"Give me a choice between creating friendships or a legacy, I'll choose a legacy every time." She snorted. "You're too naïve to understand."

"I feel sorry for you. Your legacy is that of a selfish, cold-hearted woman who wrote one good book about a remarkable woman, which you claimed was a memoir."

She snorted. "You lack the strength and determination to be a successful writer."

"Whereas *you* lack the moral compass to be a decent human being. You're feigning dementia to give yourself a plausible excuse for making false criminal charges."

She shook her head. "I'm doing this to build my platform—my back story."

"Well, I *am* recording this conversation, so your cover is blown. I'm going to write a book revealing precisely how craven you are!"

Eugena put her hands on her hips. "Do you actually think that will *bother* me? A silly book, with me as the antagonist? Shows what *you* know! That will help me sell more copies of *On the Road with Red.* Some therapist will write a case study on me in order to get on the news channels as an expert commentator. That will help me sell yet *more* books. Meanwhile, your little band of book lovers will be the hit of girls'-night-out happy hours. You'll get friend requests, interview requests, and 'oh, you poor dears.' All of that, in exchange for one lousy night in jail. You should be *thanking* me. You should be kissing my feet." She opened the door. "Get out."

I brushed past her and headed for the lobby. For a moment or two, I toyed with the notion of running to the front desk and telling the nurse that Eugena had swallowed a handful of pills and needed to have her stomach pumped. That's the type of thing *she* would have done, though. The last thing I wanted was to give her the power to lower myself to her level, even briefly.

As I signed out, the nurse asked if I'd had a nice visit.

"I did. Although she's totally faking dementia. She checked in here only so that she could claim mental incapacitation as an excuse for having knowingly filed fake criminal charges against me and my friends. If you need proof, I could email the video recording I just made of our entire conversation."

"That could be helpful. Send it to our facility email, and I'll make sure it gets to the right people. Y'all have a great day now!"

I wasn't sure if she was simply humoring me, but I thanked her and told her to have a great day, as well.

Chapter 28
Here Comes the Judge

For purposes of dramatic tension, it would have been much more exciting if we'd had a trial, with Jane acting as our lawyer, and Eugena hiring a showboating attorney that Jane could have walked all over. This was just a pretrial (probable-cause) hearing, however, and Jane was too wise to act as her own attorney. Even though I knew that this was not a full-blown trial, I was petrified. My stomach was in knots, and I felt ill. Worse, my compulsive joking could lead to my spouting off some wisecrack that could anger the judge. I didn't want to wind up being sentenced for contempt of court.

Furthermore, I was deeply disappointed that Eugena had yet to arrive. Alicia, Kurt, and Steve were in the first row of the gallery—and were seated directly behind us. When I glanced back, Alicia gave me a thumbs up and beamed at me, but I knew how worried she was. Jane sat closest to our attorney. I sat between her and Abby, with Kate at the end.

I'd only just turned to grumble to Abby about Eugena's absence when she walked through the door. At the sight of her, I had a simultaneous rush of nervous excitement and crippling anxiety. My breath caught and my vision grayed, and for a moment, I thought I was going to pass out.

The judge—who looked a bit like a pudgy, clean-shaven Tom Selleck—greeted the D.A. and our lawyer, Dave, as if they were long-time business associates.

Dave rose and stated, "My clients—Abigail Preston, Kate Ryan, and Leslie O'Kane—intend to contest their misdemeanor charges that emerged from Thursday night's brouhaha at the Walnut Cove Grill. My client, Jane Henderson, wishes to contest the charge of assault against an officer of the law."

"Which one of you is Jane?" the judge asked.

"That would be me, Your Honor." Jane rose halfway, then sat back down.   "Aha," he said, then shifted his gaze to the District Attorney.

"The State calls to the stand Officer—"

"Wait a minute," Eugena called out, rising from her seat in the gallery. "What happened to the kidnapping charges I filed? Are they all just getting wrist-slaps for what they did to me?"

The judge's eyes widened. His focus shifted from Eugena to the D.A., who rose and said, "There was insufficient evidence, your honor."

"This is a miscarriage of justice!" Eugena cried, still standing.

"Is that so?" the judge asked, crossing his arms on his chest.

"Yes, your honor. These women assaulted me!" She pointed at Jane. "That miserable woman meant to hit *me* in the face, not the officer!"

The judge looked directly at Jane. "You missed the woman and hit an officer in the face?"

She rose. "Your honor, the officer was behind me and turned around just as I brought my elbow back. I was inebriated at the time, and we'd only recently discovered that Eugena had duped the four of us. We foolishly believed that a famous writer of children's books wouldn't be so cruel as to invent a ridiculous story about our kidnapping her, purely as a means to gain publicity for her next book."

"Aha," he said. The judge peered over his reading glasses at Eugena. "You would be the writer in question, then?"

"Yes. I am Eugena Crowder, author of the Newbery Winner, *A Dog Named Red*."

"Huh. My son loves that book," the judge said.

"I'd be happy to sign a copy for him."

He raised an eyebrow. "Sit down, Ms. Newbery Winner, and refrain from speaking out of turn in my courtroom again. But I'll pass along your regards to my son." He nodded at the D.A.

"The prosecution calls to the stand Officer Davis, Your Honor."

Officer Davis walked up to the witness box and sat down. The left side of his mouth had mostly healed. He was a handsome young man, who looked like he'd been a football player in college.

"Is the defendant's story accurate?" the judge asked before the D.A. was able to speak.

"Yes, your honor. I'd been given permission to search a purse that was on the floor, and I stepped right into the blow. The defendant was intoxicated, and was being cursed out by Ms. Crowder, which is what led to the defendant's violent response. My partner and I had been giving Ms. Crowder a ride to her hotel, when she'd urged us to stop at the Walnut Cove Grill. She'd identified a vehicle with Colorado plates in the parking lot. She claimed it was used to transport her against her will from Cawker City, Kansas."

The prosecutor started to ask the officer a question, but the judge held up a hand to stop him. "So were you fixing to arrest the defendant for assaulting and kidnapping the outraged children's book writer?" He gestured in Eugena's direction.

"No, your honor. My partner and I only intended to question them. When she came to the stationhouse to file those charges, Ms. Crowder told my partner and I more than once that she suffered from Alzheimer's, and sometimes got her facts confused. We were taking her accusations with a grain of salt."

When both Dave and the D.A. said they had no questions for Officer Davis, he left the stand. Dave rose and turned to the judge. "The defense wishes to enter a DVD recording and a voice-to-text recording into evidence. The defense contends that these recordings reveal that my four clients were only trying to help Ms. Crowder. As my client said, Ms. Crowder framed the defendants and deliberately made false accusations in order to garner publicity and increase her book sales. The DVD recording was made by Leslie O'Kane during her visit of Ms. Crowder at an Alzheimer's patients' facility in town. And the—"

The judge held up his hand again and peered at Eugena for a long moment. "And what do *you* have to say about the defense's take on this, Ms. Crowder?"

"Pardon?"

"Are you guilty of filing false reports of serious crimes that never took place? Against four innocent people trying to help you?"

She got unsteadily to her feet, looking every inch the elderly, feeble, eighty-one year old that she was not. "I had gotten my heart medications mixed up and was taking the wrong doses. As a result, I gave myself dementia."

"Dementia?"

"I checked myself into an Alzheimer's facility, which I left in order to testify at this hearing."

He sighed, then gestured at her, saying, "Sit down, ma'am."

The judge took a long look at Eugena, then Jane. He then looked at Abby, Kate, and me. "Are y'all in town for a vacation?"

"Yes, your Honor," Jane said, still seated. "We're in a book club. We were on a road trip to the Laura

Ingalls Museum in Mansfield, Missouri. And to see our youngest book-club member's performance in Branson."

The judge focused on Kurt and Alicia and grinned. "I've seen y'all's show with the Missus. Very enjoyable."

"Thank you, your honor, sir," Kurt said.

The judge turned his attention to the stack of printed dialogue. "What's all this here?"

"It's the output from an application that performs like a first-rate stenographer, Dave explained. "We tested it extensively and are convinced of its accuracy. The most compelling recorded statements have tabs on them for easy reference."

He pounded his gavel once. "Fifteen minute recess." He stood up. "Gentlemen, join me in my chambers," he said to the two attorneys, "and let's review this evidence together. Stick around, Ms. Crowder. I have a sneaky suspicion I'm not done with you."

The judge, Dave, and the DA left through a door behind the stand. I finally allowed myself to relax. It felt as if I'd taken my first full breath since the hearing began. I also released Abby's hand, only then fully aware that we'd grasped hands at some point. She released Kate's hand as well. Jane smiled at us, but then faced forward and sat staring straight ahead.

The security guard kept an eye on Eugena and followed her out as she left the room.

***

Close to thirty minutes later, the judge and attorneys returned, as did Eugena and the security guard. After taking the bench, the judge nodded at the District Attorney. "The State agrees to a disorderly conduct charge for Jane Henderson, and drops all charges against Kate Ryan, Abigail Preston, and Leslie O'Kane."

We immediately made a group hug, which ended quickly at the sound of the judge clearing his throat. "Ms. Henderson, is this misdemeanor charge acceptable to you?"

"Yes, your Honor," Jane said, losing her smile.

"Ms. Henderson is hereby ordered to pay a fine of five-hundred dollars. She is also ordered to attend an AA program for six months and to file proof of her attendance to this court, at which time, her record will be expunged."

Jane's sigh of relief was audible.

The judge removed his glasses and fixed a glare at Eugena. "Now, as to *you*, Ms. Crowder, the text and video recordings make it clear that you had malice aforethought in virtually every action you took from the moment these nice ladies had the misfortune of meeting you."

I could tell at a glance that Eugena was seething; she was shaking and gripped the back of the seat in front of her with white-knuckled intensity. She turned to glare at me, then once again straightened to look at the judge.

"I checked your publisher's website," the judge continued. "Considering that your book won't go on sale for another six months, I seriously doubt all of this hullabaloo that you've created will continue, even though you've taken such elaborate steps to convince everyone of your having short-term memory loss."

"I *do* have Alzheimer's, your Honor," she growled.

"Whether or not that is true, our society has much worse memory loss than you do. I can only hope that you're not planning to generate more publicity by robbing a bank in another few months."

He pounded his gavel once. "And lastly, Ms. Crowder, I'm not interested in having your signature on my son's book."

Chapter 29
Not Forgotten...But Fuzzier

Every December, our book club meets for a Christmas/New Year's celebratory dinner. This particular dinner occurred after I'd completed the book that you are now reading. I'd purchased all five of us tickets to New York City, with my anticipated advance money from the still-in-the-works contract from a publisher.

That evening, I turned on my Pocket Stenographer App. We happened to be having a familiar conversation that warmed my heart—Jane was erroneously insisting that we hadn't ever discussed which book we would read next month.

"Don't you remember, Jane?" Kate asked gently. "We chose the book when we were waiting in the airport."

"Oh, that's right. I must have had a memory lapse."

"Me, too," Abby said. "What's it about again?"

"The title of the book is *Jane and the Unpleasantness at Scargrave Manor*. It's historical fiction, which reimagines Jane Austen as a sleuth," Susan answered.

"Which is much better than imagining her as a sloth," I said. "Or as a zombie. Or as helping Abraham Lincoln to battle zombies."

"Is Austen a zombie herself, or a zombie killer?" Abby asked.

"You're thinking of vampires," Jane said. "I don't think you can kill zombies. They're already dead."

There was a pause, during which I was trying to remember whether I'd seen a cover of Jane Austen as vampire or as a zombie, and then to consider how very weird it was to be searching my memory banks for such a thing in the first place.

"I can't wait to see your musical, tomorrow, Alicia," I said.

"It's going to seem mundane, in comparison to the Branson performance. No marriage proposals." Her eyes lit up. "Hey, we should toast to our *major* accomplishment this past year. How we finally found a book that every single one of us considers an important, well-written book."

She paused and, for a moment, had fooled me into thinking she meant my book.

"*Being Mortal*," she said. Then she laughed and put her hand on my arm.

"True, Alicia," I said. "Come to think of it, that's a book everyone in America should read, if they want to learn how to take charge of their medical care in their senior years."

"Which reminds me, we *could* read Leslie's book for our *next* meeting," Kate suggested with a big smile.

"Oh, hell, no," Abby said.

"There isn't a single likable character in the entire book," Alicia said.

"And the dialogue sucks," Jane said.

"Which reminds me," Abby said. "I've got my new business venture underway. I finished weaving a placemat from the loom at the Laura Ingalls Wilder Museum."

"You mean that tiny little replica you bought at the gift shop?" Kate asked.

"No, from the full-sized loom I bought in October that looks just like it," Abby explained.

Alicia spotted my iPad on my lap. "Wait. Is your stenographer app running right now, Mom? What happened to your promise that you'd never use that thing around me?"

"I'm sorry. You're right. It's only been on for a minute or so. I'll turn it off now." (I did as requested.) "I was feeling nostalgic and running it for 'Auld Lang Syne, My Dears.'"

"Here's to the best book club in the history of the world," Jane announced, toasting with her glass of tonic water aloft.

"That's quite the claim," I said, "although I embrace the sentiment with every fiber of my being."

"It's the truth," Kate said, lifting her own glass of tonic water.

"Absolutely," Susan and Alicia said in unison.

"Tah dah," Abby said. "Once again, we are all in perfect agreement!"

Simultaneously, we clinked our glasses.

Epilogue
Final Words from the Boob Club

Now that I've had time to reflect upon these experiences as written, I wish there was a clear moral to the story. Something along the lines of: *Crime doesn't pay,* or *Good triumphs over evil* would have been invigorating. Even: *Nice guys finish last* would have done in a pinch, for the sardonic among us.

Eugena spent zero time in jail. We did have an out-of-court settlement that I am not at liberty to reveal, but it was much less than her royalties. She makes appearances on talk shows all the time, and *On the Road with Red* is selling like hotcakes. (I asked Susan once at what point in our nation's history were pancakes ever so popular as to warrant their own cliché. The short answer is: *1839.* She asked Siri.)

Most importantly, however, none of us Boobs believes we came out of this the worse for our experiences with Eugena. (Which reminds me: Natalie Price helped me to find my agent. She and Chris broke up, and she married a semi-famous novelist. But, back to my book club.)

Primarily, I discovered that, as with every other livelihood, authors can be mean—regardless of whether or not those authors can *also* write brilliant books that contain so much emotional wisdom that they change your life for the better.

While that is all *I* have to say about this story, many moons ago, during the halcyon days of my third revision, I promised my fellow Boobs that they could provide their own wrap up and have the last word. I also promised not to contradict or edit anything that they wrote.

***

This is "Abby": Red did *too* realize that Eugena Crowder was nasty and unworthy of us. Leslie neglected to note the significance of the time Red tinkled on her ankle. I had to read this manuscript so many times I don't remember if she even included the scene in which Red peed on Eugena in the final version, but I can't think of a way of demonstrating one's dislike of a person more clearly than to urinate on them. Furthermore, Leslie asks Google questions all the time; she has an Android. I cry easily. I'm not ashamed of that. We all should cry more often and shout less. I so do NOT change subjects often. I hope you enjoyed this book. Other than her insulting my dog's slightly peaked head, I loved it.

Jane—Red pees on shoes on a regular basis. He's a dog. But, as for this book, I'd have to give it a B-. Although the main character, "Leslie," was well-developed, the rest of the "characters" weren't especially well-rounded. She also overused parenthetical statements by a factor of ten. My favorite part of this book was the scene in jail. (Love you Boobs! {Like "Leslie," I can be sarcastic, as demonstrated herein with my punctuation.})

Kate—I am nowhere near as nice as Leslie makes me out to be in this book, although it's true that I avoid confrontation and attempt to placate people when they are getting upset. I consider that a character flaw, not something to be admired. Really, all of my fellow book club members are truly the nicest, dearest people you would ever want to meet. I love them all like sisters, and I'm so proud of them.

P.S. In case anyone is curious, the second Kansas surprise was a trip to the Underground Salt Mines. It's fascinating!

Alicia—My mom has always favored my brother. That's the simple truth. Ask anybody, other than her book-club friends, who won't touch this subject with the proverbial ten-foot pole. She loves us both, however, and she's a great mom. She gets embarrassingly flattering at times in describing either of us. Believe me when I say that I'm undeserving.

In actuality, I was not the star of the 'Rockin' Oldies' show. I was one of four *equally talented* performers, and we all lifted one another's performances. My future husband never ceases to amaze me, and he is the *real* star in my little family.

My version of the events as my mother described them bears little resemblance to hers. She points out that if I read the voice-to-text printout—which, by the way, was a joint effort and not my brother's solo creation—I would discover its accuracy. My *counter*point would be that one's tone of voice, facial expressions, and body English can completely alter the meaning of a statement.

That said, among the many valuable things my mom has taught me over the years, she has taught me not to take myself too seriously, and to find as much humor as you possibly can in life. Thanks, Mom! Congratulations on your well-deserved book sale!

Susan—My role in this book is so minimal, I don't deserve an afterword. My broken leg has healed completely. I hope none of us ever again are forced to miss out on a Boob Club road trip. My own motto—for life, as well as this story is: *Good news often comes disguised as bad news.** Even though my dear friends wound up being arrested, we are all richer for the experience and have played a role in producing that which we deeply revere: a book! Hooray!!

    *Jane—I couldn't agree more, Susan. My bad news of my getting arrested ultimately resulted in my changing the focus of my practice to intellectual-property law. Also, I am now a recovering alcoholic. At restaurants and parties, I've switched to NA beer, for obvious reasons. (If your waiter announces that they've run out of wine, do *you* ask if they've got a can of grape soda?) I rest my case. :) So there, Leslie! I included another happy face and made you a liar, one way or the other!

Suggested Topics for Discussion

1. The pace of How My Book Club Got Arrested picks up markedly once the Boobs discover Eugena Crowder hitchhiking with Red. Did you find the beginning too slow for your taste? Conversely, did you appreciate witnessing their interactions and feel like Eugena Crowder hijacks too much of the Boobs' story?

2. The author chooses to fictionalize herself and her book club, and she uses the device of an invented voice-to-text software application as the source of the dialog and, later, as a plot element. How did you feel about this storytelling structure? Did it affect your reading experience one way or the other?

3. Did you see aspects of yourself reflected in any of the members of the book group? Did you enjoy hearing about their reactions to actual books that they've discussed?

4. If you were in this book clubs' position, would you have kept the on-stage proposal a secret from Leslie?

5. On a similar note, would you have knocked on Leslie's door in the wee hours of the morning to tell her that you had spoken with Alicia and she was at a casino?

6. Did you relate to the mother/daughter relationship between Leslie and Alicia?

7. How would you describe Eugena Crowder in just one word? Assuming you were suspicious of Eugena Crowder from the start, did your theory about what she was up to change as the book progressed? Despite all of her deep character flaws—and possibly because of them—she wrote a fabulous children's book that touched young readers' lives. Does this redeem her in any way? Did you feel sorry for her? Could you relate to the women initially assuming she was a wonderful person due to their enormous affection for her book?

8. In the final scene of the book, the Boobs are celebrating at a restaurant in New York City. If Eugena were to walk into that restaurant and up to their table, which character do you think would react with the most anger? Which character might react the way you would in her shoes?

9. What do you feel was the author's overall message in this book? Are you at all tempted to go on a book-club road trip?

Author's Note

I hope you have enjoyed reading this book. I've fictionalized myself a character, as I have all of the characters. My friend Claudia Mills went with me on a research road trip from Boulder to Branson. We enjoyed ourselves immensely and did not got arrested even once. I am privileged to belong to two book clubs, and while I am often repurposing various remarks and characteristics of people I know during my writing process, none of the Boobs are based on any actual book-club member of mine. Eugena Crowder is not based on any author, living or dead, or for that matter, on any one person.

At the time of this writing, the second book of the trilogy, *Book Club Brides*, exists only within my head. If I might be so bold, I whole-heartedly and enthusiastically suggest that you try my other contemporary women's novels. They are stand-alones, which means they each have their own cast of characters and complications and can be read in any order. In order of publication, the books are: *Going to Graceland, Women's Night Out, Finding Gregory Peck*, and *By the Light of the Moon*. I have also written three mystery series, the closest of which in tone to this book is the Molly Masters series, beginning with *Death Comes eCalling*. Dog lovers especially might prefer my Allie Babcock series, beginning with *Play Dead*.

Please consider signing up for my newsletter at my website *LeslieOKane.com*, which is really only an email notification that I have a new book coming out or am running an ebook promotion. I would also love it if you would join in on my interactive Book Club/Dog Blog, which I'm only just now getting up and running. I will be sharing the my book clubs' titles and a very brief review of how our discussion went, along with pictures of my dog, plus dog cartoons and doodles. (I'm getting a Sketchbook for my computer, and I want to justify its cost.) I envision the blog as my being able to get at least as many book recommendations and dog pictures from others as I post.

Lastly, please review my book on the retailer's website or wherever you feel is appropriate. Help me get the word out to readers that this book exists. Thank you!

Made in the USA
San Bernardino, CA
18 November 2017